3-00

TILDY: RADICAL WOMAN

SARA FRASER
TILDY:
RADICAL WOMAN

Macdonald

British Library Cataloguing in Publication Data

Fraser, Sara, *1937–*
    Tildy 5: radical woman.
    Rn: Roy Clews   I. Title
    823'.914 [F]

    ISBN 0–356–17481–6

Printed and bound in Great Britain by
Redwood Press Limited, Melksham, Wiltshire

Macdonald & Co (Publishers) Ltd
165 Great Dover Street
London SE1 4YA

A member of Maxwell Macmillan Publishing Corporation

Introduction

In the England of the 1820s savage laws repressed the toiling masses. Government spies, the notorious 'provocation men', incited and entrapped those hotheads among the workers who dared to form illegal combinations and demand a just return for their arduous labours. But despite the ferocious punishments inflicted on those who were entrapped, always there were others ready to step forward and take their own stand against injustice and oppression.

Tildy Crawford, young, beautiful and courageous was among that number, and she fought for the brutalized women and girls whom she worked with, and wept with ...

Chapter One

Redditch. Parish of Tardebigge. Worcestershire. January
1823 ...

The great bell of the Fountain Needle Mill began
ringing out some four hours before the sunrise, and the
massive wooden gates set in the front wall of the tall
structure slowly creaked open like a black cavernous
mouth hungry to be filled. The bitterly cold wind took the
clangorous echoes of the bell and carried them across the
snow-covered gables and roofs of the huddled clusters of
buildings that comprised Redditch Town, and within
those buildings men, women and children stirred and
groaned and yawned into wakefulness as the brassy
summons penetrated sleep-drugged minds.

In the freezing darkness of her tiny attic room Tildy
Crawford opened her eyes and lay motionless for some
moments, reluctant to leave the warm cocoon of her
narrow bed. Borne on a gust of wind the faint clangours of
the bell sounded momentarily louder, and the young
woman sighed and pushed her threadbare blankets from
her. Wearing only a thin shift she shivered as she fumbled
beneath the low cot for the steel, flint and tinderbox she
kept there, and hastened to strike sparks and kindle the
tinder so that she might light her stub of candle. The
biting cold numbed her fingers, making her clumsy, and
by the time she succeeded in lighting the candle she was
chilled to the bone.

In the feeble glow of the wavering flame she dressed,
pulling both her dark grey gowns down over her head,
and rolling both her pairs of white cotton stockings onto

her slender, shapely legs. In the small cot barely two feet distant from her own, her small child slept peacefully, and Tildy smiled down at him, wrapped in his coverings like some tiny animal in its winter lair. Moving gently so as not to disturb his rest she touched her lips to the soft skin of his cheeks, and drew the coverings close up around his head.

A wooden bucket half-filled with water stood at the foot of her bed and Tildy lifted it and grimaced when she saw the thick crust of ice that had formed on the water's surface during the night. Steeling herself she broke the ice with her palm and quickly laved her face and hands then dried herself on a strip of rough towelling, rubbing hard until her skin tingled. Using the same water she brushed her teeth with a crude powder of charcoal, woodash and salt, the water so cold that her tongue and gums became almost numb. Her toilette completed, she slid her feet into heavy clogs, wrapped a shawl about her, and with a whispered farewell to her son blew out the candle and slipped from the room.

The dark cavern of the Fountain Mill's arched entranceway was lighted now by a big lantern hanging from a hook set high on the inside wall. Beneath the lantern a tall man, heavily swathed in woollen scarves and tarpaulin watch-coat, with a broad-brimmed, low-crowned hat pulled low over his eyes, was stamping booted feet upon the cobbles and swinging his mittened hands in vain effort to keep warm. The first arrivals were entering the mill, muffled in a bizarre variety of clothing, some with blankets and sacks worn cowl-like, and many of the smaller children weeping and whining as the wind lashed them with merciless icy savagery.

'If you please, Master, I was told to speak with Arthur Conolly.'

The tall man stopped swinging his arms and growled surlily at this softly spoken young woman who had come up to him. 'I'm Arthur Conolly, what does you want with me?'

Tildy, shivering uncontrollably from the cold, told him. 'My name's Tildy Crawford, Master Conolly. I'm to start work here this morn.'

'Am you now?' The man examined her with a disgruntled expression on his long-jawed face. 'And by whose leave?'

Tildy's heart sank within her at this reception. She knew that Arthur Conolly was the senior overlooker or foreman of the mill, and if he proved to be as unpleasant as he now appeared, then her working life here could well become a misery. 'If you please, Master Conolly, Mr Robert Stafford spoke to Mr Henry Milward on my behalf, and he told me that Mr Milward said that I could have the start here this morn.'

'Doing what?' Conolly grunted.

For a brief instant Tildy's resentment at his manner caused her fiery spirit to flare, and she snapped back, 'Doing whatever work is available to be done, I would suppose.'

He frowned at her raised voice. 'You'd suppose, 'ud you?' He growled the words. 'And how would you suppose it to be iffen I was to tell you that theer's no work available for women who don't know when to keep their mouths shut, Tildy Crawford?'

Already regretting her brief outburst Tildy made no answer, only stood miserably shivering, her teeth chattering despite her efforts to still them, while men, women, and children streamed past her, clogs clattering on the cobbles as they passed through the tunnel-like entrance to be swallowed up in the dark maws of the mill.

An elderly, bent-bodied man, his head and upper body wrapped in musty sacking, came to Conolly. 'It wants but a minute to five o'clock, Master Conolly.'

'Right, get 'um shut, Ben, and keep 'um shut 'til six o' the clock.'

'I knows well enough what hour to keep 'um shut 'til,' the old man grumbled in an undertone as he exerted all his feeble strength to swing the massive wooden structures closed.

There were still people approaching the mill, and as they saw the gates closing they shouted and began to run towards them. But under Conolly's watchful eye the old man ignored the shouts and before the nearest runners could reach them the gates were closed and barred, and the latecomers could only curse and huddle shivering against the wall, trying to find what shelter they could from the cutting wind until the gates should re-open.

'That'll cost the buggers two hours pay apiece, and if anybody arn't come by six o'clock, then they'm locked out for the day,' Conolly told Tildy. 'So take heed, Crawford, and get here to time for your work.'

Tildy experienced a surge of relief. At least then, she was going to be given a job.

'Come wi' me,' Conolly grunted, and walked through the entrance archway into the big square courtyard that the mill was constructed around. In the darkness the mill was stirring like some monstrous primordial beast. Lights were appearing in its ranks of windows; shafts and cogs and wheels were screeching into motion turned by slapping leather belting and powered by a great horizontal Gin-wheel beneath which, strapped in a wooden frame, the old horse plodded round and round in its endless circles like a living carousel.

Tildy stared up at the high-storeyed walls surrounding her and grimaced at her thoughts. This mill was indeed a monster. A monster which drew its sustenance from the bodies of human beings. Consuming their strength all the days of their lives with its insatiable demands.

She followed Conolly into the building and he led her through workshops where small forges belched out choking, noxious fumes and in those fumes rows of men, women and children sat at benches fashioning needles by hand using hammers, punches, files and tongs, their bodies and heads deep-grimed with the oily filth, swarf and rust that lay thick on every surface. Even at this early hour the cold air was foul with the stench of unwashed flesh and rotten-toothed mouths; and the din of hammer-

10

ing and filing, the raucous shouts of disputes and screeches of laughter, the clamorous clattering of belting and wheels made Tildy's head pound.

Finally Conolly led her through a dark passage and into a low-ceilinged, stone-flagged room dimly lit by the fire beneath a big brick-built copper which was emitting clouds of acid-smelling steam so pungent that it caused Tildy's eyes to smart and weep and her throat to gag. The steam hung so thickly on the cold air that the women within the room were only indistinct shapes moving through the murky vapour.

'You'll be working here, Crawford,' the foreman told her, and Tildy's heart sank. She knew that this was considered to be the worst work in the mill. The lye wash shop. Where the needles were brought after the polishing process to be cleansed of the 'Coomb', the thick layer of black oily grease and particles of steel swarf and emery which covered them.

'Mary Ann?' Conolly called one of the women to him and pointed at Tildy. 'Here's a fresh 'un for you.' To Tildy he said, 'You mind you does what Mary Ann tells you to, girl.' And with that parting admonition he left the room.

The woman's plump, round face was beaded with moisture and her hair dangled in wet strands from beneath her mob-cap. Her voluminous sacking apron and clothing were saturated at the front, and Tildy's spirits sank still further when she saw the other's hands and arms in the firelight — puffy, shrivel-skinned, raw-looking, with deep cracks in the flesh caused by the harsh alkaline lye soap and the constant immersion in water. Mary Ann Avery noted Tildy's glum gaze at her hands and smiled ruefully. 'They arn't a pretty sight, am they, my wench? But there's naught any on us can do to prevent it happening. It goes wi' the job. The cracks be bloody sore though, at times, especially when the lye gets into 'um. Makes you nearly weep at times, so it does. Still, you'll get used to it, and we does get paid an extra shilling a week for our pains

11

to buy salves and ointments for to put on 'um ...' All the while she was speaking the woman's eyes were straining in the gloom to study Tildy. Now she told the younger woman, 'Come closer to the fire, my duck, and warm yourself. What's your name anyway?'

'My name is Matilda Crawford, but I'm called Tildy,' Tildy answered, and gratefully moved close to the fire beneath the great copper, holding her hands out towards the flaring coals.

'Tildy Crawford!' The three women in the room glanced at each other as they heard the name, and Mary Ann questioned, 'Youm the wench as did the pointing for Master Stafford, arn't you?'

Tildy nodded. 'That's so. It didn't last long though.'

'And it was your man that was whipped through the town by the Constable just afore Christmas, warn't it?' the woman went on.

Again Tildy nodded, and the woman exclaimed admiringly, 'By the Christ, Tildy Crawford, youm summat of a case, you be. You'se bin the talk o' the bloody town, so you 'as. And I for one am real happy to meet you, my duck. I reckon you'se shown a deal o' courage in standing up to the bloody men like you 'as. You'se got your babby back wi' you as well, arn't you?'

Tildy found this display of open admiration more than a little embarrassing. 'Yes, I've got my boy back,' she muttered and, anxious to deflect the conversation from her personal life, asked, 'how is the work done here?'

'Just as quick and easy as we can do it, my duck,' Mary Ann chuckled.

'It's the wust bloody job in this soddin' mill.' It was a woman with a cracked and querulous voice who spoke now. In the gloom with the thick steam veiling her sight Tildy could make out very little of the faces and forms of her companions, but the firelight enabled her to see that this last speaker was much older than the others, and appeared to be completely toothless.

Mary Ann started to explain to Tildy what the method

12

of work was. 'When the needles goes to be polished, they takes a piece o' new buckram and covers it with emery powder and oil, then they spreads nigh on fifteen or sixteen thousands o' needles on it and rolls it into a long tight bundle. We calls that the "purse". Then the purse goes to the polishing tables and for two days they rolls it backwards and forrards under weights. Next the purse comes to us. We unties it and empties the needles into our lye tubs and washes 'um clane, then they goes into the drying shop next door theer. They dries 'um in the bran boxes, we calls that "fanning" 'um."

'It sounds simple enough,' Tildy observed quietly, and Mary Ann nodded vigorously.

'Oh ahr, it's simple enough, my duck. It's just the things that it does to our flesh that makes it hard to bear. Apart from our hands and arms we'em forever getting colds on the chest being in this steam all the hours God sends, and wi' our clothes being so wet all the time it gives us the rheumaticks when we has to goo out into the air arter being in here. Still, like I said, you gets used to it, and we does get the extra shilling.'

'What will I earn then?' Tildy wanted to know.

'Most weeks we gets about seven shillings, give or take a few pence. It arn't much, is it, but more than we'd get from the Parish.'

Two youths came through the doorway carrying a large flat wooden board between them on which were piled rolls of buckram containing freshly polished needles. 'Come on now, ladies,' the elder of the two shouted jocularly. 'Mr Henry Milward sends his compliments and asks if you'll do him the honour of shifting off your fat arses and getting this lot washed clane.'

'You goo back to Mr Henry Milward and give him our compliments, and tell him, bollocks!' Mary Ann rejoined, and with a hoot of laughter the youths dropped the heavy board to the floor with a resounding crash. They came to warm themselves at the fire, and the elder one stared curiously at Tildy.

'Who's this sweet morsel, then?' He grinned, disclosing badly decayed front teeth.

'Her's a fresh 'un,' Mary Ann informed him, and the youth whistled appreciatively.

'From what I can see on her, her's fresh all right. Sweet and fresh enough to ate.'

Tildy ignored him, and before he could say anything more a man's voice roared from the outer passage. 'Cummon 'ere, Will Kitchen, and look sharp, or I'll strip the fuckin' skin from your back, you lazy young sod.'

'I'm coming, my lord!' the elder youth called in an affected high falsetto, and laughing the pair of them hurried out.

Mary Ann grinned amusedly at Tildy. 'He's a cheeky young bugger is Will Kitchen, my duck, but I carn't help but laugh at the sod sometimes. Mind you, he's certain sure to end up at Botany Bay, or on the bloody gallows, because he's a terrible thief. Don't you never leave aught lying about when he's in the area, because he'll certain sure lift it. Apart from that, he arn't a bad lad, and he spoke true when he said you was sweet and fresh enough to ate, didn't 'he.' Her eyes roved over Tildy's neatly plaited, glossy dark hair, smooth pale skin, and full-breasted yet slender body. 'Youm a rare good-looking girl, Tildy. You looks too soft and gentle for this sort o' work.'

'Don't worry about me being too soft and gentle for this work,' Tildy assured her. 'I've toiled hard all my life, and I've strength and to spare.'

'A wench who looks like you does, needn't ever toil hard in this mill, iffen she's ready to let the overlookers make a bit free wi' her.' It was Sarah Farr, the third of the women in the shop. In her mid-thirties, her once pretty face now was haggard from hardship, her body gaunt and angular. 'I reckon you could soon get yourself a real easy job here, Tildy, iffen you did any of the bosses a small favour now and agen.'

Tildy met the other's lascivious wink with a steady regard and then answered in an even tone. 'Whatever wages I'll be getting here, I'll be working for them. I seek no favours from bosses, and I give no favours to them either.'

'I didn't mean to cause you any offence,' Sarah Farr hastened to say.

'And I've taken no offence,' Tildy replied. 'But I always think it's best to have things straight right from the start.'

Mary Ann smiled approvingly. 'And that's a good way to have them, Tildy. You'll do well enough for me, I reckon.' She patted Tildy's slender shoulder, then added, 'Right then, I'll fix you up wi' a bit o' sacking to cover your dress wi', Tildy, and then we'll set to and get these purses emptied, or we'll soon have bloody Conolly in here screaming blue murder at us ...'

Chapter Two

At two minutes to six o'clock the portly, top-hatted, warm-clad figure of Henry Milward Esq., needle master, chapel warden, select vestryman, fanatically loyal subject of His Majesty, King George the Fourth, and sole proprietor of the Fountain Mill, appeared in the front doorway of his large house. For a brief moment he stood staring through the gloom across the broad roadway towards the left-side outer wall of his establishment, noting with satisfaction that the horse harnessed in its wooden frame which was bolted to the huge horizontal wheel of the gin above its drooping head seemed to be moving without undue difficulty. Of late, the horses Henry Milward used to power his mill had been dropping dead in their tracks with a disconcerting and expensive regularity. His sense of satisfaction abruptly disappeared when his eyes ranged along the line of dark huddled figures standing against the front walls on each side of the great closed gates.

Frowning, the needle master hurried towards the mill, and the foulness of his temper was exacerbated when his foot slipped on the icy surface of the road and he fell heavily onto his well-padded rear. As he clumsily got to his feet he heard the splutterings of laughter coming from the dim figures and his mouth tightened into a thinly compressed line. The laughter became muffled snorts and giggles as Milward reached the gates, and a chorus of respectful salutations greeted him. He ignored them, and stood in stony silence until at exactly six o'clock the great gates creaked open and a widening shaft of light from the

16

big lantern inside the entranceway illuminated the pinched, cold-pallored faces of the waiting crowd of men, women and children. When they would have surged forwards to enter the mill, Henry Millward halted them with a single wave of his arm, then shouted hoarsely, 'Conolly, be you there?'

The overlooker came out from the half-opened gates. 'Yes, Mr Milward?'

'Good job for you that you be,' the needle master grunted sourly, and gestured with his gloved hand at the people behind him. 'You can pack these buggers back off wheer they came from. If they lies stinking in their pits of a morning and can't be bothered to get here to time, then they needn't come at all.'

Exclamations of angry protest burst from the crowd, but instantly ceased when the needle master swung about to confront them. 'Mayhap you'll not be so bloody idle in the future,' he shouted. 'My mill gates opens at well afore five o' the clock, and that's the hour when I wants you here. I wun't tolerate you athinking you can come in whensoever you pleases to. If you can't come to the time I sets, then you needn't come at all. Now sod off, the lot on you, and if I hears another word from any one of you, then I'll hand the whole bloody boiling of you your sacks. Go on, piss off! Right now!'

The crowd muttered resentfully, shuffling their feet on the cobbles, but no one moved away, the loss of a whole day's wages was too serious to be given up easily. Arthur Conolly's gaze had been moving across the faces of the latecomers while his employer was ranting at them, and now he frowned unhappily and tugged at the sleeve of the needle master's thick overcoat. Placing his lips close to his employer's hairy red ear, he whispered, 'Josh Dyson is among 'um, Mr Milward. Over in the back theer.'

Milward's bloodshot eyes searched for and found the man referred to. Slightly taller than his neighbours, clad in a reefer jacket and knee-breeches, with an old military forage cap on his head, he looked like the ex-soldier he

17

was. Hard-faced, he held his thickset body stiffly erect, his eyes intent on the needle master.

Momentarily disconcerted, Milward whispered back, 'Well, what odds does that make?'

'I'm in sore need of the bugger today, Master,' the overlooker whispered urgently. 'I must needs get the last o' that Dortmund steel used up, and he's the only hardener we'se got who'll be able to make a decent job on it.'

The needle master snorted in disgust, then snapped at his underling, 'You deal wi' the bugger then.' And turning on his heel he walked on into the mill.

The crowd still waited uncertainly, and Conolly pointed at the hardener. 'You can come in, Josh Dyson. The rest on you can piss off.'

A expression of disgust passed across Dyson's features, and he answered curtly, 'I'll piss off wi' the others, Conolly. Most on 'um was not above a minute late in coming, and was here afore me, as well. It arn't right to send them away, and not me. Let us all in, or none on us, that's only fair.'

A muted chorus of approbation greeted his words and Conolly scowled, but made no instant answer. Inwardly the overlooker was in a quandary. To meet this week's production levels he needed the man desperately. If the levels were not met then his own position at the mill would be endangered. He knew from bitter experience that Henry Milward was ruthless where business was concerned, and there was always an abundance of men ready and eager to jump into the overlookers' jobs. Yet, if he now went against his employer's instructions by admitting the other latecomers, he could also find himself in dire trouble for disobeying his orders.

While he stood racking his brains for some way out of the dilemma a fat woman came from the large house across the roadway, and as she reached the gates demanded, 'What's amiss here, Conolly? Don't keep these poor craturs out here aperishing in this bloody cold! Let 'um in.'

'But the Master said ...' Conolly started to tell her, but she shouted, 'Do as I bid you, and hold your tongue.'

With a heartfelt sigh of relief the overlooker thankfully stood to one side and waved the crowd to enter. They rushed forwards, laughing in turn with their own relief.

The fat woman, who was dressed like a worker in a shabby gown, sack apron and home-spun shawl, with heavy clogs on her feet and a grimy, floppy mobcap on her untidy grey hair, stopped in front of Conolly, and questioned harshly, 'Why the bloody hell was you akeeping the poor buggers out in this bloody wind? Some o' the little 'uns was nigh on perished to death wi' the cold.'

Millicent Milward, wife to Henry Milward, had not acquired any veneer of sophistication or culture during her rise from slumgirl to needle master's wife.

'It warn't my doing, Missus,' Arthur Conolly told her sullenly. 'It was the Master. He told me to send 'um home for coming late.'

'Did he now!' The woman's broad heavy features were contemptuous. 'I'll have a few words to say to the silly old bugger when I gets ahold on him. Don't you worry your yed about it any more, he swilled too much soddin' claret last night, and it's made him liverish this morn. He'll cool his temper by and by.'

Conolly nodded gratefully. 'You'll tell him that I let 'um in because you bade me to then, Missus?'

'Ahr, I'll tell him all right,' his formidable mistress growled, and left him to finish opening the gates.

Josh Dyson did not rush through the gates like the rest, instead he walked steadily, pausing occasionally to exchange greetings and remarks with one or other of the workpeople in the shops he passed through. When he reached his own workshop he removed his reefer coat and hung it on a nail driven into the wall, revealing his leather waistcoat and plain calico shirt. He let the leather apron rolled about his hips fall to cover the front of his knee-breeches and rolled up his shirt-sleeves to display thickly-muscled forearms covered with red and blue tattoos, mementoes of his long years as a soldier.

Two other men were already in the room, both of them considerably younger than the forty years-old Dyson, and one of them gusted an exclamation of relief when the latecomer entered. 'Thank the Christ you'se come, Josh. Conolly's bin screaming for these batches already this morning, and I daren't try to temper 'um in case I buggers 'um up.'

'They'll be the last o' that German delivery,' Dyson stated, and the other nodded vigorously and spat on the floor to show his disgust.

'Bastard useless stuff! I reckon it's some o' the wust we'se ever had, and that's saying summat, arn't it? Why must Old Henry always try to do it on the chape? Iffen he'd pay the bit extra for the Hungarian we'd not have this bleedin' trouble.'

Dyson smiled in wry agreement, but made no verbal comment.

The dark, low-ceilinged room was warm from the several shallow troughs of burning charcoal, which stood on their iron legs lining one wall. Beneath some of these troughs were placed wooden tubs filled with water. Dyson's job was to take the pointed and fashioned needles and temper them for hardness by heating them to the necessary degree and casting them into the tubs of cold water. This process would bend and twist the needles, which then had to be baked to restore their flexibility and re-straightened by women using small hammers and lead blocks. After the re-straightening the needles would go on to be polished. This tempering and baking was a highly skilled task which depended on the expert eye of the hardener and his judgement of the correct degree of heat needed for each batch differing in size and type. Too much heat in the tempering would burn the needles; too little would leave them soft. In the baking the opposite maxim applied. Too much heat destroyed the tempering, too little left the needles inflexible and brittle. A first-class hardener was highly prized and could not easily be replaced, and it was for this reason that Arthur Conolly had so urgently needed Josh Dyson's skill this day. Most of the steel used in the needle manufacturies came from either Germany or Hungary. The German steel was often of poor quality and only the most skilled hardeners could achieve good results with it.

'Right then, lads, I'd best make up for lost time.' Dyson took in succession several long, flat, narrow pieces of iron bent up at one end, and on these irons he spread needles until the entire surface was covered by them, then placed the iron across the beds of glowing charcoal. Using bellows he brought the heat of the coals up and watched carefully as the needles slowly became a red hot mass. His two assistants came to stand at his side while he watched and waited and he told them, 'wi' this German rubbish it's best to wait for the yellow edging, and then in the baking use a lighter blue colour than you would for the Hungarian. Keep your eyes steady and you'll see exactly what I mean.'

Respectfully they murmured their assent and kept their attention on the glowing mass ...

At nine o'clock, three and a half hours after work had begun, the bell of the Fountain Mill clanged out again to signal the commencement of the first of the two, half-hour rest periods that were allowed during each day's labour to enable the workers to eat their breakfast and dinner.

'That's it, girls,' Mary Ann Avery shouted. 'Time for breakfast. Leave that lot for now, Tildy and come and get summat to ate.'

Tildy straightened her back, wincing at the painful stiffness of muscles engendered by bending over the tubs stirring the needles in the black-scummed oily water for long hours.

'Here,' Mary Ann handed her a piece of sacking. 'Dry your hands well on this, my duck, or you'll have the skin cracking sooner than needs be.'

Tildy took the sacking and glanced ruefully down at

the front of her clothing, already saturated with the acid-smelling water she worked with. 'I wish I hadn't put on both my dresses this morn,' she said regretfully. 'Now they'll both be ruined. But it was so cold when I woke up that I needed the extra covering.'

Mary Ann looked at the sweat beading the newcomer's soft, smooth skin and chuckled, 'Well at least you arn't feeling the cold now, my wench. You looks to be in a muck lather.'

Tildy smiled. 'That's true enough. In fact, I'm feeling a bit too warm for comfort.'

The women ranged themselves on a plank laid on the floor in front of the copper's firehole, and began hungrily to devour their bread and cheese, slaking their thirst from a jug of weak beer. Although she had eaten nothing since the previous day Tildy had no appetite for the coarse brown bread and hard yellow cheese she had brought with her to work. The fumes of the lye wash and oil coomb had caused her stomach to feel queasily unsettled, and the acid steam had made her chest and throat feel sore.

Sarah Farr watched the young woman re-wrap her food in its clean rag covering and asked commiseratingly, 'Feeling a touch sickly, am you, my duck? Pay it no mind, the stink gets us all like that to begin wi'. You'll soon get used to it.'

'I hope so,' Tildy joked wanly. 'Or else I'll be too weak from starvation to be able to work at all.'

William Kitchen came into the room carrying some fresh purses of polished needles, and he dropped them to the floor and came to sit next to Tildy on the plank. ''As you heard what happened this morning at the gate?' he enquired eagerly, and without waiting for any reply went on to relate the story of the abortive lock-out.

The three old hands chortled happily at the youth's animated description, and Mary Ann observed admiringly, 'Josh Dyson is a bloody caution, arn't he just! He don't give a bugger for none o' the gaffers, does he.' She turned to Tildy. 'Does you know Josh, Tildy? He lives

22

in one o' them cottages up the New End, at the foot o' the Front Hill.'

Tildy shook her head. 'No, I don't think so. Is he local born?'

'Ahr, he's local, but he went off soldiering for a good many years. He come back home arter Waterloo was fought. Got wounded theer, so he did. Quite a lot o' chaps from this town went off to the war, you know.'

'Ahr, and more nor a few on 'um got their bloody yeds shot off in it, as well,' the toothless old woman, Tabby Merry, put in. 'Lost me own youngerest boy, so I did, out in bleedin' Spain theer. Him and Josh Dyson was in the same regiment, and Josh saw my lad get killed at a place called Badahoos, or summat like that it sounds.' Her cracked voice became choked.

'Now Tabby, don't you go upsetting yourself by thinking on it now,' Mary Ann told the old woman kindly. 'Your lad's in a better world than this 'un, that's for sure.'

'Amen to that.' Tabby Merry muttered brokenly. ''Tis my only comfort knowing that he is, and that I'll soon be joining him theer.'

'Fuck me! Hark to holy Hannah! Does we have to listen to this agen, Tabby?' William Kitchen jeered, and the women rounded on him furiously, cursing and abusing him violently until he beat a hasty retreat.

'Theer! That's sent the young sod to the right-about,' Mary Ann gusted with satisfaction, and again turned to Tildy. 'Like I was asaying, Tildy, Josh Dyson is a fair caution, so he is. He's one o' them red republicans, you know. Hates the royalty and the high gentry, so he does, and he arn't afeared to spake his mind about how he feels neither. Bin took up afore the magistrates a few times for saying such things as well, and he's bin sent to prison for it back in 1819 when there was all the hullaballoo about the Peterloo Massacre up in the North Country theer. Him and Henry Milward has had words more nor a few times, because Old Henry is strong for King George and a real Tory.'

'Yet Dyson still works here?' Tildy showed her surprise.

'Well, Josh is the best hardener in the whole district, my duck, and Old Henry be strong for the royalty, but he's stronger yet for his own profits.' Mary Ann's plump, motherly features beamed with her good humour. 'Oh, we has some fine old shindies here atween the pair on 'um at times, I'll tell you.' She chuckled at the memory. 'Old Henry's face goes bloody purple, so it does, when Josh gets him riled up.'

'There's other folks in this town as gets riled up at Josh Dyson, and they arn't all Tories neither,' Sarah Farr put in. 'I can't say as I'm over-fond on him meself. I reckon he's got too much of a bob on himself for his station in life.'

'That's as maybe, Sarah,' Mary Ann was quick to defend the man. 'But Josh Dyson is a good-living man, and as straight as a die, and a lot o' them who carn't abide him, canna do so because he spakes the truth, and most on 'um canna abide having the truth spoke, and that's the way on it.'

'Oh yes, I'll allow you that, Mary Ann. He arn't afeared to spake out, I'll grant the bugger that. But then, it's easy for him to do so, arn't it? He's a skilled man, and good at his craft. He'll always find work hereabouts. But iffen you or me was to say one tenth part of what he does, we'd be kicked out of here on our arses and not find work in this district ever agen. We'd soon find ourselves in the bloody poor'us, 'udden't us?'

'Ahr, that's true enough, Sarah,' the plump woman sighed. 'There's no denying that for a fact.'

Tildy was intrigued by the description of Josh Dyson, and found herself curious to know more about the man. 'Is he married?' she queried.

'He was once.' Mary Ann shook her head sadly. 'And a good little wench her was, as well. One of old Snipe's daughters, from nigh the big pool. Arter he'd bin awhiles in the army Josh come home on furlough, I reckon he was a corporal by then. Well, young May Snipe thought he

24

was a real prince, dressed up in his fine scarlet coat and ribbons on his shako. Anyway, they got married and off her went wi' him to follow the drum. Soon had a couple o' kids to keep 'um company, as well. The Snipes was always good breeders. Well known for it. Then Josh's regiment got ordered out to foreign parts. But you knows how they'll only take a few o' the soldiers' women wi' 'um, when they goes abroad. Well, poor May's name warn't drawn out o' the hat, and her and the kids had to stay behind. Middle o' winter, so it was, and nowhere for the poor wench and her little 'uns to get free shelter because another regiment had moved into the quarters. Folks say that May stayed at the port trying to get a ship out to Portugal to follow Josh, until what money he'd bin able to leave wi' her had all gone, and her and the little 'uns was nigh on starving, because o' course, her'd got no settlement wheer her was, and couldn't get any relief, except for a begging pass to come back here with. So, her starts to walk back here, wi' two nippers and a big belly, because another kid was on the way. Her and the kids both got took sick on the road, and all three on 'um ended up dying o' the bloody fever down by Oxford theer.

'O' course, Josh being at the war, he didn't know what had happened to 'um for ages arter they'd died. Anyway, from what they says, it's that what's made him so bitter agen the King and the high gentry. He reckons that the wives and kids o' the men away at the war should ha' bin looked arter properly by the Government, because May warn't the only pitiful cratur left friendless and penniless when her man was sent from her. I've heard tell that there was thousands o' women and kids left in the same state, and a good many on 'um ended in their graves as well.'

Tildly nodded thoughtfully. 'Yes, I've heard that too, Mary Ann. But that's always the way of things in this country, it seems. Those that work the hardest and suffer the most, get the least provided for. I've often thought that if I were a man, I'd be a rebel myself against the King and the Government.'

Mary Ann threw up her hands in dismay. 'Don't you ever let Henry Milward hear you say a thing like that, my girl, or you'll bloody well soon be handed your sack.'

Tildy grinned mischievously. 'Well, if that's the case, I'll just think it then, and not give voice to it.'

The bell clanged out, and her companion grimaced. 'No rest for the wicked, is there, girls? Come on, let's get at it or we'll all be getting our sacks handed to us.'

As Tildy used the great iron ladle to pour freshly boiling water into the cleansing tubs she found herself wondering about Josh Dyson, and experiencing a growing desire to meet and talk with him. She'd be interested to hear how he would go about gaining a better life for the ordinary people in the country, because if there was one thing that was sure, it was time they were given some justice by their rulers.

The question of justice for the labouring masses of which she was a part had lately been increasingly exercising Tildy Crawford's mind. Although only twenty-one years of age, she had experienced more than her fair share of sufferings, hardship and deprivation, and now, alone in the world with a child dependent on her, she knew that she faced a future that could only be a bitter struggle for mere survival. She was completely uneducated, yet she possessed a fine intelligence and had managed to teach herself to read and write, and despite the grinding poverty of her daily existence she thirsted for a knowledge of things beyond the mean confines of her life and surroundings.

Now, as she bent over the tub, the choking steam enveloping her head and shoulders, a rueful smile curved her full lips. 'I suppose I'm gaining knowledge of a sort even now. At least I'm discovering how unpleasant this job is to do . . .'

In the hardening shop Henry Milward was watching Josh Dyson as the workman judged the moment and, using heavy tongs, lifted the red-hot iron plate from the charcoal and tipped the glowing mass of needles into the tub of cold water. The water hissed loudly and bubbled and a cloud of steam belched upwards. The hardener waited a moment or two then fished out a handful of the bent, discoloured needles and examined them. He nodded to his helpers. 'They'll do. Get 'um out and spread for baking.'

'How's the batch looking as a whole, Dyson?' The needle master moved forwards to stand by the hardener, and the man answered with a slight frown. 'As a whole it arn't too desperate. But this Dortmund steel is wust than most. I'm having to do the best I can wi' it, and hope for the best.'

'I pays you to make a good job on it, not to only hope that you does.' The needle master's tone was surly, and Dyson's slight frown deepened.

'And I earns my wages. You don't make me a present on 'um,' he replied sharply.

The needle master grunted, but made no answer, only remained standing scowling down at the tub of water. Dyson's helpers shuffled uneasily, made nervous by the bad mood of their employer, but Josh Dyson was unruffled.

'Well, Mr Milward?' he questioned.

'Well what?' the needle master growled.

'Why are you standing theer looking like thunder? Have you summat you wants to say to me?' Dyson demanded.

Milward's plump features suffused with an angry flush, and he shouted, 'You bin up to your tricks agen, arn't you, my buck? Conolly tells me that you was threatening him agen at the gate this morning.'

Dyson turned squarely to face his employer. 'Don't you come shouting and blarting at me, Henry Milward. If you've a grievance, then spake reasonable, and you'll get a reasonable answer from me in return.' He added warningly, 'And If we'em going to have a row, then let's

27

step back from here to have it, and give these lads room to get on wi' their work.'

Flustered, Henry Milward stepped back a couple of paces, then blustered, 'I arn't heard you gi' me an answer yet, Dyson.'

The hardener gusted a loud sigh of disgust. 'Conolly agen is it, you say?' he observed scathingly. 'Well I knows for a fact that Conolly's your cur dog, Henry Milward, and he only yaps what you wants him to yap. So don't use him to shoot your bullets. Shoot 'um yourself.'

Secretly afraid of this formidable man, the needle master shook his fist in the air and shouted, 'Arthur Conolly has got loyalty to them who gives him the work that feeds and clothes him. Which is summat that can never be said about you, my lad. You'se got no loyalty to your betters, nor to your King or country neither.'

A spasm of anger crossed the hardener's features and he stepped towards Milward, who in his turn visibly flinched and stepped backwards another pace. 'Don't you prate to me about loyalty to King and country,' Dyson hissed. 'I'se seen too many good men lying dead on the battlefield and too many fine soldiers wi' smashed bodies forced to become begging cripples for me to feel any loyalty to that fat, useless bastard you calls King. And as for loyalty to my betters,' he paused and grinned in mocking anger, 'I never once saw any o' you lot in this town who thinks youm my "Betters" marching towards the sound o' the guns.'

'I did my military service,' Milward blustered defensively.

Dyson laughed aloud. 'Military service, did you call it? The only service you ever saw, Milward, was to parade on the Chapel Green theer, once a week with all the other bloody brave Redditch volunteers, and fire a volley at the crows. If you lot had ever seen a Frenchman coming at you with his bayonet fixed, you'd ha' shat yourselves so hard you'd ha' drowned in it.'

Defeated, the needle master could only bluster his way

out of the room. 'I'll not stand here to argue the toss wi' a bloody common workman,' he shouted. 'I'se got better and more important things to do.' And he stormed away.

With a broad grin Dyson watched him go, then turned to his helpers, who were staring at him with open admiration. The hardener's grin disappeared. 'I thought I told you to get that tub emptied and the batch spread for baking,' he snapped curtly.

The two young men jumped to obey him, and the grin again quirked his lips. 'One thing you must always bear in your minds, lads,' he told them. 'You can only argue back to the masters wi' right on your side if you does your own work as good or better than anybody else can do it.'

'You told the old bugger the rights on it today all right, Josh,' one of them said admiringly, and Dyson's hard features became thoughtful.

'Old Henry arn't so bad as a good many other masters in this town, boy,' he remarked quietly. 'He's a loud-mouthed bully, but he arn't vicious wi' it, and his missus is a rare good sort. No, in all fairness, you'll meet worse nor him and her afore you goes to meet your Maker.' Again he grinned broadly. 'And when you meets Him, you'll likely find He's the worst bloody Master of 'um all. He must be to let folks endure what they has to in this bloody country ...'

There were multitudes who if they had heard his words would have agreed passionately with Josh Dyson's last statement. Ever since the war against Napoleon Bonaparte's empire had been brought to its victorious conclusion, industrial and agricultural depressions with their concomitant massive unemployment, distress, poverty and starvation had racked the British Isles, and successive governments had only offered one answer to their people's protests. Savage repression. Repression legalized by the Poor Law, the Law of Settlement, the Game Laws, the Combination Acts, the Corn Law, and the culminating punitive measures of the notorious Six Acts of 1819, known with jocose bitterness as the 'Gag

29

Acts'. With these added to a criminal law which contained two hundred and twenty-three capital offences for which death was the mandatory sentence, the ruling classes of Great Britain were able to maintain an iron grip on the country, and when starving men and women were driven by desperation to open defiance, the ruling classes unleashed upon them the Judiciary and the Yeomanry Cavalry, backed by the regular army. Then the hangmen earned extra fees and the convict ships sailed for the far-off penal colonies with full cargoes ...

The grin on Josh Dyson's face had become a bitter rictus and his grey eyes showed torment as inwardly he cursed the land that had given him birth, and grieved afresh for his own beloved dead. 'Some day ... some day I'll be avenged for what was done to you ...' he vowed silently, and then, by sheer strength of will thrust the image of his wife and children from his mind and turned once more to his work.

Chapter Three

Nathanial Farrel was hungry and footsore and when in the dusk of late afternoon he breasted high Beoley Hill and saw the lights of Redditch glimmering from the hillside across the broad shallow valley which separated him from the town he breathed a sigh of thankful relief. Crossing the crest of the hill he moved downwards to find shelter from the biting easterly wind at his back, and then paused to rest for a brief while, placing his leather valise on the ground and sitting down upon it. Of middle height and slender build, his appearance, travel-stained though it was, still bore some pretension to gentility. The black swallow-tailed coat and pantaloons and the white waistcoat were of good cut and quality of cloth, as was the brown beaver top hat. His linen was clean, his collar and high black neck-stock neatly fastened, and his leather shoes, although muddied from the road, were made to measure for his small feet.

Although a native Londoner, whose first visit this was to Worcestershire, Farrel knew a great deal about the town he was now staring at so intently. He knew that it was the principal manufacturing centre in the entire world for needles and fish-hooks. He knew that its population were noted for their propensities towards drinking and violence, even in this violent debauched era. He knew that there was much wealth in the town cheek by jowl with abysmal poverty. He knew the names and antecedents of some of the principal inhabitants, and of the select vestry-men who were its governing body. He knew also the names and antecedents of certain other inhabitants, all of which he hoped might prove useful in bringing to fruition the task he had come here to undertake. Driven by the cold he rose and lifting up his valise trudged on wearily down the steep hill.

Chapter Four

While Nathanial Farrel was crossing the Arrow Valley in the direction of Redditch, Henry Milward was seated at his desk in his office, the flame of the oil lamp casting reflections on the glass fronts of the display cases that covered almost every inch of the walls. The needle master hummed tunelessly as he pored over the open ledger before him. There came a knock on the door, and a familiar voice enquired, 'Can I come in, Mr Milward?'

Milward shouted assent, and Conolly sidled in, removing his hat from his balding head, and came to stand in front of the desk, his mittened hands toying nervously with his hat.

'Well?' The needle master did not look up from the ledger.

'If you please, Mr Milward, the order for Antwerp is packaged and ready to go. I'll be sending it up to the Unicorn fust thing tomorrow morn.'

'It should have been packaged hours since,' Milward grumbled, then looked sharply at the other man. 'What about the Paris order?'

The overlooker's long brown teeth knawed at his thin lips.

'Bugger me, Conolly! Has you lost your tongue? Speak out, man!' Milward suddenly bawled, and the other jumped nervously, his fingers twisting his hat as if he wanted to tear the material into shreds.

'No, Sir,' he blurted out. 'The Paris order arn't completed yet. I don't reckon we'll have it done by shut-gate time.'

'Bollocks to that!' the needle master roared furiously. 'I don't pay you good money to come in here and tell me that orders arn't ready when they should be. What's the delay?'

Despite the chill of the air the overlooker was visibly sweating. 'It's because o' that Dortmund steel agen, Master, it keeps on splitting under the eye punch, it was even splitting when it was being flatted.'

The needle master's fat face became so suffused with blood that in the dim light it looked almost black. The overlooker shuffled, his lips twitching, unable to stand still in his fear of his employer's wrath.

'Now hark to me, you fuckin' mawkin,' Milward's voice was half-choked with his temper. 'The carrier's waggon 'ull be leaving the Unicorn at eight sharp tomorrow morning. All the current orders from my mill 'ull be on that waggon, properly packaged. If they arn't, then you'll be looking for another position at exactly one minute past the hour of eight, and you'll be looking forever in this district, because I'll make sure that you wun't find another bloody position in the needle trade, or any other bloody trade. Does I make myself clear?'

The overlooker nodded unhappily.

'Right then!' Milward jerked his thumb at the door. 'Sod off and do what I pays you to do.'

Without another word Conolly skulked from the room with bent head and rounded shoulders. Once outside in the darkness of the courtyard his head came up and his body straightened. 'And bollocks to you too, you fat miserable bastard!' he mouthed silently at the closed door, and shook his fist at his invisible employer. 'If you warn't such a money-grubbing tight-arse, we 'udden't have this trouble to start wi'. We'd have some decent stuff to work wi' instead o' this fucking rubbish you buys all the time.'

His feelings eased a trifle by this silent castigation, the overlooker turned his thoughts towards his present problem. 'I'll have to keep as many of the buggers back as

34

needful. Even then it'll be a close run thing to get that soddin' Paris order done.' He swallowed hard as another unpalatable thought occurred to him. 'And they'll be wanting extra for working over, as well. Jesus Christ! Milward 'ull goo bloody mad about that, as well ...'

In the lye wash shop Tildy was coping well with the work despite the unpleasantness of saturated clothing and the steamy, stinking atmosphere. Mary Ann Avery was well pleased with the newcomer, and was quick to tell the overlooker so when he came to inform the women that they would be working extra time that night, and would not finish at the usual time of eight o'clock.

The man called Tildy to him and brusquely told her, 'Mary Ann is satisfied wi' the way youm shaping up, girl. To spake truly, I had me doubts about you. Still, iffen you keeps on the way you'se begun, then I'll keep you on here.'

He paused, as though awaiting a reply, and Tildy felt constrained to thank him. He nodded and left her, and she turned to Mary Ann.

'Thank you for speaking well of me.'

The plump woman smiled back. 'No need to thank me for spaking the truth, my duck. It looks like you brought a bit o' good luck wi' you as well. We'em getting some extra time tonight. Shan't get finished afore midnight, I reckon. The money 'ull come in real handy this week, I'll tell you, because my man's bin laid up in bed for a sen'night and arn't earned a penny piece.'

Tildy nodded doubtfully, her thoughts on her child awaiting her return.

'Has you got somebody to care for your babby whiles youm here?' The other woman had noticed Tildy's lack of enthusiasm for the extra time.

'Mother Readman is keeping an eye on him for me,' Tildy stated, somewhat defensively. 'I've got a room at her house, and she's really good to me. She's been a true friend.'

35

Tildy lived in a lodging house kept by Mother Readman in the Silver Square, one of the worst slums in the town. Both Mother Readman and her lodging house had a bad reputation among the respectable elements of the town's population, but Tildy had found the woman to be a good friend to her, and a good friend also to many of the tramps, transients, and homeless flotsam and jetsam who sought shelter beneath her roof.

Mary Ann smiled again, and nodded. 'Oh, I've known Charlotte Readman for a good many years, my duck. Her's all right, her is. Your babby 'ull do well enough with her. Mind you, the Silver Square arn't the wholesomest place to bring up a little 'un, is it? Theer's always a deal o' fever there, not to mention the other goings on. It's really rough theer, arn't it?'

'That's true,' Tildy was forced to agree. 'But to be fair, I've never been offered harm or insult by anyone who lives there.'

'Well, iffen youm a good friend of old Charlotte's, there arn't many who'd risk offering you harm, is there, girl? Old Charlotte can toe the line wi' any man iffen she's a mind to, and her's always got plenty to back her up in the Square, arn't her? They all sticks together theer, don't they, and I reckon when that lot comes to the boil, why it 'ud take a regiment o' soldiers to deal wi' the buggers.'

'I think you're right about that.' Tildy grinned wryly. 'There are some very tough customers about there, that's for sure.'

She went back to stirring the needles in the filth-scummed steaming tub, and her thoughts turned to the problems that faced her ...

Life had been harsh to Tildy Crawford. Left orphaned with her younger brother while still only a very small child, she had been raised by an aunt and uncle who treated her as an unpaid drudge, and gave her kicks and blows instead of caresses and kisses. Her brother had been sent as a parish pauper child to the cotton mills of the

North Country as soon as he could carry out the simplest of tasks, and she had heard nothing of him since and had long believed that he had died, like so many thousands of other tiny unfortunates sent to those hellholes to be worked to their deaths.

At eighteen years Tildy had escaped from her own dismal bondage and had entered the service of the Reverend Phillip Wren, the rector of the neighbouring parish of Ipsley, which encompassed some eastern parts of Redditch Town, only to encounter greater evils. Raped and made pregnant by Tom Crawford, her fellow servant, she had been virtually forced to marry the man. Dismissed by his employer after the marriage had taken place, Tom Crawford had taken his pregnant young wife back to his own place of birth, the nail-making village of Sidemoor in the Bromsgrove parish some eight miles north-west of Redditch.

For Tildy, life there had been a purgatory of near-slavery at the nail forges and relentless poverty and constant violence at the hands of her drunken husband. He had eventually deserted her and the child, leaving them to the mercies of the parish and the poorhouse.

Alone, Tildy had struggled to survive, her life dominated by one all-powerful motivation, the desire to raise her son to manhood, to educate him, and to see him one day accepted as a gentleman, a true gentleman who would try to protect those weaker and poorer than himself, and act always with honour.

Since her return to Redditch, Tildy had found varying types of work, and had managed to support herself and her child. Then, a few weeks past, her husband had reappeared in her life. He had tried to force her to return to him, and had ruthlessly used the child as his weapon against her. Driven to desperation, Tildy had invoked the law, and Tom Crawford had been sentenced to a public whipping and a term of hard labour in the Worcester House of Correction, and Tildy had regained her child.

But to invoke the law had cost money, and Tildy had

been forced to borrow what to her was the vast sum of ten guineas from her then employer, Mr Robert Stafford. Now, as she toiled and sweated in the lye shop, Tildy's thoughts were on that debt, and the seeming impossibility of her ever being in a position to repay it. It was not that Robert Stafford was pressing her for repayment. He was a kind-hearted young man who was strongly drawn to Tildy and would have preferred to regard the money as a gift rather than a loan, but Tildy, fiercely proud and independent in spirit, insisted on regarding it as a debt which must be repaid. The difficulty was, how? She sighed heavily and stretched herself to relieve her aching spine. 'Money is the root of all evil!' The saying reverberated in her mind, and she shook her head. 'No! Money is not the evil,' she thought sardonically. 'It's the lack of it, that's the evil.'

Chapter Five

Lack of money was also depressing Marmaduke Montmorency as he sat by the fireside in the Kings Arms tap room nursing the remains of his half-pint of ordinary. Widow Tilsley, the alehouse keeper stared at her solitary customer with a jaundiced eye.

''Ull you be wanting another drink, Montmorency?' she demanded bluntly. 'Because youm getting more benefit from my coals than I'm getting from your presence.'

The man sighed sadly. 'Indeed Ma'am, I would love another drink, but alas, I lack the necessary means of exchange at present. In short, Ma'am, I am bereft of the rhino. My pockets are empty. I have not a penny, nor a half-penny, nor a farthing, nor even the proverbial pot to piss in.' His gin-hoarse voice was that of an educated, cultured man, at bizarre variance with his physical appearance, which resembled a grotesque scarecrow, with broken boots on bare feet, ragged pantaloons, a mildewed soldier's coat covering a shirtless scrawny chest, and a huge tam-o-shanter on his greasy, shoulder-length grey hair. He grinned at the woman, and despite his black stubs of teeth and grime-grained features, there was something appealing in his smile. 'Dare I hope that you will entrust me with a sip of gin, Ma'am, the price of which I will immediately reimburse to you the very moment that my fortunes take a turn for the better?'

The buxom widow snorted indignantly. 'No, you bloody dare not hope, my bucko! Bugger me if you arn't got the hardest neck in Redditch. You still owes for that gin I give you, when Charlotte Readman showed you the door last time. Chucked you out agen for not paying your score, has she?'

Montmorency groaned loudly, threw back his head, lifted both skinny arms heavenwards and declaimed theatrically.

'I see her walking in an air of glory
Whose light doth trample on my days
My days, which are at best but dull and hoary
Mere glimmerings of decay.'

His bleared bloodshot eyes met those of the woman, and he winked slyly. 'Henry Vaughan, born 1621. Died 1695. A wondrous poet, Ma'am, truly a wondrous poet.'

'Well, he arn't wondrous enough to persuade me to give you any more o' my drink on the slate, my bucko,' the widow stated very firmly.

The street door opened and a top-hatted man entered in company with a gust of cold wind. For a moment or two he remained in the open doorway, his eyes studying the room and its two occupants.

'Jesus Christ on the Cross! Close that bloody door, 'ull you!' Widow Tilsley scolded. 'Youm letting all the heat out.'

'My apologies, Ma'am.' The newcomer's accent caused Marmaduke Montmorency to look at him sharply. 'Do you have any victuals?' The man closed the door and came to the fire as he asked the question, and putting his leather valise on the floor held his hands towards the flames. 'Dammee, but it's cruel weather we're having.'

'It is indeed, Sir,' Marmaduke Montmorency agreed heartily. 'In weather like this a man could do worse than drink plenty of hot rum toddy. Much worse!'

Nathanial Farrel's light green eyes made a quick evaluation of the scarecrow figure at the fireside, then he nodded pleasantly. 'Just so, Sir. Just so. Can you prepare me a jug of hot rum toddy, Ma'am, and some food?'

'Indeed I can, Sir. I've some fresh-cooked mutton and greens, or if you prefer I can broil you some beefsteaks, they'll not take long to cook.'

'The beefsteaks will do admirably.' The newcomer smiled at her, showing good teeth. 'And while I'm waiting I'll take a glass or two of gin, London if you have it. Bring me a half-flagon.' He turned to Montmorency. 'You'll join me in a glass, Sir?'

Montmorency inclined his head in gracious acceptance. 'I'll be honoured, Sir.'

Farrel took a golden guinea from his pocket and handed it to Widow Tilsley. 'You'll take a glass of something yourself, I trust, Ma'am.'

The woman bobbed a curtsey, impressed with the easy generosity of the stranger. 'I'll have just a taste of the gin, Sir, and many thanks to you. Now set yourself down here, Sir, by the fire and warm yourself. I'll bring you your order directly.'

In a few moments Farrel was sipping his gin, and very shortly afterwards the appetizing scents of broiling beefsteaks wafted into the tap room from the kitchen at the rear of the house.

Marmaduke Montmorency savoured the biting heat of the fiery spirit and felt its comforting warmth spreading through his wasted body, then asked his benefactor, 'You will be from London originally, Sir, that I'll wager?'

'I am indeed,' Farrel confirmed. 'But it's some years since I resided there. I've travelled a great deal.'

'Might I ask what profession you grace, Sir?' Montmorency pressed, and the other replied vaguely, 'Oh various, Sir. Various. And yourself, Sir? What is your own profession? You appear to be a person of superior attainments.'

Montmorency was too thick skinned to be upset by the mocking overlay in the other's tone, and he felt no constraint in telling him, 'I am an actor, Sir. And without brag, I may say that I am a very good one. But alas! I am at present fallen into distressed circumstances through no fault of my own. My health, Sir, my health betrayed me. Life can be cruel, can it not? Particularly to we of the Thespian persuasion.' He took a reflective swallow of gin, and smacked his lips appreciatively. 'However, there are always consolations to be found, are there not? Even in the very depths of misery and despair there yet spring up hopes of better times to come ... Do you stay long in this town, Sir? Or are you merely passing through?'

'I don't know yet how long I shall be remaining here,' Farrel answered, and in his turn asked, 'Are you a local man, Sir?'

'No, but I have lived here for some years, and I may say without fear of contradiction that despite my present difficulties I am of good name and repute in this district.'

'I don't doubt it for a moment, Sir. You appear very reputable to me.' There was now open mockery in Farrel's voice. He drained his glass and refilled it from the bottle at his elbow on the table. He proffered the bottle to Montmorency. 'You'll take another, Sir. No, I will not accept refusal. You shall join me, and you must share a beefsteak with me as well. I insist on it, Sir.'

Marmaduke Montmorency, silently blessing his good fortune, was again gracious enough to assent to the other's invitation after a suitable gesture of demurral, and during the course of the meal was only too happy to answer his benefactor's apparently casual queries about the town, its trade and its inhabitants.

Chapter Six

It was almost one o'clock in the morning when the women in the lye shop finished work, and all of them were near to exhaustion. When Sarah Farr loudly complained of this fact to the overlooker, Arthur Conolly only told her brutally, 'Shut your bloody gob, Farr. The dry shop and the packers 'ull be working for hours yet, and I'll not get any sleep at all this night, so think yourself lucky youm done wi' it for a few hours.'

When he had gone Sarah Farr lifted her forked fingers in a lewd gesture. 'That's what I says to that bastard.' She grinned tiredly. 'Ah well, let's be on our way, girls. Iffen we walks fast we can get a couple of hours sleep at least.'

'I can't walk fast, can I. So it arn't worth me going home at all,' Old Tabby grumbled. She lived nearly two miles from the mill on the road that led east towards Beoley village. 'I reckon I'll slape here. Old Ben 'ull have a good fire in his cubby. I can set down and have a nap by the side on it.'

Old Ben Wardle was the night-watchman at the mill, and spent most of his time in a deep niche in the brick-work of the entrance tunnel of the mill, which was known as his 'cubbyhole'.

'I 'udden't mind doing the same, Tabby.' Mary Ann Avery yawned and stretched widely. 'Jesus! I'm fair knackered, so I am, but if I don't goo home my man 'ull be frettin' and worritin' in case summat's happened to me.'

Tildy also was tempted by the thought of sitting down by a warm, glowing brazier instead of going out wet,

43

hungry and weary into the freezing night. But the thought of her child was a magnet, and its pull was too strong to be denied.

The four women left the workshop and made their way to the front entrance of the mill. The frail old watchman cursed their appearance in his cracked voice as he was forced to come out from his brazier-warmed niche to unbolt the great gates. 'Can't a man get to set down for a few minutes wi'out being dragged up to open fucking gates for you lot? Youm a bloody nuisance, so you am.'

'Hark to him, Tabby,' Mary Ann teased. 'Does you really want to spend the night sitting by such a miserable, moaning old sod?'

'Who says her can spend the night by my fire?' the old man challenged querulously. 'Who says I'll let her?'

'I does, you stupid old bleeder. And don't think youm agoing to be able to have your way with me neither. I arn't having your cold hands between me legs on a night like this. So you needn't think your luck's in,' Old Tabby cackled. 'I knows you of old, Ben Wardle, and what a dirty-minded old bugger you be.'

The watchman's mood abruptly transformed, and he laughed wheezily. 'Ahr, and you knows it 'udden't be the fust time I'se snuggled into your cuckoo's nest, and on colder nights nor this 'un as well, Tabby Merry.'

The old crone cuffed his skull-like head with mock ferocity. 'Don't you be atelling these innocent young maidens all our sinful secrets, you old devil.'

Despite her weariness, Tildy chuckled at the rough humour and was heart-warmed by the display of genuine camaraderie.

'You look arter our Tabby now, and make sure her keeps warm and snug, Ben,' Mary Ann told him. 'I wants to find her safe and rested when I comes in at five o'clock.'

'She 'ull be, never you fear.' The old man's voice was fond. 'Me and Tabby bin good friends for manys the long year arn't us, girl?' He turned to the old woman for confirmation, and in her turn she smiled with a genuine fondness.

44

'That we has, Ben. That we has.'

The gate creaked open and the freezing darkness enveloped the three women as they walked in company up the slightly sloping roadway that led into the town.

The centre of the hilly town of Redditch was built on a small plateau, its streets, alleys and courts radiating from a triangular green, in the south-west corner of which stood the single-storeyed, cupolad Chapel of St Stephen, overlooking the main crossroads of the town. From this plateau the land fell away to the east, west and north into the broad saucer-like valley of the River Arrow and its smaller western tributary, the Red Ditch. To the south of the town the land rose sharply in a narrow ridgeway alternately wooded and built upon. The road which ran eastwards from the main crossroads forked a hundred yards from the chapel at the Gothic arched, castellated new lock-up, the recently built town jail. The right hand fork was Red Lion Street, taking its name from the inn which stood along it on the right hand side of the roadway some fifty yards from the lock-up.

At the side of this inn was a narrow archway giving access to a long, crooked, narrow alley of mean hovels. This alley, the Silver Street, debouched into the Silver Square, a fetid quadrangle of ramshackle houses and cottages. Mother Readman's lodging house was the largest, tallest building in the square, standing some four storey high, and was licensed to shelter up to thirty bodies nightly. A legal limitation totally disregarded by its formidable proprietress. She had been known to cram ten times that number beneath her roof on Fair and Mart days. Her charges for shelter varied greatly. For a penny a night a man could lie on the floor or sit on a bench and drape his upper body across a supporting rope. For two pence he could share a bed with four or five others. For a shilling he could have a bed to himself. If he wished to spend the night with a companion, then for two shillings he could have a private room.

All Mother Readman's guests were entitled to one

same privilege. They had entrée to the great kitchen with its ever-burning fire. In winter this was the main attraction, since all other fireplaces in the building had long since been bricked up. Too many of Mother Readman's doors and floorboards had ended as ashes in those fireplaces for her to allow such amenities to continue. So the only source of heat in the building apart from the kitchen fire was whatever warmth could be got from a candle flame. It was for this reason that Tildy now went directly to the kitchen when she arrived back at the lodging house. Her sodden clothing clung clammily to her body and legs and she knew that she must dry it now or face the dismal prospect of putting it back on still icily sodden after scant hours of sleep.

The low-ceiling room encompassed the entire rear area of the ground floor, its walls thick-grimed and greased by the countless bodies that had leaned upon them. Rough-hewn tables and benches lined the walls leaving the centre space clear, and even at this late hour men, women and children crammed those benches; and bundles, baskets, dogs, and crawling infants littered the centre space, filling the air with noise, tobacco fumes, and the odours of unwashed bodies and clothing, the reek of ale, gin and rum and a myriad of foodstuffs. The rushlights guttering in their wall-brackets added their own rancid vapours and smoke to the thick fug. A huge inglenook dominated the far wall, a fire blazing in its iron basket, and a big iron cauldron of Mother Readman's notorious penny-a-bowl stew hung seething and bubbling and steaming suspended by a thick rust chain above the leaping flames.

As befitted the monarch of the domain, Mother Readman was enthroned to one side of the inglenook in a huge armchair which, capacious though it was, hardly served to contain her massively bloated body. Swathed in layers of dark petticoats and shawls, her frizzed mass of grey hair half-hidden by a grimy mob-cap, Mother Readman kept careful vigil over her guests with darting eyes slitted in puffballs of fat in a moonlike, tallowy face.

Around her were ranged her current courtiers, just as ragged and dirty as the other guests, but proudly basking in their favoured proximity to this absolute ruler of this miniature realm.

The scar-faced old harridan noted Tildy's arrival, and with a wave of her hand caused the stool next to her chair to be vacated immediately. 'Set down here, my duck. Youm bloody perished by the look on you,' she greeted the girl, for whom she had much respect and affection.

Tildy was truly grateful for the kindness, and shivering she seated herself and hunched her upper body towards the flaring coals, spreading her sodden skirts so that they might catch the heat and begin to dry out.

On the far side of Mother Readman a skinny, wizened little creature, whose grotesquely swollen belly denoted an advanced pregnancy, grinned gap-toothed at Tildy and told her, 'Davy's bin sleeping since ten o'clock, Tildy. He 'udden't rest afore because you hadn't come home, but I managed to get him off at last. His little yed was nodding, so it was.'

Tildy smiled and thanked the girl warmly. 'I'm truly grateful to you, Apollonia. I'm sorry I'm so late, but they made us work over.'

Apollonia was Mother Readman's deputy and general factotum, a fourteen-years-old parish bastard, whom the old woman had sheltered and protected for many years. But despite all her efforts she had not been able to prevent the girl selling herself to whatever clientele she could find among the dregs of the town. Apart from her sexual proclivities however, Apollonia was a good-natured, trustworthy little creature who loved Mother Readman with a fierce possessiveness, and adored Tildy's child, little Davy.

As the heat of the fire penetrated Tildy's stiff, chilled body she slowly relaxed and became aware of just how weary she really was. She could not suppress a yawn, and Mother Readman touched her shoulder and said gently, 'Listen, Tildy, you ate a bowl o' stew, and then you get on

47

up to your bed. Apollonia 'ull come up wi' you and fetch your clothes back down here, and I'll dry 'um for you.'

Tainted and unappetizing though it was, Tildy spooned the food voraciously until the wooden bowl was empty and her gnawing hunger pains stilled. Although she was immersed in the satisfying of her body's urgent needs, she still experienced an uneasy sense of strange eyes fixed upon her, and when she had eaten she let her gaze wander about the room, trying to pinpoint the source of her uneasiness.

The staring eyes belonged to a man sitting halfway along the room with his back against the wall. Even in the uncertain light Tildy could see that his appearance was considerably more respectable than the usual frequenters of the lodging house. At his side another man was sprawled across the table, snoring loudly, and Tildy could not help but smile as she recognized Marmaduke Montmorency. She turned and asked Mother Readman, 'I thought Marmaduke had been banned again?'

The old woman chuckled hoarsely. 'How many times has I banned the old bugger, Tildy? Is it one thousand, or two? I reckon I must have a soft spot for the old villain, because I always lets him in agen, and he always cadges summat more from me. Mind you,' she added regarding Tildy quizzically, 'I arn't the only one he manages to wheedle his way round, am I? If I recollects rightly he's had more nor a few shillings from you as well in his time.'

Tildy smiled wryly, remembering all the times the likeable old reprobate had wheedled money from her own scant resources. 'I'll not argue with that, Mother Readman,' she murmured.

'He's found hisself a new mate tonight, and he's come wi' money in his britches. He's even paid some of his score off. That's his mate with him, the cove who's bin astaring at you all this time.' The old woman missed very little of what went on in her house. 'Bit of a mystery man, that 'un is, arn't he? A sight too well dressed for to be here. Still, so long as he pays his way, and behaves hisself, he's as welcome to stay as the others be. He arn't bothering you is he, girl, staring like that?'

Tildy shook her head tiredly. Now that she had identified the source of her uneasy awareness she gave the staring man no further thought. Although not vain, she was well aware that many men found her physically attractive and was accustomed to their hungry stares. She yawned uncontrollably once more, and muttered, 'I must get some sleep, Mother Readman, or I'll not be able to rise from my bed in time for work tomorrow.'

Apollonia also rose to her feet, her belly jutting out monstrously from her stick-like body. 'Come on then, Tildy, let's away, and I'll fetch your clothes back here with me.'

Nathanial Farrel's light green eyes watched the beautiful, dark-haired young woman as she moved past his table with lissom grace, and thought appreciatively, 'By God, that's the sweetest piece of womanflesh I've encountered in many a day. I'll needs try to get to know her better, after all, there's naught wrong in mixing a bit o' pleasure with business, is there?'

Chapter Seven

Josh Dyson had finished his extra time at ten o'clock, and when he left the mill, instead of going to his cottage he continued on up the steep Back Hill towards the long slope of Mount Pleasant. At the top of the steep rise where the Front Hill, Back Hill and Mount Pleasant junctioned stood a large public house, the Duke of York, and a little further on up the Mount Pleasant another smaller beerhouse known as the Black Horse. It was to the smaller house that Josh Dyson directed his footsteps.

The door was closed, and the house appeared dark and deserted, but when Dyson knocked there came from inside the sound of clogs on stone flags and a nervous voice asking, 'Who's out theer?'

'Josh Dyson.'

'Are you by yourself?'

'Yes.'

The bolts were slammed noisily back and the door opened to admit him.

'I expected you an hour since. Wheer the hell as you bin?' The speaker's voice was irritable with nervous strain.

'Calm yourself, I'm here now.' Dyson patted the other's shoulder.

It was John Whateley, the beerhouse keeper, a short, thick-set, swarthy-faced man in his late twenties whose protuberant paunch was his badge of trade.

'Is he come?' Dyson asked, and the other nodded in the darkness, for he carried no light with him.

'That's why I'm closed up. I daren't let anyone see him until you gets to see him fust, and check him out.'

50

'Good,' Dyson grunted. 'You showed good sense in that. We'se got to show care.'

He followed Whateley through the darkness up to a small, shuttered bedroom where a solitary candle shed a pale weak light. The sole furnishing of the room was a low wooden pallet with blankets tumbled upon it. A man was seated on this pallet who rose to his feet when Dyson came into the room. The hardener said nothing, only picked up the candle from the windowsill and held it so that the man's features could be clearly seen. For some moments Dyson's hard eyes studied the other closely, taking in every detail of the thin, sun-tanned, pockmarked face, thick with grey stubble on throat and cheeks, the close-cropped grey hair, the deep-sunk eyes and scrawny, under-nourished, rough-clad body.

The other man's eyes betrayed apprehension and tight-stretched nerves, and skittered from side to side uneasily until finally Dyson nodded, and greeted the man. 'Hello Will Stevens, we're well met.'

The other's taut, twitching body sagged visibly as he gusted a sigh of relief, and he began to babble volubly, but Dyson placed his hand across the dry lips and silenced the spate. 'We'll go downstairs and take a sup of ale. We can talk easier sitting at a table and warming ourselves by the fire like good Christians.'

John Whately was smiling broadly now. 'Yes, lads, that's the ticket. Come on down to the tap room, I've got a good fire there.'

Only when the three of them were sitting around a table with a jug of beer apiece in front of them and horn tots to drink it from did Dyson speak again. 'Now Will, Jack here knows naught about you, so afore anything else I reckon it's best if I tells him how I come to know you.'

The man nodded assent, and Dyson turned to Whateley who eagerly leaned towards him to listen. 'You'll remember the Pentrich uprising in Derbyshire back in June o' '17?'

'I remember,' Whateley observed grimly. 'And I

remember what happened to 'um as well. Three on 'um hung and be-yedded and fourteen transported, wi' more put in jail here at home.'

Dyson grinned savagely. 'Ahr, the Government was uncommon lenient that time, warn't it?' His thoughts ranged back across the years, remembering all those other working men hung, or transported, or imprisoned when driven beyond endurance by hunger and deprivation they had exploded into violent outbreaks against entrenched authority. A violence engendered by their total lack of any peaceful recourse to get their terrible plight ameliorated. Dyson scowled bitterly, and went on with his story. 'Will here was trying to organize the Nottingham men to act together with the Derbyshire lads. I was doing the same thing in the Black Country, that's how I come to know Will, because we was delegates at the same meetings at times. After the rising was crushed, he managed to escape to America. I didn't need to run because I wasn't present at the rising, and couldn't be charged with anything. Anyway, a few months since I got a letter from Will telling me he wanted to come back home. To spake honest, I think him a fool for coming back, but then, a man's country always keeps a powerful hold on his heart, and I can understand how it can draw a man back to it, even though he risks his life by returning. Anyway, I wrote back and said I'd help, and he's back now, and going to be working wi' us.'

John Whateley offered his hand to Stevens, and they solemnly shook. 'Youm more than welcome, Will,' the publican told him warmly. 'We faces a hard row to hoe in this town though, I'll tell you no lies about that. The buggers here got no political notions at all, excepting for the masters and gentry, and they'm all true-blue Tories. King and Church men every one on 'um.'

Stevens's nervous tension had left him now, and his confidence had returned. 'Well, as to that, John, I reckon that us three has got all the political notions that be needful. All we wants of our members is that they does as

52

we directs 'um to do. Are there many with you at present?'

It was Dyson who answered. 'We arn't really recruited too many yet, Will. We'se got a few likely lads though. But while you'se bin out of the country a lot has happened to make our cause harder to fight. There's still plenty of spies and "provocation men" floating about the land, and don't forget that Thistlewood put the fear o' Christ up the Government only a couple o' years since.'

'Yes, but he ended by being hung and be-yedded as well,' Whateley remarked.

'So, Will, pay heed to what I say,' Dyson told him gravely. 'The days when we could risk public meetings and marches be over. Any union we forms must remain hidden, and be as secret as the grave. We must tread very, very careful, or we could well find ourselves hanging from a gibbet in an iron waistcoat and a black-tar shroud. Our first task is to get you fixed up wi' work, and a place to live.'

He explained now to John Whateley, 'Will was a needlemaker in a small way o' business for himself up in Nottingham, John, so he's well used to the trade, and I reckon we'll be able to get him fixed up without much bother. His name from now on is Will Stacey. His story is that he's an old comrade of mine from the army, who's bin out in America following his trade of needlemaker. His business has failed and he's fell on hard times, so is looking for work and settlement here. I reckon our best course is to be plain and open about our all being known to each other like this, because if we should try to hide it and then be seen meeting furtive-like, that'll get folks' tongues wagging the wrong way. There's nothing so well hid, as that which lies in plain sight, so to speak.'

His companions considered this for a few seconds, then nodded agreement, and Dyson went on, 'Right then, friends, just as soon as Will get's settled and becomes familiar wi' the people here, then we'll really begin. We'll get organized and strong in numbers and then—' He broke off, his eyes staring as if he saw something beyond the sight of his companions.

'What then, Josh? When we'em organized, what then?' John Whateley questioned excitedly, and Dyson blinked hard and swung to gaze at his questioner, then grinned ferociously.

'Why then, John, then we'll begin to set a few things to rights in this bloody town. We'll light a few fires under the arses of the masters and the gentry.'

Chapter Eight

The Right Honourable and Reverend Walter Hutchinson, Lord Aston, Vicar of Tardebigge Parish and Justice of the Peace of the County of Worcestershire had also been thinking a great deal about the subject of workmen's combinations and unions during the previous few weeks. Although the immediate threat of bloody revolution appeared to have disappeared from England, the labouring masses still seethed in bitter discontent with their rulers, and Reverend the Lord Aston was acutely aware of the need for a constant vigilance to be maintained. The many-headed ogre of revolutionary radicalism still stalked the land, despite the lopping off of so many of its heads during the past decade.

There were those among his fellow magistrates who scoffed at the Reverend's constant insistence on the need for vigilance, telling him that since the failure of the Cato Street plot there was no longer any possibility of an armed insurrection. That even the most rabid and obdurate Radicals had now abandoned the idea of force, and were instead concentrating their efforts on achieving a peaceful, legal mode of obtaining the reforms they sought. But Lord Aston prided himself on his percipience. He knew what he was about, and was not to be lulled into any false sense of security. Not all the 'men of blood' had yet been hunted down, there were many of them still hidden among the misguided masses, still awaiting their opportunity to unleash fire, rapine and slaughter throughout the realm.

In appearance the noble clergyman was a bulky-bodied, dyspeptic man of some fifty years who always favoured the black, full-skirted coat, knee-breeches and stockings of his calling, with a white, short-queued tie-wig perched on his shiny, bald pink pate. His heavy, sallow features were moulded in the permanent scowl of the martyr to gluttony and the concomitant chronic indigestion.

He sat now before the blazing fire in his book-lined study, and once again pored over the report he had received some weeks previously from the Clerk to the Magistrates, Joseph Blackwell, Esq. The report concerned the efforts of a young local man, Robert Stafford, to set himself up in business as a needle master during the closing months of the previous year. Robert Stafford had, according to Blackwell, acquired the patent rights for a device known as the magnetic muzzle, which was designed to prevent the murderous affliction of 'pointer's rot'.

Although Lord Aston had no financial interest or involvement in the needle trade, still he knew a considerable amount about its manufacturing processes. He knew that the needles were hand-pointed by the dry-grinding process, the needle pointers spending their days hunched over whirling grindstones, breathing in the fine dust of steel and stone. This find dust penetrated the lungs of the men and within a few years destroyed the internal tissues and brought the pointers to an early and agonizing death.

Stafford's idea had been to introduce the magnetic safety device and thus render the pointing process much safer and less harmful to the pointers. The young man had then proposed to lower the very high wages that the pointers earned, justifying this on the grounds that the men would no longer be facing almost certain early death as a result of their murderous occupation.

Lord Aston regarded the pointers as being brute beasts. They were a breed apart, violent and lawless, respecting neither God, King nor their fellow men,

56

spending their hard-won wages in drunken riot and debauchery.

The cleryman's stomach rumbled and he belched sourly, and silently called on his God to witness his sufferings. ' Tis now wonder I'm a martyr to dyspepsia, Lord. How can I hope for a sound digestion when I am beset by so many pressing problems, and none of them of my own making?' His loose-lipped mouth pouted petulantly, and again he tried to concentrate on the lines of neat handwriting. Young Stafford's proposals had received short shrift from the pointers, who had refused to use the new device. In desperation the young would-be needle master had even persuaded some women to do his pointing, but this too had been a failure. The pointers, acting it appeared in concert, had frightened away Stafford's workforce, and had forced the young man to abandon his business and smash his magnetic muzzles ...

Aston frowned thoughtfully. The pointers had appeared to act in concert. If this was indeed the case, if they had acted in organized unity, then they had broken the law, and could be brought to trial and punished with the utmost severity if found guilty.

When he had first received Blackwell's report, the clergyman, acting in his magisterial capacity, had immediately forwarded a copy to the Right Honourable Robert Peel, M.P., the new Secretary of State for the Home Department. He had received a brusque acknowledgement from that office, and had heard nothing since.

'It's a great pity that Lord Sidmouth resigned from that position, and a tragedy that Castlereagh took his own life. When they were responsible for law and order a report such as I sent would have been treated as a matter of the utmost urgency and importance. At the very least an experienced agent would have been despatched to this parish to investigate the possibility that those dammed pointers have organized themselves into a combination.' The clergyman vented an exclamation of mingled indignation and disgust. 'Ah well, at least I know where my duty lies. I must needs do whatever I can myself to keep a vigilant watch on the situation. As if I were not sufficiently over-burdened with labour already!'

Chapter Nine

As the weeks passed Tildy became inured to the pungent vapours of the lye shop. She learned to endure the discomfort of constantly saturated clothing, and to bite on her lips when the lye got into the cracks which had developed on her hands and bit agonizingly into raw flesh. She took in her stride the heavy physical work entailed by the fetching and carrying of water, the endless emptying and replenishing of copper and tubs. Her body, for all its shapely femininity, was surprisingly lithe and strong.

She was friendly with her workmates, but her innate reserve and fastidiousness of mind always restrained her from the coarseness of language and the licence of the intimate confidences that the other women exchanged among themselves. Tildy would listen, and smile or sympathize, but keep her own counsel. For their part her workmates liked her well, and although at times they would tease her for being reserved, this teasing was affectionate rather than malicious. Taking it all in all Tildy found her working life bearable, and although she wished with all her heart to better her position in life for the benefit of her child, she was wise enough to realize that compared to many women she knew her life was comparatively unstressed.

Recently she had heard news which had relieved her mind of one pressing burden at least. Her husband had been taken from the Worcester House of Correction by the Bow Street Runners and returned to London to face criminal charges arising from his sojourn in that city. It seemed that this time he could not possibly escape a sentence of transportation, and for this Tildy could only feel thankful. It meant that she could now concentrate on making a life for herself and her child without the dread prospect of her husband coming back to torture them both with his threats and his violence.

Another more recent problem remained to be dealt with, however. During the last few days the overlooker, Arthur Conolly, had become increasingly sexually suggestive towards her, and although Tildy was not a prude, she fiercely resented the man's lewd approaches. To her, one of the most unpleasant aspects of life in the Fountain Mill was the casual assumption of many of the male operatives that the women and girls working there were fair game for the gratification of their sexual appetites. Tildy accepted that there were some women and girls who encouraged the men to take liberties with them, but she knew that many of the female workers felt as she did. Unfortunately for her and them, the world they inhabited was male-dominated, and those men to whom they might turn for protection from such harassment, such as the overlookers and needle masters, were in all too many instances just as predatory as their underlings and, even more unfortunately, were in a position to exert greater pressures on the women and girls to accept their advances and to comply with their desires.

A week previously the lye shop workforce had been augmented by a new girl, Meg Tullet. She was twelve years old, but strong and well-built for her age. One of a pauper widow's numerous brood, Meg was pleasant-featured and sweet-natured, but was mentally backward and so clumsy that she could manage only the simplest of menial tasks. It was for this reason that she had been sent to act as a water-carrier for the lye shop, lugging heavy buckets from the well in the corner of the main courtyard, other departments having tried her and found her sadly wanting in the speed and dexterity necessary for the hand-fashioning of needles.

Tildy pitied the child, and tried to help her all she could, and in return Meg Tullet conceived a deep attachment for her new-found friend.

It was Monday, the tenth day of February and the morrow was Shrove Tuesday, a traditional holiday in the district. Many workpeople took the entire day off, and all had at least a half-day break. Henry Milward had issued instructions that extra time be worked that night so that the week's production levels might be maintained despite the holiday and although it was now near on midnight the mill still throbbed with activity. Several workpeople had sent out to the public houses for gin and strong beer, and had been drinking heavily while they toiled, anticipating the festivities to come. The lye shop women had also been drinking and Sarah Farr was half-tipsy, while Old Tabby was reduced to sitting down on the plank at intervals to steady her reeling head. Tildy herself, although normally abstemious, had also taken a few sips of the gin and strong beer and was feeling a trifle lightheaded.

Will Kitchen came in with several purses of needles and dropped the heavy buckram rolls by the side of the bubbling copper. Like most of his workmates he too was half-drunk, and he grinned lopsidedly at Tildy. 'Here you be, my honey-bee. These 'um the last. When they'm done you'll all be able to get off home.'

She nodded acknowledgment, and he came nearer to her. 'There'll be high jinks tomorrow, Tildy. If I wins the Shrove cock I'll give it to you for a kiss.'

'You'll do better to give it to your sweetheart, Will,' Tildy told him, smiling. 'Because you'll get no kisses from me.'

'Supposing I wins you two cocks, what then?'

'Not even if you win me twenty cocks, my lad.'

He assumed an exaggerated expression of doleful disappointment and demanded dramatically, 'Does you hear her, girls? She steals me 'eart, and then breaks

61

it like it was naught but an old clay pot.'

'Be off wi' you, Will Kitchen! We'em too busy to listen to your nonsense right now,' Mary Ann Avery, herself a little tipsy, scolded, and then asked Tildy, 'Wheer's young Meg at? This copper needs topping up agen.'

Tildy straightened up from the tub she was bent over. 'I sent her for water ages ago,' she said, and asked the youth, 'Did you see Meg by the well when you came in here, Will?'

'I saw her a while since. Johnny Brompton was talking to her, and I see'd him give her a drink from his flask o' gin.' The youth made a lewd gesture with his figures. 'Tight bastard, he is. Never gives a drop to the lads, and only to the girls when he's arter a bit.'

Tildy exchanged a look of concern with Mary Ann. Johnny Brompton was an overlooker who was notorious for his constant sexual advances towards the younger girls in the mill.

'I'm going out to look for her,' Tildy declared, and Mary Ann nodded.

'Yes, my duck, you goo and find her. No telling what that bastard Brompton 'ull try and get up to wi' the poor little cratur, her being so bloody simple-yedded her wun't know any different. I'll empty these tubs while youm gone.'

Will Kitchen leered salaciously at the women. 'What's you getting all moithered up about the wench for? Johnny Brompton wun't be the fust 'un who's got between her legs. Why begrudge him a bit o' fun?'

'Shut your rattle, you young varmint,' Mary Ann shouted angrily.

Tildy hurried out of the shop, along the passageway and into the dark courtyard. As she moved across the cobbles her eyes adjusted to the darkness which was lanced by dim shafts of light from the different workshops. At the well she found the two buckets the girl had taken with her resting on the wall of the well-housing. One bucket was filled, the other empty.

62

'Meg? Meg, where are you?' Tildy called. A muffled cry came from the open-fronted stable shed built as a lean-to against the wall beyond the well.

'Meg, is that you?' Tildy called again as she hurried towards the shed. When she reached it she could hear the sounds of heavy bodies thrashing upon the heap of dry straw that covered half the shed's floor, and again the muffled, half-choked cry came from that heaving dark mound on the straw.

'What's happening here?' Tildy yelled. 'Who's inside here?'

The black, heaving mound abruptly separated into two halves and Meg's voice shrieked, 'He's trying to shag me, Tildy! Johnny Brompton's trying to shag me!' The girl came into Tildy's arms with a stumbling rush, and she quickly led her outside into the light cast by an overhead window. The child's bodice was open and her firm young breasts were uncovered. She was near to hysteria, her breathing a series of sobbing gasps and pants.

'What has he done to you, Meg? Tell me what he's done!' Tildy beseeched the distressed girl.

'I've done naught the little slut warn't abegging me for.' Johnny Brompton came from the dark interior to face them in the light. He was lacing up the front flap of his breeches, and his coat, shirt and waistcoat were all unbuttoned, showing his chest with its mat of grey hairs.

'I didn't want to touch him wheer he made me,' Meg shrieked wildly. 'And he kept putting his hands all over me. He 'udden't stop, Tildy. I tried to get away from him, and he 'udden't stop. And then, when you come, he was trying to stick his thing in me. He was hurting me, and trying to stick his thing in me and shag me.'

'Shurrup, you little cow!' Brompton stepped towards them, and even at this distance Tildy could smell the reek of gin and beer that came from his mouth.

Meg shuddered and buried her face into Tildy's breasts, her hands and arms clinging desperately. 'Don't

63

let him get me agen, Tildy! Please don't let him get me agen,' she begged frantically.'He'll hurt me agen, so he will. I'm feared on him, Tildy. I'm sore feared.'

Tildy moved further back with the girl and glared angrily at the powerfully built, middle-aged overlooker. 'You keep well away from her, you dirty animal,' she hissed, her hot temper flaring as she felt the violent trembling of the child's body beneath her fingers.

He scowled threateningly. 'Don't you be becalling me, you fancy-speaking bitch! Me and that little slut theer was only having a bit o' fun, that's all.'

Unnoticed by either of them, Will Kitchen had run to bring others to see what was happening, and a sizeable group had congregated some yards away and were avidly watching the confrontation.

'Fun?' Tildy hurled the word like a missile at the overlooker's head. 'Is that what you call an attempted rape? To hurt a child and frighten her half to death, is that your idea of fun? If I were a man, I'd break your head for you, you vile bastard!' She trembled herself with the force of her anger.

'I warned you once about becalling me, didn't I? I'll be breaking your yed now, you big-mouthed cunt!' Brompton's fists balled and he lurched at Tildy, but before he could reach her another figure came from the watching crowd and intervened, jolting the oncoming man to a halt with a stiff-armed shove.

'Been messing about wi' the young girls agen, I see, Brompton.'

The overlooker shook his shaggy head. 'This is none o' your business, Josh Dyson, so just step out o' my way.'

'I'll step out of your way, Brompton, once I'm certain that you'll not lay a finger on either o' these wenches,' the hardener told him evenly.

The overlooker's features twisted with fury, but he made no move forwards, and Dyson spoke over his shoulder to Tildy. 'Do you need anything more here, Tildy Crawford?'

Tildy jerked her chin towards the buckets on the well-housing. 'We need water.'

'Then draw it,' the hardener said coolly, 'and then go back to your work ... Do as I say,' he urged, when she seemed hesitant to move past Brompton towards the well. 'No one 'ull lay a finger on you whiles I'm here.'

His calm confidence reassured Tildy and, ushering Meg towards the lye shop, she went herself to the well and drew the water she needed. Then, with a smile of gratitude to Josh Dyson, she returned to the lye shop.

Once there she quickly related all that had occurred to her friends. They cursed and voiced threats against Johnny Brompton until Mary Ann silenced the others curtly.

'Just let's be thankful he arn't done any real harm to the girl. He didn't manage to shove it up her, thanks to Tildy.' She stroked snivelling Meg's greasy, matted mass of hair, still covered with straw and chaff from her struggle with Brompton. 'You'll be all right, my duck. We'll all on us keep a careful eye over you from now on. None o' the bloody men 'ull get near to you agen.' She smiled ruefully at Tildy, and told her in a low voice, 'Mind you, Tildy, if Brompton had of managed to get what he wanted, it 'udden't ha' bin the fust time it's happened to this pitiful cratur. Not by a long score it 'udden't.'

'Have they made free with her while she's been working here at the Fountain then?' Tildy demanded, her anger still seething.

'Well, from what I hears, a few o' the men have had her on the quiet.' Mary Ann's plump, motherly face was sad, but it mirrored an attitude of reluctant acceptance of these matters. 'What else can you expect, Tildy? A simple-yedded wench, wi' no feyther or brother to protect her, and a mam who's naught but a simpleton herself that's had kids by half-a-dozen different chaps. Meg's bound to be chased by the men, and her arn't ill-looking, is her, which makes it worse for her in that way. It's God's own

65

mercy that her arn't bin copped for a babby herself yet. That's summat to be grateful for.'

'God's own mercy, is it?' The normally soft-toned, mild-tempered Tildy spoke with such venom that the other women stared at her in astonishment. 'I'd like to know when God has ever shown mercy on this earth to the likes of this poor little child?' She answered her own question. 'Never! Never as far as I've ever seen. But I think it's about time something was done to alter this state of affairs. Girls should be able to come to their work without having to be mauled about and worse by the men.'

'Maybe they should, Tildy, but what can we do about it? It's always bin this way, and I don't doubt that it always 'ull be, no matter what the likes of us might say.' Mary Ann's tone was both defensive, and resentful of Tildy for forcing her to face these unpalatable facts.

'Well, I'm going to have words with the Master about what's happened this night,' Tildy stated forcefully. 'I'll go direct to him when we finish work, and I'll tell him what's going on in his damned mill. He's a chapel warden, isn't he? One of the "Sunday-go-to-church" brigade, so we'll see what he intends doing to put a stop to the wicked goings-on in this place.'

Her companions were aghast. 'You can't do such a thing as that Tildy!' Sarah Farr exclaimed fearfully. 'Old Henry 'ull not pay any heed to a lye shop woman, and he'll never take her word agen that of one of his over-lookers.'

'Then if he won't take my word, supposing I ask Josh Dyson to go with me and confirm what I say?' Tildy challenged. 'Josh Dyson understood well what had been happening, that's why he protected Meg and me like he did.'

'Now Tildy, you just stay quiet for a minute and hark to me,' Mary Ann instructed firmly. 'Youm thinking like a fool iffen you reckons that Henry Milward 'ull give a hoot about what's happened here this night. Be you really so foolish as to think that he don't already know very well what's agoing on between the men and the wenches in this mill?' Her question was purely rhetorical. 'Youm a newcomer to this trade, Tildy, but all on us has spent our lives at it. I knew Henry Milward when he worked for his old dad down by Studley theer. Men chasing and tormenting wenches has always bin part and parcel of whatever men and women does that throw's 'um into close touch wi' each other. That's the way o' the world, Tildy. The only thing you'll get by going to Henry Milward is to be handed your bloody sack.

'Now I'll say no more on the matter than this, Tildy: what you does is up to yourself, but I arn't going to let you drag young Meg into it with you. Meg's mam desperate needs the money the wench earns here. If you makes the poor cratur lay complaint agen Johnny Brompton, then it's nigh on certain that her 'ull end up wi' the sack as well. It's like Sarah already told you, the masters never listens to anything said agen their overlookers. Arter all, it's them that chooses the overlookers in the fust place. They'm the masters' men. And if Meg gets her sack from here, then that'll mean the poor'us for her mam and her young brothers and sisters. So you calm yourself down and think hard afore you does anything, Tildy. I knows that you means only the best towards this pitiful cratur here, but you really don't know what a wasp's nest youm disturbing if you starts to try and make trouble for an overlooker. You arn't bin here long enough yet, my wench, to truly know what youm about.'

Twice Tildy opened her lips to make retort, and twice she closed them again without uttering the angry words that formed on her tongue. No matter how unpalatable it was to her, she was forced to recognize the truth in what Mary Ann said. Eventually she nodded and conceded reluctantly, 'Mayhap you're right, Mary Ann. Mayhap it would be best if I kept my tongue between my teeth. But it makes my blood boil to have to do so.'

'Your blood 'udden't have bin let to boil in my day. In

my day women was happy to stay in their place.' Old Tabby's voice was slurred with drunkeness. 'And the place they had to stay in, whether they liked it or not, was underneath their menfolk.' She cackled with sudden laughter. 'Theer now, I'se just said a droll thing, arn't I, our place be underneath our menfolk. Bugger me, I ought to know that all right, I spent enough bleedin' hours alying underneath my old man ... He was a reglar ram, so he was, the dirty old bastard!'

The old crone's interjection seemed to lessen some of the tension in the room, and Tildy began to untie one of the rolls of buckram.

'Well then, Tildy, be you going to let things lie? Because to my mind it 'ud be best if you did,' Mary Ann queried and advised in the same breath.

Tildy avoided answering. In her mind her familiar demon of stubbornness had arisen to torment her, badgering her relentlessly. 'Why should dirty animals like Brompton be let walk away without punishment after trying to rape a mentally backward child? Why should a condition of we women being able to work here be the men thinking they have licence to maul us about, and talk to us as if we were sixpenny whores? It's not right, and it never has been right! It's time we women stood up and demanded that we be treated with some respect by those men who work with us, and who employ us. We're not brute beasts, fit only to do as they bid or wish. We also deserve to be able to walk through our lives with some dignity. Our being poor, and female, does not mean that we are inferior in any physical or mental sense ... Then tell me, Tildy, tell me how you are going to change the way of things?' the tiny voice of doubt jeered in her mind. 'How are you, a lye wash woman, ever going to have men listen to your demands, and more importantly, pay any heed to them? You are nothing in the scheme of things, Tildy. Nothing!' For a brief while doubt almost overwhelmed her, then Tildy's stubborn courage rallied, counter-attacked, and swept on irresistibly.

'Oh yes, I'll change things,' she muttered beneath her breath. 'Somehow, somewhere, someday, I'll change things, and men will listen and pay heed to what I have to say ...'

Chapter Ten

At fifteen minutes to eleven o'clock of the morning of Tuesday, 11th February, Joseph Davis laid aside his hammer, spat the tacks from between his lips, rose from his last and took off his cobbler's apron. From its peg on the door he lifted his dark swallow-tailed coat and drew it onto his narrow shoulders. He looked appraisingly around his tiny workshop redolent with the smell of leather and fish-glue and polishes, and reminded himself that he must once more chastise his two sons for so abysmally failing in their set tasks of cleaning the numerous shoes and boots which filled every nook and cranny of the cramped room.

'Missus Davis?' he shouted in his sonorous voice, and from the living quarters at the rear his short fat wife came hurrying in dutiful obedience to her tall, thin husband's command. Wags in the town called the couple 'Jack Spratt and his wife', a fact which intensely aggravated Joseph Davis.

'Wheer's my hat and gloves, Missus Davis?' He frowned sternly at her, and she blushed and flustered defensively.

'I never knew that you wanted 'um, Mister Davis.'

His frown deepened. 'Does you mean to tell me that you don't remember what day this is, Missus Davis?'

Her bovine features showed clearly the agonized effort of thought, and then she smiled with relief. 'O' course I does. It's Pancake Day, o' course.'

Her husband snorted through his long, thin nose in impatience. 'And what happens on Pancake Day, Missus Davis? What are my official duties on that day?'

70

Again her features twisted as she racked her sluggish brain, and again she finally smiled in relief. 'Why, you must ring the batter bell, Mister Davis.'

'Exactly so, woman,' he declared sonorously. 'And would you have me go to my duties not properly clad?'

'Ohhhh, you'll be wanting your hat and gloves, won't you, Mister Davis!'

He sighed with the air of one labouring patiently under an awful affliction. 'Exactly so, Missus Davis. Exactly so.'

She bustled out and re-appeared almost instantly with the tall black hat and black woollen gloves.

While he donned these articles he issued a stream of instructions to her. 'If Charles Scambler calls, his high-lows are on the shelf there. Give them a polish when I go. If Mrs Shakles sends for her boots, tell her my parish duties have prevented the completion, but they'll be ready first thing tomorrow. If Will Gibbs passes by, stop him and tell him I'll be needing three hides for Monday, and tell him I want cows, not horses, and I want good quality. That last hide I took from him had more blemishes than Job's skin.'

She walked behind her husband to the low doorway of the shop and watched him stride across the green towards the Chapel of St Stephen, in her simplicity thinking him a very grand figure.

Joseph Davis would have agreed with his wife's opinion, for he regarded himself as a person of great consequence in the parish. He was paid five guineas a year to act as the vestry clerk, but the money he regarded as only the cream on the cake. The cake being the job itself which brought him into close and intimate contact with the leading inhabitants of the entire district. The clergy, the gentry, the needle masters and most prosperous farmers, the chapel wardens, the select vestrymen, the overseers to the poor, the constable, in short, everybody of any importance in his small world.

On Sundays in particular Joseph Davis was in his glory, sitting on the elevated seat beneath the high pulpit from which the Reverend John Clayton preached the word of God. From his perch Joseph Davis kept an eagle eye on the congregation, and on the sidesmen, whose duties included using their long wands to prod awake those misguided souls who had the temerity to fall asleep during the longer sermons. Woe betide any mischievous urchin who might dare to chatter or giggle during the service, because then Joseph Davis himself used the rod of chastisement on their soft flesh after the service was over. So, although the ungodly and the wicked might make mock of him, Joseph Davis was complacently aware of his own importance, and well-armoured in righteousness.

On his way across the green the vestry clerk encountered a remarkably handsome young man who was dressed in an ultra-fashionable dark brown frock-coat, buff kerseymere waistcoat and light blue merino trousers with a military-style peaked cap set rakishly on his silky blond hair and a froth of lacy cravat at his throat. Tall and well-built, with bright blue eyes, a fresh complexion and elegant side-whiskers Doctor Hugh Taylor caused many female hearts to flutter. In partnership with his father, Doctor Charles Taylor, the young dandy had the largest medical practice in the district.

Joseph Davis, who disapproved of handsome young dandies on principle, nodded curtly. 'Good day to you, Doctor Taylor. It's pleasant to see the sun shining, is it not?'

The young man smiled broadly, well aware of the other's sentiments regarding him. 'Yes indeed, Mr Davis, even though the wind is chill. Just off to ring the batter bell, are you?'

The clerk confirmed this fact, and could not resist adding, 'Mind you, Doctor, I think it smacks of heathenism. There's naught in the good book to justify the ringing of chapel bells so that housewives might know it's time to get the mixing started for their pancakes. I reckon it's a pagan custom, and that's a fact. It arn't mentioned anywheres in the scriptures, is it?'

Hugh Taylor in his turn could not resist baiting the other man, who was well known for his dourness and lack of humour, 'But it is a fine old English custom, Mister Davis. In these modern days so many of our ancient customs are falling into disuse, and it's a damned shame that should be so. No doubt you'll be joining in the sports this afternoon, will you not?'

'Not I, Sir!' the clerk stated forcefully. 'I disapproves of shying at the cock, and climbing greasy poles and all the rest o' such nonsense as that. And to tell truth, I'd not be ringing the bell neither, if it warn't for the fact that Reverend Clayton insists on me adoing so.'

The doctor grinned. 'Yes indeed, the Reverend Clayton certainly shares my own views regarding the keeping up of our old customs, and a grand thing it is too. They are what help to give us our sense of national identity, Mr Davis. Without them, we would be in danger of forgetting who we English are.'

'Well, that's as maybe,' the clerk rejoined grudgingly. 'I'd best be on me way, or I'll have the Reverend awondering what's happened to the bell.'

A crowd of children had gathered around the chapel door, and they cheered lustily when the bell in the cupola tower began to peel out, and in shrill-voiced unison shouted the chant:

> 'Ding dong, pan on.
> Pull the little 'un off,
> Put the big 'un on.
> Ding dong, pan on,
> They can hear us at Malvern even,
> Say the bells of old Saint Stephen.
> The frying pans be on,
>   And the pancakes be done.
> Ding dong, pan on.
>   Pull the little 'un off . . .'

On one corner of the main crossroads stood the shop of

Timothy Munslow, the pie man and confectioner, who was also a blacksmith with a forge at the rear of his shop. At the door of his shop a queue composed of elderly paupers had formed earlier that morning. They too cheered when the chapel bell peeled. Inside the shop Timothy Munslow had long since prepared his batter-mix and now, aided by his wife and aged father, he began to make pancakes on his charcoal cooking range. He marked the first three pancakes from the big iron pan with a cross and sprinkled them with salt, then his father recited over them:

> 'Good pancakes made o' milk and beer,
> be made for no one present here.
> There's one for Peter
> And one for Paul,
>   An' the third 'un's
>   for Him as made us all.'

'Amen to that, Feyther,' Timothy Munslow and his wife Elizabeth chorused. As the old man carefully wrapped the pancakes and put them aside his burly, red-faced, bluff-mannered son told his wife, 'That'll keep Old Nick from our door, my duck. Now let's get on wi' feeding them poor old sods out theer.'

It was Munslow's own private charity. Each year on Shrove Tuesday he presented a free, fresh-cooked pancake to any aged pauper of the town who came to his shop.

Tildy Crawford had come to buy pancakes and she waited patiently while the old people received their savoury gifts, enjoyed the expression of keen anticipation on their faces, the rough banter they exchanged among themselves.

Next to Munslow's shop was a small tavern, the Malt Shovel, kept by the jolly-natured, rotund Billy Bray, and he also had his own private charity. On a trestle outside his tavern he had set up a cask of strong ale, and as each old person came from Munslow's with their pancake, Billy

74

Bray served them a free horn-tot of the potent drink.

When the last of the old people had been served Tildy was able to make her own purchase, and set off towards Silver Square carrying the greasy, hot, succulent delicacies in the covered crock-pot she had borrowed from Mother Readman. Just as she was turning under the Red Lion arch her name was called, and she looked back to see Josh Dyson. She smiled with genuine pleasure at seeing the man, and when he came up to her told him, 'I'm really glad to see you, Mr Dyson. I wanted to say thank you for helping us last night. If you hadn't been there I fear it would have gone hard with me.'

He returned her smile, disclosing teeth surprisingly good and white for a man of his years, and for a brief instant Tildy had the visual illusion of a young boy in the man before her.

'Don't think no more on it, Tildy Crawford.' He waved aside her thanks. 'I was pleased to be able to help you, and if Brompton tries to give you any more trouble then you come straight and tell me. I don't like to see a decent girl blaggarded by the likes of him.'

On impulse she said, 'To be honest, Mr Dyson, I did want to talk to you about something, about the way we're all of us treated by the masters.'

His eyes became suddenly wary. 'What about it, Tildy?'

She noted the transition of mood in the man and hesitated, made uncertain by it, but, driven by her complusion, she went on.

'I wanted to ask your help to do something about what happened to young Meg, and about the other things at the Fountain as well.'

He glanced about him as if to see if anyone was watching their exchange. Then he tapped the crock-pot she carried, and asked at a tangent, 'What's in here then?'

'Pancakes,' she answered, puzzlement in her voice at his manner.

Again he grinned at her, but the wariness still hovered

in his eyes. 'You'd best get 'um home, Tildy, afore they gets cold.'

'Don't you want to talk with me, Mr Dyson?' She could not resist pressing him, but in return he said only, 'You get off home now. I'll be around the town all day. There's a cock-throwing and some backsword play 'ull be taking place on the green later. I'll probably be having a try at both. Iffen you should by chance be there, and I should by chance meet you, then I expect we'll be exchanging a few words, won't us?'

Still puzzled by his attitude, Tildy was forced to leave the matter for the time being, and hurried on along fetid Silver Street with her crock of pancakes.

Back in the lodging-house kitchen Mother Readman, Apollonia and little Davy were awaiting her return, plates already laid out in anticipation of the pancakes. While they ate, Tildy kept her eyes on her small son. He was now just over two-and-a-half years of age, and she adored him with all the fervour of her warm heart. Although secretly ashamed of what she did, she still could not help but surreptitiously examine him while he ate, searching for any resemblance or similarity in manner to his father, Tom Crawford. As always, with thankful relief, she found none, except for his thick mop of dark curly hair, which bearing in mind her own dark colouring could equally well have come from her. Although Tildy accepted the incontrovertible fact that Tom Crawford was the child's father, she preferred to think of the man only as the purely mechanical means by which the fetus had been engendered. She preferred to believe that her son, in mind, temperament and all physical and spiritual attributes was her creation, and hers alone; and in all truth little Davy was a loving, sweet-natured child, and had never betrayed any traits of his father.

While she looked at him now Tildy's love for the child whelmed over her, and a lump came into her throat as she watched the dark curly head bent above the huge pancake, which with endearing, childish clumsiness he was carefully dissecting with his huge spoon and his fingers. The physical act of eating suddenly became an impossibility to Tildy, and she laid down her own knife and spoon. The shrewd eyes of Mother Readman observed, understood and smiled fondly.

Tildy had refused to accept any money from Mother Readman towards the cost of the pancakes. 'No, let me treat you both. It's only such a small thing in return for what you both do for me,' she told the old woman and the stick-legged girl. Not for the first time Tildy blessed her own good fortune in finding two such true friends in what most respectable people would regard as a most unsavoury milieu. She paid Mother Readman two shillings a week for her tiny attic room, which was a large amount to deduct from her six or seven shillings of earnings, but Tildy considered herself lucky. She knew that at the busy times of year the old woman was actually losing money by allowing Tildy to have the room for herself and her child alone. Also, there was the inestimable boon of having Davy cared for by the pair while she herself was at work at the Fountain Mill. A further real blessing for Tildy was that when towards the end of the week her money began to run out, she was allowed to eat as many bowls of the penny-a-bowl stew as she wished on credit. Admittedly, the stew would not tempt a fastidious eater, but hunger made the best sauce, a fact that Tildy knew from harsh experience, and she counted it her good fortune that she needn't fear actual starvation for days on end. There were many among the poor for whom this fear was a weekly reality. A smile of thankfulness touched her full, moist lips. 'All in all, things could be worse for me,' she thought. 'Much, much worse.'

Chapter Eleven

The black-feathered cockerel sqawked and jumped with a frantic flurry of wings to avoid narrowly the short wooden stave that came hurtling at its head, and the thrower cursed his luck, while the crowd jeered and cat-called. The cock-keeper walked to the stake to which the bird was tied by its leg with a ten-foot length of cord and retrieved the three wooden staves the thrower had shied. As the cock-keeper returned the twenty-odd yards distance to the throwing-post he bawled, 'Come now, three shies for tuppence! Three shies for tuppence! Win the fine Shrove-cock for tuppence! Three shies for tuppence! Three shies for tuppence! You can fill your belly, or breed a flock, all for tuppence! Three shies for tuppence!'

'Give us 'um 'ere.' A drunken young needle pointer, still wearing his working rig of leather waistcoat, checked shirt and apron rolled about his hips, with knee-breeches, thick-ribbed stockings and heavy clogs, a bright-coloured kerchief knotted around his throat and a square, brown-paper hat on his long hair, stepped to the throwing-post and handed over his two copper pennies in return for the three short staves. His mates in the crowd encouraged him vociferously.

'Goo it, Ned!'

'Knock the fucker's yed off!'

'Come on the pointer!'

'Show 'um how it's done, bucko!'

'Show 'um how a pointer lad can do the business!'

The young pointer bowed, clowning for the crowd's benefit, and then squinted blearily at the tethered bird, which in its turn stalked and scratched and pecked at the ground. With a wild yell the pointer hurled the first stave, and almost as if it taunted his poor aim the bird ignored the tumbling shaft of wood, its beak tearing savagely into the squirming body of the worm its claws had grubbed from the earth.

Tildy stood hand in hand with little Davy and joined in the general laughter at the pointer's discomfiture. Her son tugged at her hand.

'Mammy, why is the man throwing things at the hen?'

'Well, if he can hit it, and catch it up in his hands before it can rise again, then he will keep it,' Tildy explained.

'Does the man want it to play with him?' the child asked, and she smiled at his innocence.

'Yes honey, he wants it to play with him.'

Tildy, like the vast majority of her generation, saw nothing cruel or unnatural about the practice of cockthrowing. She had been raised in a savage world, and from childhood had been taught to believe that animals were merely soulless things put on the earth for the use of mankind, and consequently were to be treated without consideration. Of course, there were those who considered themselves to be animal-lovers, but they were mainly concerned with what were regarded as the nobler species of beasts. Barnyard fowls were not included in that category.

Tildy's eyes ranged across the crowd. It consisted mainly of needle workers, but here and there a blue or grey or white smock denoted the farm labourer, and there were some fine coats and gowns of gentlefolk, and the broadcloth and leather gaiters of farmers also. Unwillingly, Tildy was forced to admit to herself that she was disappointed not to see Josh Dyson here. She was strongly drawn to the man for reasons she could not explain to herself, and she felt an ever-strengthening desire to talk with him.

'Come on, lads,' a man standing near to her said to his

companions. 'They'll be starting the backsword matches down by the Crown any minute now.'

Tildy remembered that Dyson had said he would be competing in those matches, and she walked slowly after the group towards the tavern which stood at the far end of the green on the brow of the Fish Hill, where the road plunged steeply downwards to the north.

'Where are we going, Mammy?' Little Davy was reluctant to leave the cock-throwing. 'I want to throw a stick at the hen. I want to play with it and keep it for my ownself.'

'You're too small yet to be let throw at the hen, my darling.' Tildy soothed him with a promise. 'Be a good boy now and walk with me nicely, and I'll get you a piece of sugar cone or some ginger-snap, if there is any.'

In happy anticipation he came willingly then, his chubby legs thrusting against the long skirt of his dress. Tildy smiled down at him with just a hint of sadness in her eyes. 'You'll soon be wearing breeches,' she thought. 'And then you'll not be my baby any longer, but a boy growing fast to manhood.'

People were sauntering from many directions towards the rough platform that had been erected outside the front door of the tavern. Fashioned from planks set on wooden barrels, its surface was a small square without any ropes or guardrails. Around this platform the first of the contestants were limbering up and whirling their basket-handled, yard-length ash staffs through the air like cutlasses or sabres as they practised the cuts, thrusts and parries of the sport. Despite the fact that they were mostly young men in the prime of their strength, the contestants were known as 'old gamesters'.

As Tildy neared the platform she was able to recognize some of the shirt-sleeved gamesters, and was surprised to see certain of them there. The Reverend John Clayton, curate of St Stephen's Chapel, an exceptionally ugly young man, but possessed of a remarkably muscular physique, had discarded his black clerical coat and short-queued tie-wig and was lustily swinging his ash staff, clad in his shirt-sleeves and black knee-breeches, his close-cropped brown hair ruffling in the breeze. Near to him was Doctor Hugh Taylor, a blond Adonis clad in lavender shirt and pantaloons, and next to him was young Henry Milward, old Henry's son, down from his university for a visit.

Hoisted atop a slender pole rammed into the ground some distance from the platform was an ancient, gold-laced tricorn hat. This was the prize to be fought for. The overall winner of the match would be allowed to take the hat away with him and wear it for a year. Despite its battered shabbiness, the winner always wore the hat with immense pride, as the visible token of his prowess.

'Mrs Crawford, what a pleasant chance to have met you!'

For a fleeting instance Tildy thought it was the man she sought and she turned gladly, only to find it was Nathanial Farrel staring appreciatively at her.

'I'm glad you do not wear a mob-cap, Mrs Crawford. Your hair is a glory that should not be hidden.' His light green eyes swept up and down her neat grey gown and rested on her hair, which was coiled upon her head and was glossy in the sunlight. 'You are a picture of neat charm, Mrs Crawford, but I declare that if you were to let your hair fall loose around your shoulders, you would then present a picture of rare beauty.'

'I would present the picture of a wild gypsy woman, Mr Farrel,' Tildy answered evenly, and her expression was ambiguous as she regarded him. Tildy's opinion of the man to whom she had been introduced by Marmaduke Montmorency some days after his arrival at the lodging house was uncertain. His manner was always friendly and courteous, but his openly expressed admiration of Tildy's good looks and the fulsome compliments he paid her both gratified her natural vanity and at the same time irritated her intelligence. She always experienced the uncomfortable feeling that his pleasant smile was a mask behind

81

which his true expression was a vicious sneer.

'Do you intend watching the backsword matches, Mrs Crawford?' the young man asked, and she nodded.

'For a while, yes.'

'Then pray permit me to keep you company while you watch.' He lifted his brown beaver top hat and bowed gallantly, and despite the ambiguity of her feelings towards him, Tildy could not bring herself to be rude to the man.

'Very well, if it pleases you to do so,' she acquiesced, and slowly they strolled on towards the platform.

'You'll needs explain the rules to me, Mrs Crawford,' Farrel smiled, 'For in London these rustic bumpkin sports have all but died out and I've not seen this backsword play before.'

Tildy's resentment sparked as she thought she detected a sneer against the locals in his voice, but then she checked and silently castigated herself: 'Damn you for constantly seeking for sticks to beat this man with. You are forever fancying slights where in all truth there are probably none intended. It was a perfectly innocent thing for this man to say. There is no call for you to take offence at it.' Her sense of guilt caused her to make the effort to reply in a friendly tone. 'I know little enough about it myself, Mr Farrel. But I think the rules are simple enough. I believe in fact that the backsword play is beginning to die out in these parts also. But some of the local men enjoy to keep up the old customs.'

'And a very good thing too. I applaud them for doing so,' Nathanial Farrel agreed heartily. 'I'm all in favour of maintaining traditions. And speaking of traditions, I was forgetting an old London tradition myself ... Hold fast for a moment.' As they halted he bent to the child and from a concealed pocket in his black swallow-tailed coat produced a stick of garishly coloured candy-rock. 'The tradition from where I come from is that on a Shrove Tuesday we old gentlemen present you young gentlemen with a big stick of candy-rock, Master Davy.'

Davy reached eagerly for the sweet, and Farrel said laughingly, 'You must give me a kiss in return for it though, young gentleman, for that also is part of the tradition.'

He presented his smooth-shaven, scented cheek to the child who, after a momentary hesitation, kissed it. Farrel laughed pleasurably. 'There now, here's your reward, young gentleman.'

Davy immediately began noisily sucking his prize.

Tildy could not help the perverse imp of jealousy which suddenly goaded her to snap curtly, 'Say thank you to Mr Farrel for his gift, Davy, and don't let him think you to be nothing more than an ignorant yokel boy.'

With a hurt expression the child gravely thanked the man, and Tildy felt a pang of remorse that she should have spoken harshly to him. Farrel smiled at her.

'He is a credit to you, Mrs Crawford. He's a bonny boy, and I'll wager he'll grow to be a fine man.'

Farrel, by accident or by design, had breached the weak spot in Tildy's defences by his kindness to her child, and now she allowed her guarded caution to relax a little. 'I pray that may be so, Mr Farrel, for truly he's the entire world to me.'

The man's expression was very serious and sincere when he told her, 'That's plainly seen, Mrs Crawford, even by a comparative stranger to you both, such as myself. I've never been wed, and consequently have no experience of parenthood, but I would imagine that the love of a mother or father for their child transcends all other emotions. Mayhap it could prove both joy and pain at the same time. But I would venture that the joy far outweighs the pain, and perhaps even the pain is touched with a tenderness and concern that ennobles that unhappy emotion.'

Tildy found herself in total agreement with what he said, and for the first time since she had met Farrel found herself completely at ease with him, even experiencing a tentatively burgeoning liking for him. 'Perhaps I have been sorely misjudging this man,' she thought, and that thought gained in strength and certainty as they slowly sauntered on in a companionable silence.

James Bray, the town crier, resplendent in his official uniform of gold-laced tricorn hat, full-skirted canary-yellow coat, plum breeches and white stockings with silver buckled shoes on his feet, mounted the platform and rang his brass handbell loudly.

'Oyezzzz, Oyezzz, Oyezzzz,' his deep voice sounded out across the green. 'All gamesters wanting to fight for the champion's hat, attend now and draw lots. Oyezzz, Oyezzz, Oyezzz. All gamesters attend now and draw lots . . .'

As he shouted, a group of men issued from the front door of the Crown. Old Henry Milward, plump face ruddy with the effects of brandy and claret, led the group together with three other needle masters, William Hemming, Abel Morral and Charles Bartleet, who was William Hemming's partner in their mill which was only a few yards from the Crown. The leaders were followed from the tavern by a stream of men, and among these Tildy saw Josh Dyson. Like the other gamesters he was shirt-sleeved and knee-breeched. On impluse Tildy said to her companion, 'Could you do me the favour of holding Davy here for a moment.' He nodded smilingly, and she told Davy, 'Mammy will only be a moment away, honey. Be a good boy and stay nicely with Mr Farrel.'

Engrossed in the candy-rock, the child only nodded, and Tildy slipped through the rapidly increasing crowd around the platform until she came to the side of Josh Dyson, and touched his arm. When he turned to her she said hastily, 'I just wanted to wish you good luck in the match, Mr Dyson.'

He looked at her gravely, but his hard eyes softened. 'My thanks, Tildy Crawford for your good wishes. Luck must play its part in all things, must it not?'

Embarrassingly aware that she was blushing, Tildy hurried back to where Farrel and her child were waiting. The man regarded her keenly.

'Is he a good friend of yours, Mrs Crawford, the man you spoke with?'

She paused for a moment, then said off-handedly. 'I don't know him well enough to call him my friend, Mr Farrel. But he works by me at the Fountain and he did me a good turn a short while back. I wanted to wish him luck today, that's all.'

Farrel's light green eyes fixed speculatively on the hardener's muscular, erect figure, and he remarked casually, 'His name is Dyson, Josh Dyson, is it not?'

'That's so.' Tildy was faintly surprised that he should know that. 'You know him then?'

Farrel shook his head slowly. 'No, not to speak to, at any rate.'

Then he lapsed into silence, but Tildy noticed that his attention remained on Josh Dyson and the man who came now from the tavern and spoke to the hardener.

'Who is that fellow? The one now speaking with your friend?' Farrel asked, and this time it was Tildy who was forced to shake her head after examining the thin, sun-tanned features and cropped grey hair of the stranger.

'I've no idea who he is, Mr Farrel. I've never seen him before.'

'Is he a newcomer to this town?' Farrel pressed her, and again Tildy shook her head.

'I don't know.' Her voice sharpened impatiently. 'I've already said that I've never seen him before.'

Her companion nodded thoughtfully. 'He's got a bronze to his skin that was put there by hotter climes than this,' he observed, then appeared to thrust the matter from his mind. 'Now, tell me, who d'you fancy to win the champion's hat? I'll put a wager on whoever you name.'

Tildy shrugged smilingly. 'I've not the foggiest idea who'll win it.' And the tiny voice in her mind whispered, 'But I hope it's Josh Dyson.'

The draw was quickly completed. Names of contestants were written on scraps of paper and placed in a hat, then drawn out in pairs. Abel Morral, thick-set and heavy-featured, his hair still worn in the old-fashioned queue and his face still showing the old scars of his brawling youth as a needle pointer, was appointed umpire, and he took his place on a tall stool set on a huge, upended barrel to bring him level with the platform.

The first two gamesters, the younger Henry Milward and a burly farm labourer, climbed onto the rough boarding. They came to stand facing each other at two paces' distance, each man with a backsword in his right hand and left arm held behind his back, left thumb tucked into the rear of his breeches. If either freed that left arm then it meant an automatic disqualification for him.

'You knows the rules of backsword, gentlemen,' Abel Morral bellowed. 'The fust man to get cut anywheres above the line of the eyebrows loses the match. No striking below the waistbelt, no kicking, no biting, no butting, no spitting. Does you both understand me, gentlemen?'

The burly labourer nodded without any change in his stoical expression. His boyish, much weaker-bodied opponent swallowed hard, and with pale, set features nodded nervously.

'Very well then ... Salute your opponent!'

The gamesters lowered their ash staves then raised them high, touching the basket hilts to their lips, then lowering them once more.

'Take your guard!' Morral bawled.

Both men came to the fencer's on-guard position.

'Lay on!'

Morral's command was all but drowned in the roar of the crowd. In seconds the contest was over. A quick flurry of movement, a rattle of stick on stick, a cry of pain, and young Henry Milward went sprawling to the boards, half senseless, blood pouring from the long lacerations on his scalp.

The crowd jeered the youngster's poor showing, and old Henry Milward flushed with angry chagrin.

'Drag the useless young bugger out on it. He fought

86

like a soddin' dolly-mop, so he did,' Abel Morral shouted loudly, slyly watching his old rival, Henry Milward, out of the corner of his eye, and equally slyly grinning at his discomfiture.

Milward's lips tightened, then he forced a laugh, and told Morral, 'You'll not get me to rise to that 'un, Abel.'

By Tildy's side, Nathanial Farrel scoffed sneeringly, 'By God, I can see now why this bumpkin sport has died out in London. One touch of a stick and they lay down. It wouldn't do where I come from, we produce real hard chaws there.'

A man standing in front of Farrel overheard him and swung about. Tildy recognized the man, and her heart quailed. It was Richie Bint, needle pointer, poacher and local prize-fighter and brawler, squat-bodied and solid as oak, with long, uncombed sandy hair, and a nose punched almost flat.

'I takes it that you don't think much to our local lads then, cully?'

Farrel was instantly wary, sensing the violence simmering in the man fronting him.

'I meant no offence, mate. I spoke hasty, that's all,' he offered placatingly. 'I was a mite upset because I'd wagered heavy on the young 'un.'

For what seemed to Tildy an endless stretch of time, but was in reality only a few moments, Richie Bint stared hard at Farrel, then with an expression of contempt he lifted one meaty hand and, setting his palm against Farrel's face, he pushed hard. 'You'd best go and stand elsewheres, my Cockney nancyboy,' he warned. 'Because I don't like having cunts like you standing near to me.'

The Londoner staggered back a couple of paces, unbalanced by the strength of the push. Regaining his balance, he stood facing Bint for a second or two, and his eyes were murderous. Then he turned on his heel and walked away through the crowd without a word or backward glance.

The needle pointer jeered at his retreating back. 'All bloody wind and piss, that 'un,' he told his neighbours, and they were quick with sycophantic plaudits.

'He run like a cur dog, didn't he?'

'You scared the shit out on him, Richie.'

'Ahr, I could smell the stink on it in his britches when he went past me.'

Tildy heard the gibes about Farrel's apparent cowardice, but with a strange inner certainty knew that whatever it was that had caused the Londoner to walk away so meekly, it was not fear. She had seen and experienced enough violence in her life to be able to recognize cowardice in men and women in all its guises. Despite what had just happened, there was one thing of which she was sure, and that was that Farrel was no coward. His eyes had held blood-lust, not fear. She shivered involuntarily, and thought to herself, 'If I were Richie Bint, I'd not be becalling that man. Instead I'd be very careful to watch my back from now on, indeed I would.'

The next contestants were on the platform, and the incident between Farrel and the needle pointer was forgotten in this new excitement, because the two gamesters now saluting each other were counted to be the best in the district.

Reverend John Clayton and Josh Dyson came to the on-guard position, and on the shout of command the match began. The ash staffs swished and clattered with lightning speed and the two men moved with the sure-footed grace of dancers, round and round, now backwards, now forwards, thrusting, cutting, parrying, attacking, defending, counter-attacking. Near to Tildy an ancient, bent-bodied veteran gamester was hissing a constant stream of instructions through his toothless gums:

'Moulinet, right sweep, right rear volte. Strike right flank, right cheek moulinet, left cheek moulinet, flank, flank, flank. Head attack, head parry, two hand parry, head attack, hand in quarte, thrust, thrust, thrust, thrust ...'

The shouts of the crowd quietened as they became absorbed by the skill of the contest, and Tildy herself felt hypnotized by that skill and dexterity. Her eyes were dazzled by the whirling arcs of the staffs, and she lost all track of time and all awareness of anything other than the platform before her and the men locked in combat upon it. Then, suddenly, a scarlet streak appeared on the right temple of Josh Dyson and, as the crowd groaned in concert, blood jetted from that streak to stream down his face and spatter onto the white shirt. John Clayton immediately stepped back and raised his weapon in salute, and Dyson grinned ruefully, and acknowledged the other's victory with a bow.

The crowd clapped and cheered lustily and excitedly argued and disputed the finer points of the fight with each other at the tops of their voices. From what Tildy could hear of the comments it appeared that the encounter had been an epic one, and both victor and defeated had gained ample glory. She experienced acute disappointment that Dyson had lost, but as he pushed his way through the dense throng towards her she saw by the broad smile on his bloody, sweating face that he was taking his defeat in good spirit.

Before he reached her other gamesters had taken position and Dyson was all but ignored by the crowd as fresh wagers were offered and taken on the new match.

Davy stared at the hardener's bloody face with mingled interest and apprehension, and the man told him gently, 'There's no call for you to be frit o' me, little fella, this is only a bit of a leak from here, see, that's where all this nice bright paint comes from.'

He pointed to the gaping wound in his temple, and Davy's interest overcame his apprehension.

'Does it hurt?' he asked. 'Will it all run out, all the paint?'

'It only hurts when I laugh,' Dyson chuckled, 'and it'll stop running out very soon, I'm sure.' To Tildy he said,

'Well, Tildy Crawford, I'm feared the luck didn't hold for me today, did it? They tells me you knows a fair bit about treating wounds, my wench.'

She nodded. 'I know something of it. I did some work as a sick-nurse for a while. How did you know I had?'

He lifted his forefinger and placed it against the side of his nose, then executed a deliberately owlish wink, and she laughed and told him, 'No, don't bother to tell me, I know well enough that there's little stays secret in this town for long.'

'Well now, you said afore that you wanted to talk wi' me, Tildy, so if youm agreeable to fixing up this cut, then come to my house wi' me now, and we can talk while youm stitching me up.'

She hesitated only a moment, then agreed, 'Very well, Mr Dyson, I'll do that with pleasure.'

'You'll do summat else as well, Tildy, you'll stop calling me Mister, and use my given name. It's Josh, if you don't know that already.'

She nodded. 'Very well then, Josh it shall be.'

As they walked towards the crossroads on the southern edge of the green they passed the cock-throwing post and saw that the wily bird was still evading all efforts to hit it. Tildy chuckled as the bird caused yet another thrower to miss widely, and asked Dyson, 'Have you thrown at the cock yet?'

He grinned ruefully. 'No, and I'll not be doing so neither. I've just found out how it feels to be clouted on the yed with a heavy stick, so I'll not subject the poor cratur to that treatment. Not this year, at any rate.'

They chatted casually as they passed through the crossroads and went south along the Evesham Street towards the long terrace of cottages in the area known as the New End which covered the first slopes of the Front Hill.

Tildy found herself completely at ease with this man and her spirits rose high so that she chattered and giggled excitedly like a very young girl, and was forced to pause and remind herself mentally that she was a full-grown

90

woman, married and with a child to boot, and it was not proper to behave so like a silly child herself.

Dyson, while not appearing to do so, drew a great deal of information from Tildy about her past life by a series of shrewdly worded questions. In his turn he was feeling the strong attraction her physical beauty exerted on him, but more than that, he found himself liking her as a person also. He had admired the way she had intervened to protect simple Meg Tullet, and was pleased to find that this earlier good opinion of Tildy was being so strongly reinforced by her now.

The interior of his terraced cottage was like the man himself, immaculately clean and rather austere with no clutterings of ornaments or furniture, just the few, simple necessities of table, stools and cookpots and, surprisingly for a working man, a shelf filled with books, some of which were bound in expensive, gold-tooled leather.

He took tinder and steel and flint and after some moments had kindled a fire in the grate on which he placed an iron kettle of water to heat. Tildy sat on one of the stools with Davy on her knee, content to watch Josh Dyson at his tasks in the small white-washed room.

From a wooden wall-chest he took a clean shirt and laid it ready for use. 'Once I'm cleaned up I'd best change into this,' he smiled. 'Otherwise folks might think I've only the one shirt to my name.'

When the water was warmed Tildy got up and put Davy onto her seat. She filled a crock-bowl with the water and placed it on the table while Dyson seated himself on a stool beside it. With a wet rag she washed the dried blood from the man's face and carefully cleansed the immediate area of the wound. The blood had by now almost completely clotted in the torn flesh and only a tiny trickle still oozed. Tildy examined the cut closely. It was about an inch and a half in length and seemed fairly shallow, but the swelling caused by the blow was causing it to gape.

91

'How does it look?' Dyson asked, and she frowned slightly.

'I think it might be best if you got it stitched.'

From a drawer in the table the man took a small looking-glass and held it so that he could see the wound. 'Youm right, Tildy, it's gaping a bit too wide to be left like it is. Here ...' From the same drawer he lifted a small hank of fine silk thread and a long, curved needle. 'Just put a few stitches in,' he instructed. 'Here, here and here.' He pointed to the places.

Tildy had sewn up wounds before and she felt no squeamishness as she deftly placed and tied the threads, drawing the edges of the wound firmly together. When she bit the thread to part it she was forced to bring her head close to him, and she was very much aware of the clean, warm smell of his body.

For his part Dyson forgot the pain of the needle and thread passing through his flesh as he felt Tildy's full, firm breasts touching his shoulder, and he fought down the sudden urge to fold her in his arms and draw her closer to him.

'There now, it's done.' Tildy finished tying the last stitch, and stood back to examine her handiwork. Davy, who had been watching in silent enthralment, now piped up, 'Mammy, can I have my head sewed as well?'

Both adults burst out laughing, and Tildy lifted her child and kissed and hugged him before setting him back on his stool once more.

'Have you any bandage here?' she asked the hardener. 'It might be better to cover it.'

Dyson regarded the dressed wound in the looking-glass, and said approvingly, 'That's a neat job, Tildy. It seems a pity to hide such good work from view. Mayhap you should think of becoming a surgeon, because you've done a better job of stitching than some of those gentry that I've come across in the past.'

She smiled, gratified by the compliment, and burst out impulsively, 'Do you know, Josh, if I were a man that's what I would have enjoyed to be. A surgeon, or a physician. I've long had great interest in the treatment of wounds and illness.'

His grey eyes were kindly as he studied her flushed, happy face. 'Who can tell what the future might yet hold for you, Tildy. There are hundreds of goodwives who treat the sick and make a good job on it as well. Why should not a woman become a surgeon or physician?'

'I could give you a hundred reasons,' Tildy replied wryly. 'But never mind, we can always dream, can't we? That at least is not forbidden to us.'

'By God, Tildy!' he ejaculated in a hoarse whisper. 'Even if it were forbidden on pain of death, we still must dream. Because without our dreams we are nothing. It's dreams that'll change the world we live in, and it's the dreamers like us who will bring those changes about.'

She became suddenly pensive. 'Can things ever change for the likes of us, Josh? Or must we forever sweat and toil merely to survive one day to the next, knowing that our future more than likely will only ever hold a bench in the poorhouse and a grave in the Potter's Field?'

For a while he sat silent, staring hard at her, then, as if he had come to a momentous decision, he drew a deep breath and asked quietly, 'Can I trust you, Tildy? Can I trust you to tell no one what I might now say to you?'

She did not answer immediately, but instead pondered his question. When she did finally reply it was hesitantly, but without timidity. 'You ask me if I can be trusted not to tell things you might now tell me, Josh? In all truth, I'm not sure. It would greatly depend on what it was you told me. If it were something that I thought to be wicked and evil, something that might bring harm to helpless people, then, to be honest, I would probably tell others of it to warn them ...'

'Do you consider it to be a wicked thing, or an evil one, to wish to raise your fellow man from the level of a brute beast? To want to put an end to the virtual slavery of our children in the coal-mines and factories and mills? To

93

want all men to have a voice in the governing of this country? To want to see our old people with full bellies, and a fire in their own hearths and their own roofs above their heads?'

Tildy smiled and shook her glossy head. 'Of course not.'

'Well, it is these things that I want to see brought about in our country, and anything I might now tell you is to do with bringing them about.'

'Go on,' she told him, and he began to talk ...

He talked of the laws that bound men, women and children in an iron-fettered servitude to the ruling classes. He talked of the attempts of men to break those fetters, to unite and gain strength enough to demand justice from their rulers. He told her of Tom Paine, and his book, *The Rights of Man*. He told her of the Radical Hampden Clubs, and the Spencean Societies, of the Pentridge rising, of the Spa Fields and Ely riots, the Cato Street conspiracy, of the march of the blanketeers and the massacre at Manchester known as Peterloo; and lastly, he told her of his own part in the struggle to achieve justice for the labouring masses of Great Britain.

When he had finished she sat in silence, her mind battling to comprehend fully the import of what she had heard. At least she sighed, and asked quietly, 'And how could I be of any help in such a struggle, Josh? What would you have me do?'

'I would have you with me, and not against me, Tildy,' he murmured. 'Nothing more than that.'

'Oh, I'm with you all right,' she answered fervently. 'If only for the sake of my Davy, I would be with you in what you seek for. But from what you have told me and what I have read and heard myself, it seems a hopeless task.'

'I should imagine that when the first labourer tried to move the first great stone to build Stonehenge with, then he too thought it was a hopeless task,' Dyson said dryly. 'But if that man could eventually learn to work with his mates and so build Stonehenge, then I'm sure that you and I and others like us could also work together and eventually help bring about what we seek for.'

'Then tell me how?' she urged him eagerly. 'Tell me how people like us can bring about these changes?'

Chapter Twelve

Meg Tullet was afraid. She hurried down the lane towards the isolated, tumbledown cottage she lived in with her mother on the fringes of the Pitcheroak woods lying south-east of the town. With her she had three ragged, snot-nosed infants, younger brothers and a sister, and try as she would to make them move faster, their tiny legs could not manage the pace.

The cause of her fear was gaining fast on her now, and she could hear the sounds of his harsh-panting breath as he drew nearer and nearer to her. For a moment or two she thought of leaving the track known as the Red Lane, and plunging into the thick woodland undergrowth to hide from her pursuer. But even her slow mind was forced to understand that with three small, squalling children, hiding would be an impossibility. A sob choked her throat as she looked fearfully back over her shoulder.

Behind her, Johnny Brompton grinned in cruel delight and blessed his good fortune in spotting the girl as he had when leaving the Unicorn Tap to go home to his nagging shrew of a wife. Everything seemed to have conspired to be in his favour. It was dusk. She was encumbered with kids. Nearly everyone who would normally be likely to be travelling this trackway was up in the town where the holiday festivities were still in full swing with dancing on the green now that the backsword matches were finished. Even the normally bustling brick-kilns set further off in the woods would be deserted on this afternoon.

Suddenly, the girl in front of him halted, and stood with bowed head and heaving shoulders, her face buried in her hands and the ragged children crying and whining around her. Johnny Brompton slowed his own rapid pace, glad of the chance to regain his breath. He knew now that she would no longer try to escape him and already the sight of her helpless, beaten posture was powerfully exciting him. His manhood was already starting to engorge and stiffen before he had even laid a hand on her.

Meg still had her face covered by her hands when he came up to her, and for a few moments Brompton stood grinning down at her small figure. Then he said, 'It arn't no use you skrawking, girl, there's no one here to pay heed or to help you, is there? Come now, I arn't agoing to harm you, Meg, so dry your eyes. I just wants a little bit of a chat wi' you, that's all.'

The younger children were all crying in unison with their big sister and Brompton felt the urge to smash them into silence. But he restrained himself, knowing that by displaying a little patience now he could achieve all he wanted, and achieve it without the danger of possibly unpleasant consequences for himself afterwards. He fumbled in his coat pocket and produced a large piece of dirty rag which he pressed into Meg's hand.

'Here, blow your nose and dry your eyes, girl. I arn't agoing to hurt you.' To the smaller children he showed a bag of ginger-snaps which he took from his other pocket. 'Who'd like a bit o' this?' he asked them and instantly their tears were forgotten as they clamoured around him, grubby hands reaching out for the sweetmeat. 'Hold hard, damn you!' he cursed irritably, and they instantly hushed to fearful silence and drew back from him, faces already beginning to crumple with fresh sobs. 'Listen, you children,' he forced himself to speak kindly to them. 'I'm going to give each one o' you a piece o' my ginger-snap. But you'se got to set yourselves down in the bushes over theer and wait for Meg to come and fetch you. Iffen youm very good and very quiet while youm waiting for her, then I'll give you all another piece, as well.'

Quickly he distributed the sticky, brittle wafer among

them and ushered them off the track and into a thick clump of bushes. They seated themselves obediently and, satisfied that no casual passers-by would see them there, Brompton grinned and in an unusual outburst of generosity gave them each a little more ginger-snap. 'Theer, that's for being good, and now you must wait here for Meg to come and fetch you, and she'll bring you some more sweeties then. But you'll only get it iffen youm really good and quiet betimes. Does you understand me?'

The three small, dirty, runny-nosed faces nodded solemnly at him, their pieces of oily golden sweet clutched tight in grubby fingers. Satisfied, Brompton left them and went back to Meg. She had stopped sobbing now and only hiccupped at intervals and sniffed noisily.

'Blow your nose, girl. I told you once already,' he ordered, and she obeyed without demur. 'Come on, we'll goo up theer a little ways.' He pointed into the woods on the opposite side of the track to where the children were hidden. 'Now I arn't agoing to hurt you, girl, but I wants to tell you summat very important to you, that's all.'

Like some defeated captive Meg walked behind him, and as they walked he told her, 'Now you listen careful, Meg. Old Henry Milward wants to gi' you your sack because of the ruction you kicked up the other night. But I udden't let him, even though you'd bin so nasty towards me. I told him you was a good girl really, and you was just feeling a bit off colour that night. So, he's agreed to let you keep on working at the Fountain, just so long as I wants you to be theer.'

Meg stared at the back of his head with dumb misery in her eyes as he went on. 'I knows what 'ud happen to your Mam and your little brothers and sisters if you got your sack from the Fountain, Meg. They'd all be put in the poor'us 'udden't they? And what 'ud become on 'um in theer, Meg? Aye? Tell me that? They'd suffer dreadful, 'udden't they? And it 'ud be your fault, 'udden't it, for being so bad as to lose your work at the Fountain.' He swung to look at her, and saw that her eyes were brimming with tears, and impatiently he said, 'Don't start bloody shrawking again, girl. Arn't I already told you that I'm agoing to let you stay on at the Fountain?'

She nodded wordlessly.

By now they had got to a small glade, its surface a mixture of thick, dried grasses and moss, and Brompton grinned. 'Right, this 'ull do, it's nice and dry and sheltered from the wind.' He turned to face her. 'Now, Meg, you knows that if I'm to be good to you, and let you keep your job, then it's only fair that youm nice to me in return, arn't it?'

When she only stared down at the ground and made no reply a note of exacerbation entered his voice. ''Ull you give me an answer, or have I to go to Mr Milward, and tell him to get rid of you?'

She looked up at him in alarm, and he realized just how much he was enjoying what he was doing to this helpless girl, and felt a frisson of acute pleasure as he thought of what was yet to come. 'Well?' He scowled at her. 'What's it to be?'

Twice her lips opened as if to speak, and twice only a meaningless sound issued from them, then she coughed nervously and managed to tell him, 'I'll do whatever you wants me to, Mr Brompton.'

Her features were all but hidden by her matted mass of hair, but Brompton didn't need to see her face clearly to know that he had won.

'That's better, girl.' By now the lust was thickening in his throat so that his voice sounded curiously strained. 'You'se got to be nice to me now, Meg, and be nice to me whenever I wants you to be in future as well, and then I'll make sure that you keeps your work in the Fountain, and your Mam and the little 'uns 'ull not have to goo to the poor'us. Does you understand that well?'

She nodded dumbly and the tears welled from her eyes and fell down her cheeks, but by now Brompton was too excited to care. Impatiently he gripped the skirt of her dress and pulled it off over her head. She made no resistance, only stood trembling violently in her sole undergarment, a ragged, dirty shift. Breathing harshly, Brompton lifted this shift from her body also, and when she moved her hands to cover herself he pulled them roughly to her sides and stared avidly at her high, rounded breasts and the prominent dark triangle at the top of her pale thighs.

'By the Christ!' he grunted, and his tongue ran along suddenly dry lips. 'Girl you might be, but youm built like a full-grown 'ooman, and a fine-bodied 'un at that.'

He tore at the lacing of the front flap of his breeches and let the flap fall to reveal his erect organ. He grabbed the sides of her head between his hands and savagely crushed his mouth on hers, bruising her lips with his force. Then he took his mouth away and pressed her head down towards his throbbing maleness. 'Take it in your mouth, girl,' he panted. 'And suck it nice and gentle. That'll do for starters.' As he felt the warm wetness of her lips enfold him, he groaned with pleasure and then with one hand began to unbutton his shirt.

It was full night when Meg at last came back for the children, and they were cold and hungry and very afraid of the darkness. She made no answer to their babble of words, only whimpered softly with the pain of her ravaged, violated body as she led them on towards their home. She could still hear Brompton's parting threats in her mind and, terrified, she could only keep on repeating silently, 'I won't tell anybody what you did to me, Mr Brompton. I swear I'll not breathe a word about it. Not to anybody. Not to me Mam, or to Tildy, or even to God hisself ... I swear I won't tell.'

Chapter Thirteen

John Clayton was in the study of his home on the Fish Hill, facing his vicar and father in Christ, Reverend the Lord Aston. All the pleasure of the day made memorable for him by having won the champion's hat at backsword was now irrevocably soured by what his employer was telling him.

'I confess, my lord, that this news you bring greatly disturbs and saddens me,' he stated now. His attractively ugly face, bearing the welts left by his opponents' backswords, was sorely troubled, and he began to pace restlessly up and down the book-lined room, as if the physical movement would relieve his mental tension.

'Dammee, Sir, will you kindly cease from stamping about the room like an enraged bull,' Reverend the Lord Aston complained pettishly.

His curate came to a standstill. 'My apologies, my lord. It is my habit when I am disturbed by anything.'

'Then get quit of it, Sir, for it makes me feel positively vertiginous.' The sallow features scowled. ''Pon my soul, Sir, do you think yourself to be the only mortal disturbed by this news? I was at breakfast when the letter from Peel's office reached me this morn. I've been suffering most painfully from indigestion ever since, I do assure you. Still, I have told you now what is afoot here, and it behoves you to act as a loyal subject of His Majesty. Remember, John, in my absence you stand in my place, just as I stand in place of the Earl when he is absent from the parish. I rely on you to do your duty, young man.'

'I trust that I have always vindicated that reliance, my

lord.' The curate's tone held a note of resentment which caused his superior to look sharply at him.

'Then be careful not to fail me now, John,' he snapped. 'Remember, there are a good many young men in holy orders who would be more than grateful for the curacy of St Stephen's.'

The vicar took his leave shortly afterwards, and John Clayton sat down in his study to think on what he had been told. An agent of the Government, a spy, a 'provocation man', had been sent by the Department of the Home Secretary to the needle district to investigate whether or not illegal combinations of working men were in existence among the needle workers. He was to pay particular attention to the pointers, following their concerted effort during the closing weeks of the previous year in defeating young Robert Stafford's attempt to introduce a new safety measure to the pointing process which would have enabled him to lower the very high wages demanded by the pointers.

Clayton found the knowledge that a Government spy was in the town to be abhorrent to him. Although a Tory himself, and an anti-radical, he disagreed strongly with the way successive governments had dealt with the problem of unrest among the people. He did not like what he had read and heard of the activities of Government agents such as the notorious 'Oliver the spy', and Castle and Edwards, and others like them who had deliberately encouraged working men to break the anti-combination laws and then informed on those men for pay. He pondered on the possible identity of the spy who had come into this district. All the Home Secretary's office had told Lord Aston in its letter was that an agent had recently been sent to the town. The curate decided that he must try to identify that agent. Aston's information had been that the man would make himself known to the magistrates once he had uncovered any illegal combination. John Clayton felt very unhappy about this secrecy. Who could guarantee the probity of this unknown agent? Who could tell just what hurt might be inflicted upon the town by someone who might deliberately set out to foment trouble for his own eventual rewards? Clayton knew only too well that the unruly Redditch people would need little enough encouragement to engage in violent protest.

'I don't want to see bloodshed on our streets.' The young curate recoiled from that dread prospect. 'I don't want to see the Yeomanry Cavalry sabreing men, women and children here, as they did in Manchester. If I can identify this agent, then mayhap I'll be able to nip any trouble in the bud.'

Thoughtfully he rose and started to pace up and down the room.

'Now how best to go about the business?' he wondered, and for long hours his footsteps echoed on the polished floorboards as he puzzled over this problem far into the night.

Chapter Fourteen

The bell of the Fountain pealed out its summons, and the in-workers came in reluctant, fuddle-headed, sick-stomached obedience to the call. Brawl-bruised men, love-bruised women, parent-bruised children streamed through the great arch in the darkness of early morning, and Arthur Conolly stood watching them enter.

The overlooker's expression was sour. As far as he could judge, a full third of the workforce had failed to come to time. This was always the case following a holiday, as inevitable as Old Henry's liverish outburst of anger when Conolly reported the number of absentees to him.

'He'll roast me good and proper agen,' the overlooker whined mentally. 'As if it's my bloody fault! Every year it happens, and every year the bloody old fool gives me the roasting for it. Why can't he do like other masters and give the sods only a half-holiday? That way mayhap there 'udden't be so many get so drunk that they can't bloody well rise up in the morning. But no! The old sod keeps on blethering about him being a true-born Englishmen, and true-born Englishmen must have the full day's holiday, and then he gives me the bollocking when the bastards don't come to time next day. What does he expect me to do? To goo and drag 'um from their bloody pits, I wonder?'

His gloomy train of thought was interrupted by the sight of Tildy Crawford coming under the entrance arch. Even at this hour there was a freshness about her appearance that caused the overlooker's lust to awaken. He made a great show of holding his pocket-watch up to the lantern light and checking the hour.

'Youm cutting it very fine, arn't you, Crawford? Another few seconds and the gate 'ud ha' bin shut to you.'

Tildy nodded, and would have walked on, but the man stepped in front of her, forcing her to halt.

'Now Crawford, has you give any more thought to what I said last week?'

She looked steadily at him, dislike for the man openly showing in her luminous brown eyes. 'I haven't needed to think any more about it, Mr Conolly. My answer is still the same. I'm not wanting other work at your price.'

His long, yellow teeth were wolfish in the lantern light. 'I wouldn't ha' considered that you and me having a bit o' fun together 'ud be a hard price to pay for getting out o' the lye wash and into a clean, easy little job, Crawford. Youm not living with any man, am you, and you must be missing having a prick between your legs of a night. A good-looking 'ooman like you needs to be well-fucked, and I'm the man to give you all you needs in that line.'

Tildy's quick temper rose in hot resentment of his crudity. 'Do you talk to your wife like this, Conolly? Because if that's the case, then save all your filth for her. I don't want to hear it.'

Sexual frustration drove the man to act as he did now. 'I knows what you needs, you stuck-up bitch,' he growled. 'Come here!'

His hands grabbed for her breasts and buttocks and he jerked her towards him. Tildy reacted instinctively and her knee shot upwards with stunning force and accuracy. Conolly squealed in agony, cupping his testicles with both hands as his body doubled over.

No one was entering the arch by now, but from his niche in the wall old Ben Wardle the night watchman had seen the incident.

'That's the way to do it, Tildy.' His cracked old voice was gleeful. 'I see'd what happened and what he tried on

105

wi' you, girl. So iffen need be I'll tell the gaffer what I see'd.'

Tildy smiled gratefully at him and hurried on towards the lye wash shop, knowing that she would find the added security of allies and friends there and, if driven by dire necessity makeshift weapons of defence in the shape of boiling water and heavy iron ladles.

Once in the steam-filled shop she told the other women what had occurred and they cackled with congratulatory laughter, but Tildy herself was now undergoing a reaction to the violent interlude and to her chagrin found that her hands were shaking. Mary Ann Avery noticed, and told her reassuringly, 'Never you mind about Conolly, Tildy. If the bugger comes arter you here, then he'll have us lot to deal with as well.'

Tildy experienced an onrush of pure gratitude. 'I'm truly thankful for that,' she said quietly. 'But I don't want you to go getting into trouble on my account.'

'Don't you moither your yed about that, Tildy,' Sarah Farr put in. 'What else be friends for, if not to stand by each other in face o' trouble.'

Tildy could only voice her thanks once more, then she saw that there was an absentee. 'Hasn't young Meg come yet?'

'No,' Mary Ann frowned. 'The silly little cow's probably still laying in bed. Bloody little mawkin! If her starts to keep bad time her'll end up wi' her sack in double-quick time, because noddy-yeds like her are ten a penny. It's only the skilled workers who can risk taking any liberties wi' the gaffers.'

The mention of skilled workers brought Josh Dyson to the forefront of Tildy's mind and as she toiled, cleansing the filth from the needles, she thought about their conversation of the previous night. At the time, with his enthusiasm to fire her own imagination, the ideas he had projected had seemed both exciting and feasible. Now, in the cold, dark morning hours the excitement was still there, even if a little muted, but the feasibility of what he

106

had proposed appeared increasingly unlikely. To form a secret Combination or Union of operatives firstly in this mill, and then gradually throughout the entire district had seemed possible last night. Today she was doubtful as she mentally examined the venture. Secrecy was not the major problem initially, she thought. When the numbers were small, they could choose their fellows very carefully, and the fearful knowledge that discovery would mean at worst, transportation for life, at best, imprisonment at hard labour in this country, would go a long way towards ensuring closed mouths.

Tildy frowned in concentration. She considered now that the major problem would be the actual recruiting. There were many hundreds of stop-tap rebels in the district; men and women who, in their cups, were ready to defy King and Government, magistrates and Yeomanry Cavalry. But to find men and women who would be equally defiant at six o'clock on a cold wet morning would be a different kettle of fish altogether. Such courage was hard to find, and those who possessed it were few and far between.

As Josh Dyson saw it, sheer volume of numbers was essential for any union or combination to succeed. Tildy now found herself differing from that view. She thought rather that it was quality, not quantity, that was essential. A few, dedicated, resolute individuals acting with complete accord and trust in each other could do far more to advance their chosen cause than thousands of loud-mouthed tap-room supporters.

With a shock of surprise Tildy suddenly realized that by thinking in this manner she had in her sub-conscious mind already committed herself to taking an active part in the attempt to form a secret union in this district.

'It's as if I've been waiting for someone to set me on this road,' she thought wonderingly. 'And yet when the nailers ceased from work back in the Sidemoor I refused to join them.' Her lips twisted ruefully as she remembered the violence finally used against her to stop her working. She still bore the round, puckered scar of a pistol ball on her body as a visual legacy of that violence. 'Why is it then that I should now be so strong for this union? I still have my Davy to support, as I did then, which was why I went on working. Yet now I can face the prospect of striking from work with hardly a tremor?' She pondered this for some time and came to the conclusion that now she had sufficient experience of life to know that unless matters were radically changed, she faced only a lifetime of drudging poverty.

She thought afresh about Josh Dyson, and of the undoubted attraction he exerted upon her. Although Tildy possessed great depths of physical passion, she was too fastidious in her tastes to indulge her considerable sexual appetites with the licence many other women in her position displayed. She had only ever slept with two men apart from her husband, and that had only been on a single occasion each time.

With her husband she had known only a brutal congress of the flesh, more akin to rape than to love-making. She longed for a tender, sexual, loving relationship which would be part and parcel of a permanent union based on mutual trust, respect, and understanding, but she had long since realized that she could contemplate such a union only if she met a man who possessed very special qualities of mind and character. She had also long since decided that until she met such a man, then she would live without physical loving, and when driven by the remorseless cravings of her body she would satisfy her own needs in the lonely hours of the night. She was determined above all else to maintain her own sense of self-respect, and she knew that if she were to surrender to her own powerful sexual needs, and sleep with any of the men who chased her, then inevitably that self-respect she clung to would be mercilessly eroded.

During the second half-hour break of the long day Johnny Brompton came into the lye wash shop. Tildy was

108

nearest to the door and she could not help but feel a
nervous tremor as he stood next to her, his eyes searching
through the steam.

'Wheer's Meg Tullet?' he asked Mary Ann, and the
woman shrugged.

'Her arn't turned in today.'

He nodded acknowledgment, and as he swung to leave,
his eyes met Tildy's. He grinned at her with an air of
mocking triumph, but said nothing. There was something
in his expression which struck an unease about Meg
Tullet into Tildy's mind, and when he had gone she said to
Mary Ann, 'I wonder if Meg's all right?'

Again the elder woman shrugged. 'She might be
unwell, my duck, that's a common enough thing, arn't it?'

Tildy nodded pensively, and decided that when she left
the Fountain that night she would walk to the Tullets'
cottage and find out why the young girl had not come to
her work. The visual image of Brompton's triumphant,
sneering grin kept returning to her constantly, and
she had a strong foreboding that in some way or other
it was Brompton who was responsible for the girl's
absence.

Periodically also Tildy gave some thought to her own
immediate problem, Arthur Conolly. She was sure that he
would try to revenge himself on her, but could not decide
how, or when. She ruthlessly crushed down the impulse to
go and unburden her problem to Josh Dyson. It was her
battle, and she would fight it herself, her own pride
demanded that of her.

At about six o'clock in the evening there came a slack
period in the work, and the women stood around the
copper's fire to try and dry out their sodden clothing a
little. It was then that Tildy casually brought up the
question of a combination existing in the district.

'Do you think that the pointer lads have got such a
union? Because they all seemed to act as one against
Robert Stafford, didn't they?'

'You should know that better than anyone else here,

my duck,' Mary Ann smiled ambiguously. 'It cost you your pointing work, didn't it?'

'That's true enough,' Tildy confirmed, then added reflectively, 'but to be honest, Mary Ann, I think that in a way they did me a favour by causing me to lose that work. It was terrible hard on my lungs. I still feel at times as though there's stone dust in them, even now.'

'Ahr, it's a killer of a job, so it is,' Mary Ann observed. 'And I think youm right in saying that the pointer lads did you a favour. But why be you asking if they'm in a combination, though, Tildy? You knows it's forbid to form such things.'

'I was just wondering, that's all. Because they did all act together, didn't they?'

'The pointers always sticks together,' Sarah Farr joined in 'But they'm allowed to get away wi' doing so. Iffen we was to try the same thing, then we'd bloody soon be out on our jobs.'

'But why should that necessarily be so?' Tildy challenged. 'Surely if all the women in this mill stuck together, then they wouldn't be given their sacks for doing so?'

'Wouldn't they though?' Sarah Farr scoffed. 'By the Christ, Tildy, but you'se got a lot to learn about factory life, I'm buggered if you an't.'

Tildy's stubbornness was roused and would not allow her to leave this matter now she had raised it. 'I still think that if all the women here would only stand together, then we could improve things for ourselves.'

'But we 'udden't be let to stand together, Tildy,' Sarah Farr declared forcefully. 'Youm talking foolish, my wench. You knows already that there's laws agen us doing such a thing. We'd find ourselves on the way to Botany Bay afore you could say "Jack Robinson".'

'But suppose that we organized secretly, and the masters didn't know that we were a combination?'

Sarah Farr stared at Tildy as if the girl were a simpleton. 'How could they not know such a thing, if we all on us acted together?' she exclaimed impatiently. 'It

110

'ud be bloody plain that we was acting in combination 'udden't it! Be you too yampy-yedded to understand that, Tildy?'

'Of course I understand that.' Tildy in her turn showed impatience. 'But what I'm saying is that if no ringleaders could be identified and picked out, and if no actual proof could be discovered of the existence of an organized combination, then there's not much the masters could do about such a situation, is there? They couldn't send hundreds of women to Botany Bay just because they suspected those women of having formed a combination. They couldn't put hundreds of women in jail, just because those women had individually decided that they were not prepared to work in a needle mill for any longer.'

'I take your point, Tildy,' Mary Ann interjected. 'But there's one small matter youm forgetting, my duck, and that is that the women are here working because they've only got two choices. Work here, or bloody starve.'

'We could all apply for parish relief.' Tildy realized deep down the essential fallacies of her argument, but still she could not help but persist in it.

'Oh yes, we could all apply to the overseers for relief,' Mary Ann nodded. 'But who are the overseers to the poor in this town, my duck?' She lapsed into silence, knowing that she had won the argument, and Tildy could only smile in defeat.

'Of course you're right, Mary Ann. The overseers are the same men who are the masters and the gentry. I know you're right, all of you, and that I'm probably speaking foolishly. But still I have to say it. I think it's time that all we women did band together in some way or other, and demand justice for ourselves.'

'So does I think that, my duck, and nigh on every other woman in this town thinks it as well, I shouldn't wonder,' Mary Ann agreed sadly. 'But the only snag is, we've no chance of ever doing so. Look at all the men that have tried to do such, and have been beaten down. If men can't succeed, then how can us women ever hope to do so?'

Tildy allowed the argument to lapse, and the brief period of respite was soon ended by the advent of William Kitchen with more purses of oily buckram in his arms.

Chapter Fifteen

'My darling, says she, I think it no surprise,
For I know what you want, by the look that's in your
eyes.
My mother has told to me what all young men do seek,
And you'll try to put your hand,
In me cuckooooo's nesssst ...'

The tendons stood out in Marmaduke Montmorency's
wasted, grey-stubbled throat as he sang to the tune played
by lame Ben Mitchel on his fiddle, and John Whateley
came roaring in to join the chorus:

'Some like a girl who is pretty in the face,
And some like a girl who is slender in the waist.
But I like a girl who can wriggle and can twist.
At the bottom of the belly
Lies the cuckooooo's nessssst ...'

Nathanial Farrel, still sober despite the considerable
amount of ale and gin he had drunk in company with his
companions that afternoon and evening, sat silently
smiling and tapping with his fingers on the table top in
time to the music.

'And I often puts me hand on her
cuckoooooooo's nesssssssst!'

The song came to a close with uproarious self-applause
from the two singers, and Whateley invited, 'Come now,

lads, sup up,' and shouted loudly, 'Bring us another jug-full here, Missus.'

His wife, a buxom, dark-eyed woman, came from behind the bar counter and with obvious bad grace slammed down another foaming jug of ale on the table. Two young girls seated with them in the tap-room of the Black Horse giggled behind their hands at Mrs Whateley's show of temper, then tried to flirt with Nathanial Farrel, but he paid them little heed. His light green eyes were watchful and missed nothing of what was happening around him.

In the opposite corner of the room three Yeomen Cavalrymen were talking quietly among themselves, their over-fed, bucolic features not matching the dashing gallantry of their scarlet tunics, black-and-red striped overalls, white crossbelts, splendid silver epaulettes and gold and scarlet waist-sashes.

'Come all you sweet charmers, come give me your choice,
    For there's nothing to compare
    with a ploughboy's voice,
For to hear the little ploughboy sweetly sing,
All the hills and the valleys,
He makes for to rinnnng . . .'

The singers struck up again, and as the two girls joined their high-pitched voices to the rest, Nathanial Farrel took the opportunity to move across the room and speak to the soldiers.

'Your pardon, gentlemen, might I enquire your regiment? I've not seen this uniform before.'

'We'em in the Earl o' Plymouth's troop o' the Worcestershire Yeomanry, Master, the Tardebigge troop.'

'Yeomanry Cavalry?' Farrel exclaimed in innocent surprise. 'You are not regulars then? 'Pon my soul, gentlemen, I took you for such. You have the stamp of the regular service.'

The three farmers visibly preened at the compliment to their martial appearance, and their spokesman said, 'Well, as to that, our adjutant is Captain John Emmot. He was an officer of the Light Horse for many years, and he's trained us to the standards of the regular cavalry.'

'Judging by your bearing and turnout, he has succeeded well,' Farrel flattered fulsomely. 'Come, gentlemen, will you do me the honour of taking a glass with me? I've a strong wish to drink to the health of the Yeomanry Cavalry.'

They accepted with alacrity, and while drinking the fresh pots of ale chatted with their new-found admirer.

'Have you been on duty?' Farrel asked.

'No such luck, we've been to Droitwich to send one of our comrades off on his last journey. 'Tis always a sad thing to see a good friend buried.'

'Indeed it is,' Farrel sympathized. 'I've buried many good comrades myself. But when they fall in battle, at least we have the consolation of knowing they died for their King and their country. Did your friend die on service?'

The fattest of the trio chuckled salaciously. 'You might say that, friend, he were serving his missus, and his bloody heart conked out.'

All four men laughed, and then Farrel said casually, 'Mind you, there have been many opportunities for rough service for the Yeomanry these last years, have there not? What with all the troubles in our country. Do you find that there is much unrest in these parts among the labourers?'

'Well, not really. Not like it was a couple of years since in the nailing villages up around Bromsgrove. No, the needlemakers hereabouts am an unruly lot, but in all truth they mostly fights among themselves only.'

'You've had no trouble with Luddites or Radicals then?' Farrel pressed.

'No, not really. There's bin little o' such nonsense in this parish, and iffen there ever should be, well, we stands ready to deal wi' it.' Three plump red faces scowled in fierce unison.

'Ahr, I'd like to see the Radicals who could stand against the Tardebigge troop.' The youngest trooper gripped the pommel of his sabre and shook it so that it rattled in its scabbard. 'We'd soon be giving the buggers a taste o' cold steel up their arses.'

'Like you did at Peterloo, aye, my bold buckoes.' It was John Whateley who spoke so loudly and aggressively, and the room hushed. The landlord was drunk, and his swarthy features were dark with anger.

'Now then, John, what's amiss wi' you?' the youngest trooper challenged, and Whateley deliberately hawked and spat onto the man's shiny, polished riding boot. 'Youm amiss wi' me, Charlie Wadcoat. You and all the rest o' you murdering bastards that thought it such fine sport to chop down helpless women and kids up in Manchester theer.'

Wadcoat's youthful face became sullen in resentment. 'None on us were at Manchester, Whateley, and you knows that bloody well. It warn't the Worcester Yeomen who did that business.'

'Maybe not.' The landlord was unabashed. 'But it was buggers like you, warn't it? Bloody farmers and shop-keepers, bloody lick-spittles to the bloody gentry . . .'

'Damn you, John, will you hold your tongue? You'll get yourself into sore trouble one o' these bright fine days.' Whateley's wife, Jean, came between the bridling men. 'You'd best get to your bed, you drunken pig!' she stormed at her husband, her face deathly white with temper.

John Whateley was always a little afraid of his wife when she was in the grip of the sort of passion she was now displaying, and he tried to justify himself.

'Look, Missus, all I said was —'

'Shut your big mouth, 'ull you, for the love of God, shut it!' she shrieked wildly, cutting him short. 'You'se lost us too much trade as it is, wi' your forever cursing your betters. And what's so good about you, might I ask? What entitles you to becall men who can make a profit from their work? All you ever does is waste money by sitting and swilling wi' useless layabouts and sluts like this lot here.' She stabbed her forefinger at Marmaduke Montmorency's bemused face, and then at the faces of the tipsy girls. 'Look at 'um, 'ull you!' she shrieked furiously. 'Drunken scums and whores, every last one on 'um!'

With an offended expression, Marmaduke Montmorency lifted his floppy tam-o-shanter from his long, greasy hair and rose from his seat to stand swaying giddily. Then he struck a theatrical posture, one hand high above his head, the other clutching his hat to his shirtless chest, and declaimed sonorously:

'Pray Goody, please to moderate the rancour of your tongue.
Why flash those sparks of fury from your eyes?
Remember, when the judgement's weak,
The prejudice is strong ... *Midas*, Act One, Scene Four.'

Without a moment's hesitation Jean Whateley picked up the half-filled jug of beer from the table and hurled its contents into Montmorency's face.

'Jean Whateley!' she shouted, almost beside herself with rage. 'The Black Horse tap-room. February the twelfth!'

Everyone in the room, except for the two protagonists, burst into roars of laughter. Marmaduke Montmorency made no attempt to wipe away the beer that streamed down his head, instead he bowed with a flourish of his tam-o-shanter and moved towards the door. When he reached it he turned and smiling sweetly at the enraged woman he lifted both his hands towards her, and recited mellifluously:

'One kind kiss before we part.
Drop a tear, and bid Adieu.
Though we sever, my fond heart,
'Til we meet shall pant for you.'

He ducked through the door as the jug shattered against it.

Even while Nathanial Farrel laughed with the rest, one part of his mind was already giving thought to the words and behaviour of the landlord, John Whateley. 'Could he be one of those I'm seeking for? Surely he's a likely enough prospect ...'

Chapter Sixteen

The wattle and daub cottage was in darkness and Tildy stood for a few moments in the frosty moonlight mentally taking stock of the broken, rag-stuffed shutters, the sagging, mouldering thatched roof and the general tumble-down look of the building. She smelt no smoke, and could see none issuing from the stub of chimney even though the night had turned very cold so that her own breath plumed whitely in front of her face.

'Is there anybody inside, I wonder? Well, there's only one way of finding that out.' Stepping up to the door she rapped sharply with her knuckles.

'Meg?' she called softly. 'It's only me. It's Tildy. Tildy Crawford.' Again she knocked and listened, her ear pressed against the rough, unplaned planking. 'Meg? If you're in there, then open the door. It's Tildy Crawford ... Meg?'

Suddenly she heard a shuffling within the cottage and then the door slowly creaked open, and the moonlight silvered Meg Tullet's forlorn face.

'Oh Meg, what ails you?' Tildy exclaimed pityingly. 'Why do you look so sad? Are you ill? Is that why you didn't come to work today?'

For several seconds the simple-minded girl only stared at her in mute misery, then, abruptly, her face crumpled and she came sobbing into Tildy's arms.

For a long time Tildy only held the girl and spoke soothingly to her, and eventually the sobs died away to snuffles and hiccups. Tildy shivered, and said gently, 'Do you think it better that we go inside, my honey, out of the cold air? Do you have a candle handy?'

Meg shook her head, and burst out sobbing again, and Tildy grimaced wryly. 'There now, dry your eyes, it doesn't matter. It doesn't matter. The moonlight is candle enough.' Slowly she calmed the girl, and then asked, 'Is your mam here?'

'No.' The tousled head swung dolefully from side to side. 'Theer's only me and the little 'uns. Me mam went to Studley to see her sister, and ask her if she can lend us a few pence.'

'And she's left you without light or fire?' Tildy spoke as if to herself, wondering what sort of mother Mrs Tullet was, to leave her children alone in a cold, dark house, and Meg said defensively, 'Her don't trust us wi' fire when her's away, Tildy. The little 'uns plays wi' it, and twice now they's nearly set the house afire.'

Tildy nodded, silently accepting that perhaps the woman had reason enough to leave them in darkness. Aloud, she said, 'Well, never mind that now, but for the love of God go and get something to wrap yourself in, child. You'll get perished with the cold else.'

Meg disappeared into the darkness to re-appear muffled in an old blanket. 'The little 'uns be all sleeping sound, Tildy, so let's move a bit away in case we wakes 'um. They'm buggers to get settled again if they wakes in the night.'

Tildy was happy to walk and generate some warmth in her chilled body. 'Now Meg, are you poorly?' she questioned as they moved from the door.

'No, I'm all right.'

'Then why didn't you come to your work today? We were all worried about you.'

The girl made no answer, only hunched her shoulders and bowed her head, and again Tildy's former forebodings burgeoned.

'Has something happened to you, Meg? Tell me!' She brought the girl to a halt and with her fingers gently lifted the trembling chin so that she could see her expression. Meg Tullet's small face was a silver mask of torment in the moonlight, and Tildy's forebodings became conviction, and she spoke sharply in her anxiety. 'Listen, Meg, I think something's happened between you and Johnny Brompton?'

'I never told you!' The girl shrilled out so unexpectedly that Tildy physically started with shock.

'I never said nothing! I never said nothing about it to you! I never said nothing!' Again and again the girl wailed her denials, and without conscious volition she began to jerk her body grotesquely. 'I never said nothing! I never did!' Hysteria was in her voice, and Tildy reacted instinctively by grabbing and shaking her hard.

'Be quiet, Meg! Stop shouting!' An iron determination to find out the truth had gripped Tildy now, and she steeled herself to act roughly. 'You'll tell me what's happened, or I'll clout you myself, and hard too ... Now!' Her voice was like a whiplash. 'What has happened between you and Johnny Brompton?'

For a long moment the two of them seemed frozen in time and motion, then the tight-clenched fists of Meg Tullet slowly opened and her stiffened body swayed and sagged. With fresh sobs shuddering through her she choked out the story of her brutal violation. As Tildy held and cuddled the grief-stricken child, her own anger burned fiercer and fiercer within her, and she felt the red lust to wreak vengeance on the man who could subject this simple-minded, unprotected girl to such a terrible ordeal. She waited until the girl had sobbed herself out then asked gently, 'Did you tell your mam about it when you got home, Meg?'

'No, I was feared to, and I'm feared now, Tildy. Johnny Brompton said that he'd know the minute I told anybody what he'd done to me, and then he'd come and kill me.'

Tildy clutched the shaking girl hard against her breasts. 'Don't be feared any more, Meg. Johnny Brompton will not harm you again, I promise you that. I'll protect you from him.'

'But how can you, Tildy?' the child asked doubtfully. 'He's a man and stronger than you. Youm naught but a woman.'

'Don't I know that well enough already,' Tildy thought sardonically, then her anger against Brompton swept over her once more. 'Listen Meg, I want you to come with me straight to the constable, and tell him all about what happened.'

'Oh no! I couldn't. I'd be too shamed to,' Meg protested tearfully. 'Besides, I darcn't leave the little 'uns by themselves. Suppose summat bad happened to 'um, and me not here?'

Her distress was such that Tildy had not got the heart to badger her further. 'Well then,' she asked softly, 'supposing I was to go and tell the constable on your behalf? Would that suit you better?'

'Oh yes, Tildy, you tell him for me. He'll listen to you, but he'd not pay any heed to me. He's shouted at me and me Mam afore. Called us dirty beggars, so he did, and said we was naught but trampers' whores.' She hesitated, and then a fresh wave of fear broke over her. 'But what about Johnny Brompton, Tildy? I'm so feared on him. He swore he'd kill me iffen I told on him, and he said that nobody 'ull be able to stop him from getting me.'

'There's plenty can stop him, don't you fret,' Tildy assured her grimly. 'And anyway, he won't know that you have told anyone until it's too late for him to try anything, will he? When I tell the constable what he's done, why then, Brompton will be in the lock-up before he can draw breath. You'll be safe, my honey. I promise you, you'll be safe from him.'

'Will I, Tildy?' Doubt was still hovering in the girl's face. ''Ull you sure I'm safe? 'Ull you promise?'

'I will,' Tildy promised fervently. 'You may depend on that, Meg. I swear on my baby's life that I'll keep you safe from Brompton.'

Reassured by this Meg Tullet allowed Tildy to lead her back to the cottage.

'Now you go inside and bar the door fast,' Tildy instructed. 'And don't open it to anyone until I come back myself.'

'But what if me mam comes?' Meg questioned anxiously, and Tildy could not suppress a faint smile. 'Yes, let your mam in, of course. I'll try not to be long now, honey.'

Tildy hurried back to the town. Although the hour was not late the streets were deserted and many of the houses in darkness. The after-effects of the holiday debauchery had sent most people to an early slumber and only an occasional light glimmering through a window-pane denoted that anyone still remained astir.

Joseph Cashmore, the parish constable, lived midway along the Evesham street in a house set back from its neighbours. Tildy was relieved to see that a light still burned within. She knew the man's inflammable temper, and dreaded to think of his reaction should she have had to raise him from his bed. Her knock was answered by the constable's wife, Janey Cashmore, a small, timid-faced, timid-voiced, timid-mannered woman who was completely dominated by her formidable husband.

'I want to speak with the constable,' Tildy told her. 'It's very urgent.'

The woman stood with her hands nervously fluttering up to her chest and down to her hips. 'I don't rightly know as how you can speak with him at this time,' she said at length.

Tildy was in no mood to be gainsaid however. 'Look, Mrs Cashmore, I'm sorry to come at such a late hour, but I haven't come here for any little matter. It's very serious, and I must speak right now with your husband.'

For another seemingly interminable length of time Janey Cashmore hovered at the door, then she whispered, 'Wait here a minute, 'ull you.'

The door closed in Tildy's face, and for one mad instant she was sorely tempted to hammer on it with both fists. Then it re-opened and the woman beckoned her to enter.

123

The candle-lit room was stiflingly hot and steamy and reeked with a mixture of pungent smells. When Tildy saw the burly-bodied constable she also saw the origin of the smells. He was half-lying in a big wooden armchair by the side of the fire hob, on which a large, shallow, open pan bubbled and steamed. His shirt and waistcoat were pulled open and a great poultice covered his hairy chest. Tildy knew this remedy for sore throats and chests. Cabbage leaves and leeks boiled in vinegar then wrapped in a cloth and slapped hot onto the affected parts. Her heart sank. If the constable was ill with his chest then he'd not be likely to spring into action on Meg Tullet's behalf.

He scowled at his unwelcome visitor and in a voice so hoarse as to be almost unintelligible croaked, 'What brings you here, Tildy Crawford? More bloody trouble, is it?'

Tildy tried to be diplomatic. 'I'm sorry to come pestering you when you're not well, Master Cashmore, but it's a very serious matter I've come about.'

'Well?' he croaked, and his sweaty, flushed features remained grim.

Tildy drew a deep breath and launched on her story. When she had finished relating the account of Meg Tullet's ordeal she asked, 'Will you be arresting Johnny Brompton tonight, Master Cashmore?'

A fit of coughing racked the man, and it was some moments before he had recovered sufficiently to answer her. Then, his breath wheezing noisily, he said, 'No, Tildy Crawford. I'll not be arresting Johnny Brompton tonight, nor tomorrow night neither.'

Tildy could not believe she had heard him correctly. 'Are you saying you'll not arrest him?' she queried in puzzlement.

The constable slowly nodded his head. 'That's what I'm asaying, my wench.'

'But why not?' Tildy burst out. 'The man has raped a young girl. He must be arrested and punished for it.'

'Has you got proof that Brompton raped her?' Cashmore wanted to know.

124

'What do you mean, have I got proof?' Tildy riposted. 'I've just now left the girl. Her distress is awful to see, and she's in fear of her life besides.'

'Ne'er mind her bloody distress, that's easy put on,' Cashmore wheezed, and coughed again. 'Goddam this bloody chest o' mine.' He sounded half-strangled. 'When I says proof, Tildy Crawford, I means has you got any witnesses to this so-called rape?'

'Of course I haven't, you know that well,' Tildy replied scathingly. 'How could there be witnesses? He took her deep into the woods, didn't he, where no one was likely to see or hear what took place. He left the smaller children hidden among bushes and gave them sweets to keep them quiet.'

'And the girl? Has her got bad injuries like cuts or bruises or broken bones?'

Tildy began to experience a sense of failure. 'No, none that could be termed as bad injuries, at least, none that are outward. There are some small bruises on her thighs and shoulders ...'

'Which her could have got in the normal way o' loving?' Cashmore finished the sentence for her.

Tildy's expressive features showed clearly her growing dismay, and Cashmore was sensitive enough to recognize what she was feeling. In a kindlier tone he wheezed hoarsely, 'Listen to me, my wench. I arn't saying that I doubts you personally. I think you to be an honest woman. But because you believes this story o' Meg Tullet's, then it don't really signify that her's atelling the truth, does it?

'Her's simple-yedded, like her mam, and the two on 'um bears the names of whores round about these parts. They'm both on 'um well known for it. Perhaps Brompton did have a bit o' sport wi' the girl up in the woods theer. But he arn't the fust married man to ha' done so, if he did, not by a long score he arn't. And iffen I was to go and arrest every married man who had a bit on the side, well I'd have half the bloody parish in the lock-up, 'udden't I?'

Tildy's anger had re-ignited while he spoke, and again she demanded, 'Will you arrest Brompton, Master Cashmore?'

He spread his hands in a gesture of helplessness. 'I can't do that, Tildy Crawford, not on the unsupported word of a known whore. The magistrates 'ud never commit a man to sessions on a hanging charge like that 'un is, wi'out a deal more proof than you'se got to offer.'

'If you do not arrest Brompton now,' Tildy said heatedly, 'then I shall go directly to the magistrates myself this very night, and lay complaint against that animal.'

'You mun do as you pleases, my wench,' Cashmore told her, and then erupted in coughing and waved his hands at her in dismissal.

Knowing that she would obtain no satisfaction from him, Tildy went from the house. Outside in the chill night air she drew her shawl closer about her shoulders and slowly walked along the street debating her next move. She had already put Davy safely to bed before going to Meg Tullet's home and had given Apollonia a penny to watch over him. Her own evening meal she could do without.

'So there's naught to stop me going direct to a magistrate right now. But perhaps it's better that I go and see Parson Clayton before I go to Lord Aston's house ...'

Candle held high, clad only in a long night-shirt and tasselled night-cap, the Reverend John Clayton peered in surprise at his caller.

'What in heaven's name do you want with me at this hour, Crawford? What have you been up to now?'

The cleric had very mixed feelings about this young woman before him. Although he admired the way she struggled to support herself and her child and to maintain her respectability, he disliked her attitude towards her betters, which he considered to be sadly lacking in the respect due to them. Also, he felt that she was a deal too

126

ready to challenge the authority of those whom God had placed above her. All in all, she was a damn sight too proud-natured and independent-minded for her own good, and seemed insufficiently aware of her own lowly station in life.

'I'm sorry to have roused you from your bed, Parson Clayton ...'

Despite himself, John Clayton found her soft voice with its underlying rustic burr very pleasant to the ear. He was also honest enough to admit that her large dark eyes and pretty face framed by glossy hair made an appealing picture in the candle's glow.

'... but I must speak with you on the matter of a very evil man.' She stood staring at him intently, and after some thought he nodded reluctantly.

'Very well, you'd better step into my study, Crawford. You've ruined my night's rest already, so you may as well continue to disturb me for a while longer.'

He left her waiting without a candle in the dark, fireless study until he returned fully dressed some half-an-hour later. He put his candlestick on the mantel and seated himself in a large leather armchair to one side of the cold hearth, then indicated that she should take the chair opposite to him.

'Now, Crawford, I am prepared to hear the reason why you have so rudely disturbed my night's rest.'

His ugly features were stern, but Tildy knew from past experience that he was not as harsh and unyielding as he liked at times to portray himself as being. As simply as possible she retold her story, and this time also related what had transpired between herself and the constable.

When she had done Clayton steepled his forefingers in front of his chest and rested his chin lightly on their tips as he considered what he had heard. Then he told her, 'My Lord Aston is presently in London, Crawford, and during his absence I normally stand in his stead in the parish. Do you, I wonder, realize the gravity of these charges you are levelling against this man, Brompton? If brought to trial

127

and found guilty he will be sentenced to death, and will most certainly hang. His Majesty does not normally exercise the royal prerogative of mercy in this type of criminal conviction. How would you feel if this man, whom I believe has a wife and three children, were to be hung as a direct result of your laying these charges against him?'

Tildy did not make an immediate reply. In her turn she gave the question deep consideration. When she had done so she looked at Clayton with troubled eyes, but spoke firmly.

'Parson Clayton, the man would not be hung because of the charges I bring against him. He would be hung for having committed a most cruel and brutal assault on a defenceless girl. You ask how I would feel about him being hung, I will tell you frankly, Parson Clayton, I would think he well deserved to be so hung.'

'Then even though you are a mother yourself, and should possess the gentle heart of your sex, your conscience still would not distress you at the sight of the grief you would cause his innocent wife and children, and the eternal shame you would have brought down upon their name?'

His sanctimonious tone irritated Tildy, and she gusted a sigh of impatience. 'Are you forgetting that Meg Tullet is still but a child?' she challenged hotly. 'Are you forgetting the grief and shame she is suffering? And what of the terror this man has instilled in her, so that she was too feared even to tell what was done to her until I practically forced it from her? Tell me this, Parson, if Johnny Brompton had raped a woman of your class, a woman of the gentry, would you be asking her kinsfolk about their consciences? I think not! And would their consciences be troubled at the sight of his grieving wife and children? Again, I think not!' She gave him no chance to interrupt but swept on, lost to everything other than her burning desire to avenge Meg Tullet. 'The consciences of the gentry are not troubled by the sufferings of the pauper children sent to slave and die in the mills of the North Country, as my own small brother was sent. They are not troubled by the women and girls who toil like brute beasts of burden, and are continually maimed and killed in the coal mines.

'Tell me then, what gives you the right to expect me, a pauper woman, to display a tenderer conscience than the gentry? Your gentry-made laws failed to protect Meg Tullet. At least then, let those same laws avenge her by removing the animal who attacked her from the face of the earth. That way we can be certain sure that he can never use another helpless soul so wickedly.'

John Clayton was a fair-minded man, and now, despite his self-righteous indignation at Tildy's attack on himself and his class, he could still accept that there was some inherent truth in what she had said. Therefore, instead of reacting hostilely, he kept a rein on his own fiery temper.

Already Tildy was regretting her own inability to control her emotions and keep a curb on her tongue. She realized that her outburst could well prejudice Clayton's reactions to the accusations she had made against Brompton.

'Damn my temper,' she thought ruefully. 'Damn my loose tongue! Why cannot I ever control myself and act calmly when I seek for justice?'

Then, with a mingling of relief and disappointment she heard him proposing, 'I will have John Brompton brought before me, Crawford, and I will question him myself about these allegations you are making.'

'Well, at least he has not disregarded me entirely,' she thought, and asked aloud, 'Would you wish me and Meg Tullet to be present when you question Brompton, Parson Clayton? Because to my mind that would be best. I am more than eager to accuse him to his wicked face.'

'I do not doubt that fact, Crawford,' he remarked dryly, with a hint of an ambiguous smile quirking on his lips. 'But your presence will not be necessary.'

Instantly, Tildy flared up again. 'But how will it not be

necessary?' she burst out. 'If we are not present, then he will be able to make a denial without challenge. Surely it is necessary for us to be here to fling his lies back in his teeth.'

By now John Clayton was beginning to feel that he was being badgered beyond all reason by this volatile young woman. 'Hark to me, Crawford,' he gritted through clenched teeth. 'You have roused me from my bed. You have kept me here in this cold room for nigh on an hour. You have insulted my class and myself, and now you continue to rant and rave and badger me even after I have agreed to take action on your wild accusations. You try me too sorely, Crawford. So now, let me advise you that it is in both your own and this girl, Tullet's, best interests, that you now leave me in peace. Now, this very instant.'

Tildy rose to her feet, and even in his foul temper, Clayton was forced to acknowledge that she was very beautiful with her fine breasts heaving and her eyes so hugely dark in the pale oval of her face.

'I'll go, Parson Clayton,' she declared. 'But when will you question Brompton?'

The cleric's control finally snapped. 'When I damn well choose to do so, woman!' he shouted and, springing up from his chair, he grabbed her arm and forcibly propelled her from the study, along the passage and out of the front door. 'Get away from me, Crawford. I've seen and heard more than sufficient of you this night.'

Shaken and shocked by his violent outburst, but still defiant, Tildy stood her ground on the frost-rimed pathway.

'When will you question Brompton?' she repeated, her voice a trifle unsteady, but her whole posture radiating a determination that the man was forced to give way to.

'Tomorrow. Tomorrow morning ... early.'

'And shall I come here with Meg Tullet, Parson Clayton?'

'Goddamn you, yes. Come then!' he bellowed. 'Now go, before I strangle you with my own hands ... Go! For the love of God, Gooooo!'

130

The door slammed so violently that the casements of the front windows shook and rattled, and Tildy found herself giggling in a nervous excitement and venting of tension.

'Well, it's not exactly what I looked for,' she accepted. 'But at least it's something. I'd best go back now and tell Meg to be ready for me to fetch her tomorrow morning.'

Tildy's nervous energy pulsated through her, and she felt that even though her body was aching with weariness she could drive her flagging muscles and tendons without respite through the night. She felt intoxicatingly charged with an excitement that she could not really identify.

'Perhaps this is how a soldier feels when going into battle?' she fancied. 'If this is truly how he feels, then if I had been born a man I think I would most surely have become a soldier.'

Undaunted by the prospect of the long walk to the Tullets' cottage and then back to her lodgings, Tildy hummed a lively tune as she stepped out across the iron-frosted ground.

Chapter Seventeen

While Tildy had been walking from the Tullets' cottage to the constable's house, other people were moving stealthily through the Pitcheroak woods that stretched out from the Red Lane. These other people were all male, and they came singly, entering the woods from many different directions but all heading for the same objective, the brick kilns that were in a great clay hollow at the end of a winding lane known as the Muskatts Way which debouched onto the Red Lane some distance nearer to the town than the Tullets' cottage.

The kilns resembled big square boxes in the moonlight, some three-and-a-half yards cubed and were grouped together at one end of the elongated pit. To reach them each approaching man was forced to leave the protective shadows of the trees and cross a moonlit expanse of flattened, hard-packed clay. Hidden at the edge of the tree-line a man lay watching these other men as they crossed the flat expanse, their heads wrapped in scarves or rags so that their features could not be recognized. The watcher noted that as each newcomer neared the kilns he was brought to a halt by a low-voiced challenge, and each time two hooded men stepped from among the deep shadows of the kilns and approached the newcomer. Once they had appeared to verify his identity the three of them would go into the clump of kilns.

The watcher cursed softly to himself, and gave grudging credit to the planning of this clandestine meeting. No one could approach nearer than thirty yards to the kilns under cover of the trees, then that cover must be broken. If any attempt was made in force to cross that space the hidden sentinels had ample time in which to raise the alarm and enable all those in the kilns either to fight or flee. The watcher glanced quickly around the top of the great pit. It would take half a regiment to cover its perimeter, and even then men could still get through the lines and into the trees.

The man shivered with cold as he lay in the dead bracken, but he stoically endured for more than an hour until the masked men began to slip away singly from the kilns and disappear once again into the trees. He smiled grimly to himself; whoever had organized this meeting was displaying considerable intelligence and cunning. Using this means of dispersal prevented any would-be spy from entering the kilns after a meeting was finished in search of clues to the identity of those present. There was no way of knowing if anyone had remained behind in ambush. A further problem for the watcher was that during this cold weather the kilns also attracted trampers and homeless people to sleep near the warmth of the fires which during working periods were kept burning throughout the night-time hours, and of course, the brick-workers themselves would be tending those fires, so how could any stranger find out who had rightful business on the site without drawing unwelcome attention to himself?

The watcher again smiled in grudging respect. 'Whoever it is running this combination certainly knows what he's about, I'll give the bugger that.'

He groaned softly as he moved his cramped limbs, stiff and painful with the cold, and stealthily moved away from the great clay pit himself.

Tildy had seen Meg, and told her to be ready for Tildy to call and take her somewhere early in the morning. She had no wish to worry the girl with the prospect of a confrontation with Johnny Brompton, so had not told her where they would be going. Happily for Tildy's own peace of mind, Meg had accepted what she was told without

133

question. Her mother had not yet returned to the cottage and Tildy decided that if the woman had still not returned by morning, then she would take the smaller children with her also to John Clayton's house. She felt very tired, but was content enough.

'After all,' she told herself, 'perhaps tomorrow I'll see young Meg get justice done to her for once in her pitiful life.'

As she came up to the entrance of the lane known as Muskatts Way, she was surprised to see a man she knew come from the woods in which lay the brick kilns, quickly cross Red Lane and disappear into the undergrowth on the oppposite side.

'What's he doing wandering abroad in the woods at this hour?' she wondered. 'Surely he can't be going poaching? He doesn't seem the poaching type. He's a city-bird, Nathaniel Farrel, not a country-bird.'

City bred or not, she could hear no noise of him blundering through the undergrowth as she passed the spot where he had crossed the lane. 'He moves very quiet, he must have cat's eyes to see his way in the dark.' She smiled as she recalled his light green eyes. 'Indeed, when I think of it, his eyes do look like a cat's, don't they?'

Then her own affairs came to fill her mind once more, and Nathaniel Farrel's mysterious night-prowlings disappeared from her thoughts ...

Chapter Eighteen

The noise coming from John Clayton's study could be heard even in the roadway outside his house. Meg Tullet came to a halt, and the three small children grouped behind her skirts like fledglings cowering beneath the mother-bird's feathers.

'Come now, Meg,' Tildy coaxed persuasively. 'Don't be feared of people shouting. No one will harm you. I'm with you, and the parson and the constable will be there as well.'

The young girl's face was pale and drawn with apprehension and she flinched physically when the front door of the house opened and John Clayton shouted to them, 'Come inside, will you? Don't waste any more of my time than needful, by standing there like petrified mawkins!'

Tildy took Meg's hand and half-led, half-dragged her into the house.

The study was a bedlam of angry, raised voices, and crying, wailing children. Johnny Brompton's wife, a meaty-armed, loud-mouthed virago had brought her own brood of children with her, and was now berating her husband.

'You'se brought shame on me, you bloody hound! And you'se brought shame onto your poor kids' yeds as well!'

The dirty, snotty-nosed, ragged children wept and whined noisily as their mother roughly rammed them towards their father, who was standing between two deputy constables, while Cashmore leaned on his crowned staff, coughing hackingly and grumbling bitterly to himself between each painful, racking bout.

'Look at these innocent babbies, you bloody sod! God ought to strike you down dead for bringing such disgrace onto 'um.' Sally Brompton's voice was gratingly shrill and penetrating, and rasped on the nerves of all her hearers.

The moment they entered the room the Tullet children added their own wails to the hubbub, and Sally Brompton rushed towards Meg as if she intended physically to attack her. The girl squealed out in fright, and Tildy pushed her back and stepped in front of the raging woman.

'You dirty little whore! You wicked, stinking trollop!' Sally Brompton shrieked ferociously at Meg, but made no attempt to push past Tildy. 'Leading men into badness wi' your sinful, lustful body, and them wi' wives and innocent childer awaiting for 'um at home. My man 'udden't goo wi' you, 'ud he, you dirty little bitch? That's why youm atelling these wicked lies about him now ...' Then she shrieked into Tildy's face, saliva flecking from her mouth, 'And you? What the fucking hell does you think you am, amaking up such wicked stories about my husband? He's a good-living man, so he is. A God-fearing, good-living man. Youm as bad as this other bitch, you be, you fancy-speaking cow, you!'

Tildy, although her heart was pounding, showed none of the fear she was feeling at the ferocity of the woman's attitude. Instead, she drew a deep breath, then stepped forwards and pushed Sally Brompton back, telling her, 'Your husband is an evil brute, and if you refused to see that with your own eyes before, then you'll have to see it now. Meg Tullet is no whore. It's filthy animals like your husband who force her into sexual acts that are the whores, not Meg!'

'Be silent, all of you!' John Clayton roared, and rounded on Cashmore. 'Get Mrs Brompton and all these children out of here. And the rest of you, be silent. If I have to tell you again, then I'll put the lot of you into the lock-up, and keep you there until you learn to obey me.'

Not ungently, Cashmore ushered the wailing children

and the bitterly protesting Sally Brompton out into the passage, then came back into the room and after closing the door stood with his back against it to prevent any re-entry by those evicted. Even so, the wails of the children and the curses of Sally Brompton still kept resounding hollowly from the passage, and though this matter was of such grave seriousness, Tildy experienced an almost insane desire to burst out laughing. The preceding scene had an element of farce in it, and she found sardonic humour in the way Sally Brompton had swung from berating her husband to praising him so fulsomely. Then, at John Clayton's next words all elements of farce abruptly metamorphosed into a deadly grim seriousness.

'We are here to ascertain whether or not John Bromp-ton should go on trial for his life,' he told them harshly. 'So there will be no more caterwauling like damn fish-wives, no more hurling of insults at each other's heads. You will speak only at my direction.' He looked at each of them in turn. 'Do you understand me?' He kept his gaze on each individual until in turn they affirmed that under-standing. 'Very well.' He seated himself behind the leather-topped table that served as his desk and when Tildy opened her mouth as if to speak, he scowled so fiercely at her that abashed, she stayed silent and bowed her head. 'Each of you present knows why this enquiry is taking place,' the clergyman stated. 'Therefore I shall waste no time in needless preamble. What have you to say about the allegations made against you, Brompton?'

The burly, grey-haired overlooker's expression was devoid of any anxiety that Tildy could detect, and she was surprised by this absence. Although he had stood shifty-eyed and hang-dog while his wife had been berating him, now his manner radiated a steady-eyed confidence. 'They'm bloody rubbish, Parson!' he declared ringingly, and as Clayton frowned, hastened to add, 'Pardon my language, Master Clayton, Sir, but o' course I'm feeling a bit het-up that I should ha' bin brung here on the word of such a dirty little whore as that 'un theer.'

'Then you deny raping Megan Tullet?' Clayton queried, and the overlooker answered heatedly, 'O' course I denies it! Who 'ud need to rape a tuppenny whore, Parson?'

'It is me who is asking the questions, Brompton,' Clayton snapped curtly. 'All I require from you are answers to those questions, not any comments of your own.'

'I beg pardon, Sir,' the overlooker said humbly, and Tildy wanted to shout at Brompton that he was nothing but a mealy-mouthed hypocrite acting in such a meek way, but she ruthlessly kept hold of herself, knowing that any intervention on her part could only prejudice the clergyman against both herself and Meg.

'Did you have sexual congress with Megan Tullet when you went into the woods with her?' Clayton asked next, and Tildy saw the shiftiness come back into Brompton's eyes.

He dropped his head, and for some seconds his hands twisted together and his facial expression was that of a man labouring under tremendous strain. At last, in a halting, broken voice, he almost whispered, 'May God forgive me, but yes, I did lie with that whore in the woods, Parson Clayton.' He drew in a long shuddering breath and closed his eyes, his features working furiously as if he were deeply distressed. 'I met her when I was aleaving the Unicorn Tap to goo home for me supper. Her had bin in a bit o' trouble at work, and I managed to have her keep her job by promising Master Milward that I'd keep me eye on her. I felt sorry for her, you see, Parson. I knew that if her lost her work wi' us, then her and her family 'ud have no money at all coming into the house, and they'd be forced onto the parish.

'I was talking to her like a father, and telling her that she must improve in her work. Then she asked me to go deeper into the woods wi' her. Her told me that her didn't want the little kids to hear what she was agoing to tell me, so, I give 'um some sweetstuff to keep 'um contented until we could get back to 'um. I never thought no harm in doing that, Parson. I thought I was only doing the poor little souls a kindness ...' He drew in a long shuddering breath. '... Well, when we got deeper into the woods, her started to talk dirty to me, and to ask me if I'd like to feel her tits, and kiss her, and stuff like that.'

Tildy stared incredulously as a sob tore from Brompton's throat, and he began to rub his hands against his eyes as if to brush away tears. In a choking, groaning voice he told his hushed audience, 'I'd bin drinking, you see, and you know how drink takes a man, even a God-fearing man like meself. It excites us, don't it, and turns our mind to carnal, unclean thoughts. I just couldn't help meself when her started kissing and fondling me ... I lay wi' her, Parson ... May God forgive me for it, but I just couldn't help meself.' He broke into loud, harsh sobbing which lasted until Clayton told him sharply, 'Pull yourself together, Brompton, and act the man, will you!'

'I'm sorry, Parson,' Brompton slurred, and rubbed his teary eyes until they reddened. Then, appearing to regain some control of himself, for the first time since beginning his recital he looked Clayton straight in the eyes and told him falteringly, 'Arter we'd done, her asked me for money. I only wanted to get away from her then. I felt so shamed at having give way to such sinful temptation, you see. All I'd got wi' me was a single shilling, and I offered her that. She took it, and then said that it warn't enough, and that I must give her more, or else she'd tell everybody that I'd taken her by force. Well, I got angry meself then, and I told her that if she told anybody what her had tempted me to do wi' her, then I'd break her bloody neck for her.

'I left her then, just as quick as me legs could carry me. And ever since I bin apraying our Saviour, sweet Jesus Christ, for his forgiveness for me sin in laying wi' an whore for money, like I'd done. That's all there is to tell, Parson Clayton, I swear to God, and I'll swear so on the holy book itself that what I'se told you is the truth, the honest truth. May God strike me dead this instant if I'm lying to you ...'

Clayton stared sternly at Meg Tullet. 'Let me hear what you have to say to that, girl?' he ordered.

With a sickening dismay Tildy saw the dawning conviction in the faces of the men about her that Brompton was indeed speaking the truth when at her side Meg Tullet buried her face in her hands, and her shoulders heaved spasmodically.

'See her now, Parson!' Brompton exhorted righteously. 'See how her's acarrying on now because her's bin caught out in her lying.'

Tildy could no longer contain the maelstrom of emotion raging within her. 'You cunning bastard! It's not Meg who's lying, but you!' she cried out, and appealed angrily to Clayton, 'Cannot you understand what he is doing here? He is confessing to the lesser sin, to hide the greater one ... Meg, speak out now,' she begged the weeping girl. 'Tell the truth of what happened to you up in the woods. Tell the parson what really happened, and show him that Brompton is lying.'

She attempted to draw Meg's hands away from her face, but the girl wrenched violently away and shrieked, 'Let me goo home! Let me goo home! Let me goo home! Let me goo home!' Over and over again her agonized screams buffeted the ears of her listeners, and Clayton ordered the constable, 'Take her outside to the street, Master Cashmore, and let her go from here. She is too deranged to state anything that could be given credence.'

Crying hysterically Meg was taken out through the passage and her appearance there provoked a fresh outburst of loud abuse from Sally Brompton and a tumult of wailing from the children.

The cleric shook his tie-wigged head disgustedly, then told the overlooker, 'You can go, Brompton. Stay well away from Meg Tullet and you'll hear no more about this. I would most strongly advise that for the good of your immortal soul you fight against the temptation to commit adultery in the future.'

140

'I will, Sir. I've seen the error and evil of my ways, Sir, indeed I have,' Brompton assured fervently. 'May God bless you, Sir, and praise Him for having shown you the truth, that's all I can say. Praise Him for all His tender mercies.' He looked at Tildy. 'I forgives you also, Tildy Crawford,' he said with an air of regretful reproach. 'I'm prepared to believe you was acting in good faith. If you warn't, then I knows that in His own good time God 'ull punish you for your wickedness. I suggest you searches in your heart and prays to Our Blessed Saviour to show you His mercy as He's showed it to me this day. God Bless you all.' With a look of pious joy on his face the overlooker went from the house, his wife and brood of children straggling noisily after him up Fish Hill.

'Could you not see how he was lying?' Tildy challenged the clergyman and deputy constables. 'Could you not tell? Could you really not tell?'

The two deputies shuffled uneasily and averted their eyes, but Clayton met her accusing stare full on. He gestured to the other men to leave and when he and the young woman were alone he frowned unhappily at her.

'It is not my personal opinion as to Brompton's veracity that matters, Crawford, and you must remember that in strict fact I have no judicial powers. I merely act on behalf of Reverend the Lord Aston during his absences from the parish. I can only recommend to his Lordship whether to hear a case or not. But I can tell you this, that even if I were to recommend to his Lordship to have Brompton brought before him, it would make no odds as to the eventual outcome. On present evidence even if Lord Aston was to commit Brompton to sessions for trial, undoubtedly a ruling of 'no true bill' would be given at the preliminary hearing.'

'What you are saying then, Parson Clayton, is that Johnny Brompton has been allowed to brutally rape a young, defenceless girl and walk freely away,' Tildy stated hotly, and Clayton's expression hardened.

'I am saying only what I have just told you, Crawford.

141

No more, and no less. Do not try to put words into my mouth, or to attribute opinions to me other than those I have just now voiced. My advice to you now is to put this matter from your mind, and to concentrate instead on your own affairs.'

Too angry and disgusted even to answer the man, Tildy went from the study. Outside the house she found Joseph Cashmore and his two deputies staring perplexedly at the three wailing Tullet children. Of Meg there was no sign.

'Where is she? Where is Meg Tullet?' Tildy asked anxiously, and Cashmore shrugged his beefy shoulders.

'Buggered if I knows, my wench. One minute her was asetting on the wall theer sobbing her heart out, and the next minute she ups and goes running like a bat out o' hell down the hill theer.'

Tildy peered down the Fish Hill but could see nothing of the girl. She bit her full, moist lower lip, and a sense of dread clutched her as she visualized the fast-flowing River Arrow with its deep holes and treacherous currents. 'I hope she comes to no harm.' She looked uncertainly at the children. 'They can't be left here by themselves,' she told Cashmore. 'I'd best take them back to their home and see if their mother's got back there yet.' Again she stared worriedly down the hill. 'I'm feared about Meg, she might do harm to herself, the state that she's in.'

The constable's taciturn features softened a trifle, for he was not a cruel man at heart. 'I'll tell you what, Tildy Crawford,' he offered. 'Me and these lads 'ull go down and look for her, while you takes these kids home.'

'Would you do that? Oh, thank you.' Impulsively she reached out and squeezed his muscular forearm in a surge of gratitude. 'That's really good of you, Master Cashmore.'

He reddened slightly, as if embarrassed, then the next instant erupted in a fit of coughing.

The two deputies were not pleased to be going in search of Meg Tullet, however.

'I needs to get back to me shop. I'se lost enough wages this day already,' the taller of the two grumbled, while his sallow-faced companion stated sullenly, 'I don't reckon her 'ull come to any harm. Her's bloody simple-yedded maybe, but all them simple-yedded buggers knows how to look arter themselves all right, don't they?'

Cashmore wiped his streaming eyes with a huge piece of rag and scowled at his deputies. 'You'll both on you help me search for that wench, whether you likes to or not, so just come on,' he wheezed and led the reluctant pair down the hill, while Tildy gathered the forlorn children together and coaxed them to accompany her.

To her relief Mrs Tullet was now back in the cottage. She was an older version of Meg, dirty and unkempt, but not unhandsome for all that her body was beginning to sag and her teeth were decaying badly in front.

She heard Tildy's account of what had taken place in her absence without any great show of interest or concern and Tildy's exasperation at the woman's manner steadily mounted, but she refrained from taxing Mrs Tullet with her apparent lack of concern about what had happened to her eldest daughter.

'God help poor Meg. What chance has she ever had with a mother like that,' Tildy thought sadly as she hurried back to the town and on down the Fish Hill to join in the search for Meg.

She reached the Pigeon Bridge at the very bottom of the long decline where the Red Ditch flowed west to east towards its junction with the River Arrow. She followed the shallow stream along its bank past the ancient wattle and daub cottages that some said dated from the days when the Cistercian Abbey of Bordesley had flourished in the nearby fields, still known as the Abbey Meadows and dotted with the hummocks of its buried ruins.

There were no people to be seen around the cottages, and Tildy wondered at the absence of even a small child or pottering old crone in the gardens. She came in sight of the Forge Needle Mill, its two separate buildings linked

143

by an overhead walkway, beneath which the great water-wheel trundled to power the machinery. The uneasy dread that had gnawed at Tildy since Meg's disappearance suddenly hardened to an awful certainty as she saw that the water-wheel was motionless, which meant that the mill-race had been cut off at the sluice.

She ran round the side of the nearer building and saw the silent crowd standing at the edge of the long, wide expanse of the big mill pool. Along the banks the men and boys from the Forge Mill were prodding the bottom of the deep pool with long poles, and by the sluice gate itself she saw Joseph Cashmore talking with a man clad in a dark frock-coat and top hat, whom she recognized as George Chillingworth, the master of the Forge Mill.

Tildy hurried to join the two men, but in her mind already knew what had happened. One glance at Cashmore's grim expression confirmed it for her, and she stated, 'It's Meg, isn't it, Master Cashmore? She's done herself a mischief, hasn't she? She's in there!' She pointed at the dark, muddied water.

Cashmore nodded wordlessly. A sickening faintness engulfed Tildy and she swayed and would have fallen had not the constable's powerful arm surrounded her in support.

'Theer now, girl. You set down a minute and gather your senses,' he told her gently, and lowered her to sit on a stack of old round grindstones.

A sudden attack of nausea brought bile into her mouth and she retched and vomited helplessly, but since she had eaten nothing for more than twenty-four hours all that she voided was a spattering of bitter-tasting stomach acids onto the gravel. Gradually the nausea passed leaving her feeling cold and clammy-skinned. She was still light-headed and giddy, but she dragged deep draughts of air into her lungs and fought to regain control of her body. When she had recovered sufficiently she stood up and asked Cashmore, 'Are you certain that Meg is in the pool, Master Cashmore?'

The constable asked her in return, 'Be you really feeling all right now, girl?'

'Yes, I'm all right now, I thank you,' Tildy acknowledged, and only then would he confirm, 'Yes, the poor little cratur's in theer, right enough, Tildy. One of Mr Chillingworth's workmen was out here at the sluice gate, when young Meg came arunning and acrying out like a demented soul and threw herself in the water over theer by the bridge.' He pointed to the wooden footbridge which spanned the Red Ditch where it entered the mill-pond. 'The wheel was working, Tildy,' the constable explained. 'And o'course, wi' the sluice gates being full open there was strong undercurrents warn't there? So the poor little soul was sucked right under. The chap had the wits to close the sluice gates straight off, but we arn't bin able to find the wench. Her could be snagged in the bottom weeds anywhere along the bloody pool really, because that sluice sets up some wild swims in the water.'

A terrible sensation of anguished guilt assailed Tildy, and she choked out, 'It's my fault this has happened. If I hadn't brought her to Parson Clayton's this morn, she'd still be alive. It's all my fault!'

Once more the constable's strong arm came out to her, but this time his powerful fingers gripped her shoulder painfully hard. 'Now just you cut that bloody sarft talk, Tildy Crawford,' he scolded vehemently. ''Tis no use you ablaming yourself for what happened here. I might just as well say it was my fault for not helping you as I should ha' done when you first come to tell me what that bastard Brompton had done to the poor little simpleton.'

Tildy's eyes fixed on him accusingly. 'Are you telling me now that you believe he did rape her, then?'

The man shrugged. 'I believed it afore, Tildy,' he admitted shamefacedly. 'But wi' only her word to go on I knew well that there was naught to be done about it in the way o' bringing him to trial, her bearing the name of a tuppenny whore, like her did.' His manner became defiant. 'Anyways up, if anybody is to blame for what her's done to herself, then it arn't neither me nor you. It's bloody Johnny Brompton who should bear the blame, and the shame on it, not us! I only wish her could come back from the grave and haunt the bugger for the rest on his life.'

A fearful dread struck Tildy at his words. 'Oh no, God forbid that!' she exclaimed in horror. 'You shouldn't say such wicked things.' Her inbred superstitious nature quailed at even the thought of the dead girl's spirit wandering restlessly.

'You needn't goo moithering yourself about Meg rising from the dead, Tildy.' Cashmore spoke bitterly, and his broad features were full of an angry distaste. 'Because when we buries her I'll have to do that which 'ull stop her acoming back to haunt the bastard, God rot him.'

'What do you mean? What is it you'll have to do?' Tildy questioned nervously.

'You'll find out, girl, all in due course,' he told her grimly, and refused to add anything more.

The search went on for another hour or longer, and during that time the crowd was being continuously augmented by new arrivals. As always, in its own mysterious fashion the news of the tragedy had spread through the district like wildfire, and as was their custom people laid aside their tasks and came to watch, even from the mills and workshops.

The Reverend John Clayton had come, and pale-faced stood with Cashmore and George Chillingworth. He spoke only once to Tildy.

'Truly I'm sorry for this tragic happening, Crawford. We must all pray for her soul.'

Tildy was sorely tempted to tell him that if he had believed the living girl, then perhaps they would not have needed to pray for the dead one, but distressed and shaken as she was she held her peace, knowing that displays of rancour would not serve Meg Tullet now.

George Chillingworth was becoming increasingly restless as time went on and the search met with no success.

'I'm losing production because o' this,' he announced disgruntedly. 'I can't afford to have my mill at a standstill all bloody day. I'll have to open the sluice-gates again and get my lads back to their work.'

'You cannot do that, Master Chillingworth,' Clayton remonstrated. 'What if the poor child's body should be dragged into the water-wheel and mangled?'

'Well, at least then we'd have found her, 'udden't we?' the needle master pointed out with a reasonable air. 'And her certain sure 'udden't feel any pain if a few of her bones got broke, 'ud her?'

'By God, but you shock me, Chillingworth!' the clergyman declared angrily. 'For the sake of your damned profit you would be prepared to see a human being's remains desecrated? You shock me, Sir!'

'Look, Parson,' the needle master said in an equable tone,' a drownded body won't raise itself to the surface until arter the seventh, eighth or ninth day, that's well known, that is. Which means that according to your way o' thinking I must keep my sluice gates shut for all that time. So that 'ud mean that my mill 'ud be closed down for that length o' time as well. It arn't only my profit I'm thinking about, Parson Clayton. It's my workpeople's wages as well. Be you prepared to pay 'um while they'm laid off from here? Because if you am, then I'll do as you want, and I'll stand my loss of profit.' A grin of triumph lurked in his eyes as he spoke, for he knew that his argument was unanswerable and that even the most tender-hearted of his operatives would prefer to risk a dead body being mangled, rather than lose a week's wages, with the consequent hardship that that would entail for themselves. 'Well, Parson, what d'you say to my proposition?' the needle master baited.

'I doubt that you'll need to keep the sluices closed much longer anyway, George Chillingworth,' Cashmore intervened. 'Look and see who's coming over theer.' He pointed to the footpath which led over a small, hilly rise directly south of the millpool. 'It's the cunning-man from Red Lion Street, Jack Smith.'

Tildy was startled to hear that name. She herself had had dealings with a woman named Esther Smith who was a local witch-woman, and she wondered now if the approaching man could be related to the old woman.

'Jack? Jack Smith?' Cashmore shouted as the man drew within earshot. 'Cummon over here, Jack, we'd like a word wi' you.'

The man came up to them and Tildy recognized him from having glimpsed him at times in the town. Once seen, Jack Smith was not that easy to forget. He stood only five feet in height, with a massive, barrel-like body, tremendously broad shoulders, and so short a neck that his big head seemed to grow directly from his torso. His dark hazel eyes were peculiarly piercing as if they could penetrate the very depths of anyone he looked at, and the ugliness of his swarthy features was compounded by a lower lip so thick and pendulous that it looked a deformity. His dress was as eccentric as the rest of him: a threadbare black waistcoat in the style of the previous century and a coat of the same colour, the tails of which brushed the ground at his heels. His shaven cannon-ball head was covered with a low-crowned black hat, the brim so broad that it drooped to touch his shoulders.

'I take it you'se heard what's happened here, Jack?' the constable asked him, and the pendulous lower lip twisted into a rictus grimace.

'O' course I knows.' His voice was low-pitched and husky. 'I seen the blue corpse-candle passing backards and forrards across this pool three nights back. I knew a drowning was nigh, but I couldn't know the name.' He sighed sorrowfully. 'Poor bairn. Poor, benighted bairn.'

Tildy warmed towards this eccentric figure for his obvious pity for the dead girl, while at the same time she felt a superstitious awe that he should have seen the mysterious small, pale blue ball of flame known as the 'corpse-candle' that denoted the coming death of a child. If it had been an adult who was to die, then the ball

148

of flame would have been larger, and of a yellowish hue.

Her agile mind also grasped the implication that if the cunning-man had seen Meg's corpse-candle some three nights previously, then the child's death must have been pre-ordained. 'But who by, and for what reason should Meg have had to die?' Tildy pondered in a mingling of sorrow and fear-tinged awe.

'Well Jack, we can't find her body.' Cashmore appeared now to be quite cheerful and hearty. 'Has you got any suggestions that might help us bring the poor little cratur up to the surface?'

'It's wiser that you should wait 'til the pool chooses to give her up agen.' Jack Smith's expression was wary. 'Arter all, when the waters claims a life, they likes to keep the body wi' 'um for a week or more, so as to draw all trace of the life force from it.'

As the man spoke John Clayton's manner became increasingly and aggressively impatient, and now he broke in to snap at Cashmore, 'Why do you waste your time listening to this sinful, superstitious nonsense, Master Cashmore? Surely you would be better engaged in having some sort of vessel procured by means of which the centre of the pool could be reached and the bottom searched.'

The piercing eyes of the cunning-man locked onto Clayton, and he grated out, 'I 'udden't be too quick to call the "old knowledge" a nonsense, Parson. There's knowledge in this land which is older and wiser by far than the teachings of the Hebrew that you bows your head to. You seems to have forgot, that's if you ever knew o' course, that "Wicca" has bin the religion o' this land of our'n for thousands o' years, right back into the dawn o' time, it arn't some foreign muck from the deserts o' Palestine brought to these shores by foreign priests. If you wants to mock what I believes in, Parson, then let's make a match on it. Let's see who can find the child's body, shall us? You, wi' the help o' your foreign God, or me, wi' the help of the "old knowledge"? What say you to that, Christ man?'

For a few moments the young clergyman was rent by inner struggle. Confident in his faith, he itched to take up the verbal gauntlet of challenge thrown down by the cunning-man. But, on the other hand, would he not be displaying credence in the other's powers if he, Clayton, were to enter into such a matching? He decided that he would exercise a degree of cunning himself. By doing so he saw a chance to discredit this man before him, and also to strike a blow against the rampant superstition in the needle district, where the vast majority of the people believed implicitly in the supernatural powers of the local witch-women and cunning-men. He now told Smith in apparently placatory tones, 'I fully accept that you have a right to your beliefs, Master Smith, and I would hope that you accept my own right to worship God in whatever way I choose to so do. But frankly, in the light of our modern scientific knowledge, I fail to see how any mumbo-jumbo of this so-called Wicca will enable you to discover the location of the child's body.'

The pendulous lower lip quirked grotesquely, but this time it was into a smile and although Tildy at first thought it a smile of bravado, the longer she looked at Jack Smith's eyes, the stronger became her conviction that the smile was not bravado at all, but rather a smile of absolute confidence in the superiority of his own knowledge.

'All right, Parson, I'll find the bairn. The pool has claimed her life from her, so perhaps it will be contented enough with that and not try to keep her body to itself for any longer than needs be. We must just hope that by taking the bairn from it we don't end by angering it, so that it 'ull claim another life afore very long.'

He appeared unconcerned by the now openly contemptuous sneer on the face of John Clayton and said to George Chillingworth, 'Your house is nigh to the mill, arn't it, Master Chillingworth?'

The needle master nodded. 'That's well known, Jack.'

'Right then,' the cunning-man instructed. 'Fetch me a well baked loaf wi' a good, thick crust to it. A small 'un 'ull do. And a pot o' butter, it don't signify if it be salt or fresh, it makes no matter.'

Chillingworth called one of the mill boys to him and sent him scampering away on the errand. While they awaited the boy's return, Jack Smith drew a little way away from the others and lapsed into profound silence, his hands clasped behind his back, his pendulous lower lip jutting out, his piercing dark hazel eyes roving constantly across the muddied surface of the pool.

An excited buzzing of talk ran amongst the watching crowds as they realized that the cunning-man was going to use his mysterious arts to make a search for the child's body, and the men and lads with the long poles drew them from the water and laid them aside.

Cashmore smiled at Tildy. He now appeared unusually cheerful, in bizarre contradiction to his normal grim taciturnity. 'Be you feeling better now, my wench?'

She nodded, but could not smile. 'Yes thank you, Master Cashmore. But naturally I'm still upset about poor Meg.'

'It was no fault o' yourn that this happened to her, girl, and I don't want to have to tell you that agen. You heard what Jack Smith said. That he'd seen her corpse-candle well afore this happened. Her death was meant to be, girl, that's as sure as that God makes little apples.'

Tildy found herself accepting that statement, and drawing additional comfort from the demonstration that her vague beliefs in pre-ordination were not singular to herself, but were shared even by hard-headed people such as Joseph Cashmore.

'What does Jack Smith intend doing now?' she asked.

The constable shrugged. 'Buggered if I knows, girl. I'se heard tell of 'um firing cannons over the water to bring up a drownded man, but there arn't no cannons to be found hereabouts, so I don't know what he's agoing to do. But I'll tell you summat, young 'ooman, that's just atween you and me and the gatepost. I hopes that he does bring the girl up or mark where she lays, if it's only to spot John

Clayton one in his eye. These foreign incomers who's bin to university and such places, am a bit too ready to mock at what us local folk believes in. It'll do John Clayton a power o' good to be shown that we arn't entirely the thick-yedded mawkins he takes us for.'

For the first time since her arrival at the mill Tildy now suddenly thought of Mrs Tullet and the rest of the Tullet children. 'Dear God, who is to tell her mother what has happened to Meg?' she wondered aloud. 'What will become of her and her children now?'

'That'll be one o' my tasks, Tildy.' Cashmore's features resumed their customary glum, taciturn cast. 'But I'm very well used to having to break bad news to people, so I can't in all honesty say that it 'ull affect me too much.'

'What will happen to her and the children now though?' Tildy persisted. 'Because as I understood it, Meg was their main support.'

'Well, if her makes application to the vestry, they'll assign her and her little 'uns to the poor'us. At least they wun't starve to death in theer, and it 'ull be a roof over their yeds, wun't it?'

Tildy, remembering her own grim days in that establishment, shook her head involuntarily. 'No,' she murmured. 'They won't starve, but what kind of future do those pitiful children face now?'

'Whatever future is fated for 'um, my wench,' the constable replied simply.

By now the boy was running back with a small round loaf and a white crock-pot of butter. A hush fell on the crowd, and the only sounds were the soughing of the wind and the splashing of the thin jets of water escaping through the warped planks of the sluice gates to fall into the wheel-pit.

Jack Smith wasted no time, but took the loaf and nodded in satisfaction as he examined the brown, hard-baked crust. With his spatulate fingers he gutted the loaf so that it resembled a hollow bowl and threw the innards of it into the pool.

'That's the offering,' he said, as if to himself, then he clawed out the butter and spread it thickly all over the outside of the loaf, and afterwards, did the same to the inside. He wiped his greasy hands on the grass and took from his pocket a small stone bottle. 'This is quicksilver ... mercury ... a most powerful seeker.' Again it seemed as if he were speaking only to himself. Carefully he poured the shimmering silver liquid into the loaf where it collected into a big shiny globule on the base of the hollow. Muttering unintelligibly he knelt at the water's edge and launched the loaf as if it were a small toy boat onto the surface of the pool.

Every eye in the crowd was intent on the loaf, every breath was held in anticipation. The loaf drifted gently out, rocking and bobbing slightly, then the crowd vented a concerted gasp as the loaf appeared to change course of its own volition, rotating slowly round and round as it went. Then it began to travel in ever-decreasing circles and although it could only have been scant seconds since its journey had begun, to Tildy it seemed that an eternity had elapsed. Slowly, slowly, so very very slowly the loaf's rotations ceased and it came to a halt only a couple of yards from the bank, directly where a fruitless search had already been made.

A groan compounded of disappointment and chagrin rumbled from a hundred throats, but before anyone could speak Jack Smith hurried to the bank opposite the loaf, taking up from the ground one of the long, slender poles discarded by the searchers.

John Clayton openly scoffed. 'There! What did I say? That man deals only in superstitious mumbo-jumbo. That area has already been most thoroughly searched, and nothing found there. The man is at best a self-deluding fool, and at worst a rogue and a charlatan.'

While the crowd seethed around him, poised to turn their angry disappointment against the cunning-man, Jack Smith himself was confidently prodding the invisible pool bottom beneath the loaf. After a moment or two he nodded sharply to himself as if in satisfaction, then made two or three slow sweeps with the pole, not taking it from the water. Another nod of apparent satisfaction and he suddenly thrust hard and released the pole so that it stuck in the mud at the bottom and remained leaning at a drunken angle above the water's surface.

'The bairn is there, at the base of the pole,' he stated quietly. 'Be gentle with her as you fetch her out. The poor cratur has suffered enough already.' He swung on his heel and his grotesque figure moved quickly up the rising footpath that he had first travelled down.

Even before the cunning-man had disappeared from view two of the younger men had stripped down to their skins and plunged naked into the pool. The muddy, red-brown-black waters bubbled and swirled and then a great shout rent the air as, spluttering and gasping, the two men surfaced supporting between them the limp, muddied, weed-entangled corpse of Meg Tullet.

At sight of the dead girl all Tildy's guilt and grief returned instantly to torment her. At her side Joseph Cashmore could not suppress a taunting directed against the clergyman.

'Theer now, Parson, it looks like Jack Smith knows a powerful sight more than you was prepared to gi' him credit for. There's no arguing wi' that over theer, is there? He knew what he was about, didn't he just? We arn't such mawkins hereabouts as some folks 'ud like to take us for. There's knowledge here that can't be found in any bloody college.'

The clergyman looked mystified and more than a little annoyed, but made no answer, except to tell the constable, 'You had best go over there and have them cover her decently.'

Tildy, fighting to hold back useless tears, asked the clergyman, 'Where will they take Meg now, Parson Clayton? Will she go back to her home?'

He appeared momentarily uncertain. 'I'm not sure that it would be permissible to allow the corpse to be taken back to its home in this case, Crawford. After all, she killed herself. In law, that is termed self-murder. There will have to be a coroner's inquest to determine a verdict, which means, I suppose, that her corpse must be kept in the custody of the rightful authority until such time as the coroner has given his judgement.' He frowned, and added pettishly, 'It's a damned nuisance, this. It will cause much inconvenience for we who hold positions of responsibility in the parish.'

Too heartsick even to resent his selfish attitude, Tildy walked around the bank towards where Meg was lying. The crowd was densely packed about her, jostling and squabbling with each other in their efforts to get a closer view of the body. Sickened by their callousness, Tildy halted, unable to face the prospect of fighting her way through to Meg's side, and she turned away.

Again she thought of Mrs Tullet and decided that she herself must go and break the news of Meg's death to the woman. Distasteful as that action promised to be, Tildy felt that it was her obligation to do it.

'It may well be that poor Meg's death was fated to happen, just as Jack Smith says it was,' she pondered. 'Yet still, I am one of the instruments that were involved and contributed in one way or another to her death. If guilt there is, then I must bear a piece of it.'

Chapter Nineteen

'Drownded? Our Meg? Drownded?' Mrs Tullet appeared as though she could not comprehend the word. 'Drownded?' she repeated again, her eyes dull and puzzled in her dirty face with the lank, greying hair hanging down on her cheeks in tangled, greasy tendrils. She shouted back over her shoulder through the doorway of the cottage, 'Bocker? Bocker, cummon here 'ull you?'

Tildy knew by sight the man who now came to the door, for he lived in one of the mean hovels of the Silver Street.

Bocker Duggins was barely above twenty years of age, but looked twice that. His skin was deep-grimed with filth, and his face, framed like Mrs Tullet's with tendrils of greasy, lice-ridden hair, was a mass of pockmarks, tiny scars and virulent looking pimples. He scratched vigorously beneath his rags as he grinned at Tildy, showing a mouthful of black, rotting teeth.

'I knows you, don't I, Missus? You lives at Mother Readman's, don't you? Your name's Tildy, arn't it? Tildy Crawford.'

'That's right,' Tildy acknowledged, and the grin broadened.

'Ahr, I allus recalls a face once I'se sin it once,' he told her with evident pride.

'Her says our Meg's bin drownded, Bocker,' Mrs Tullet told him as calmly as if she were announcing the delivery of a pound of candles, but unlike the woman he appeared shocked at the news.

'Fuck me blind!' he explained. 'Her never has, has her?'

'Yes, she has. I'm truly sorry to have to tell you,' Tildy confirmed sadly, and again the stocky man cursed his surprise.

'God fuck me blind! Well! Meg drownded, is her? Well, 'ud you credit it! Bloody drownded! Wheer was that at then?' he asked eagerly, displaying appreciative interest, but not a sign of grief or regret.

Drawing deep breaths to steady her voice and calm her jangled nerves Tildy told them both the full account of what had occurred. Doubt in the evidence of her own senses inexorably increased as she saw the dull apathy with which Meg's mother listened to the dreadful story. Tildy could hardly believe that any mother could take the news of her child's death so unemotionally. Bocker Duggins on the other hand was anything but apathetic. He listened to her with avid attention, his eyes so sharp and cunning that they irresistibly reminded Tildy of the feral stare of a hungry rat.

'Wheer's her at now?' he demanded, when Tildy's halting account drew to a close.

Tildy could only shrug. 'I don't know. Parson Clayton wasn't certain that she could be brought back here. He said there must be a coroner's inquest on the poor child.' Once more a lump choked her throat and tears stung her eyes as she thought of the pathetic little figure brought out from the muddy waters of the mill pool. 'God rest her soul,' she muttered. 'God rest her poor soul!'

'It arn't her soul we needs to worry about now,' Bocker Duggins declared, and he rubbed his black-stubbled chin with his black-nailed fingers as he thought hard for a few moments. 'We'll have to goo and get her brought back here,' he said finally. 'Her's no use to us alaying in some other bugger's shed.'

Tildy stared at him in puzzlement. 'What do you mean? No good to you laying in someone else's shed?'

The man's cunning eyes raked Tildy's face and he ejaculated contemptuously, 'By Christ, but youm bleedin' green, Tildy Crawford! Fuck me blind iffen you arn't the

157

greenest apple that ever come out on the bleedin' orchard!'

'Haven't you understood me?' Tildy challenged incredulously. 'Poor Meg is dead! She can be no good to anyone now, can she?'

'That's all you knows about it,' Bocker Duggins dismissed her words scathingly. He gripped Mrs Tullet's arm.

'Goo and get the little 'uns quick. I'se thought of a way to make a few shillings for us,' he ordered brusquely. 'We'll all on us goo down and find out wheer they's got your Meg. And now, listen hard to what I'm atelling you, woman. Youm agoing to ask for Meg's body, to bring it back here, and youm not to be denied, not even if you has to scream the bloody place down. Youm going to bring Meg back here, and youm not to let anybody deny you that. Does you get me? Nobody, no matter who, nobody must stop you having your own daughter back here at home.'

Dully she nodded. 'All right, Bocker.'

'Good! Just you remember it.' He pushed her into the cottage. 'Now look sharp and fetch them kids out. They's got to be crying for their sister to be brought back home as well.'

Tildy could see no good reason for the man's determination to bring the dead child to this cramped hovel.

'But why are you so anxious to have Meg brought back here, Bocker? There's little enough room for the living ones, as it is. Where can they put Meg?'

He grinned, and told her, 'We can put her right in the middle of the room, or use her mam's bed, because that child 'ull be worth a small fortune to us, missus. The "dead man's hand" is allus a good earner, but this is the best 'un of all. A ded child that's done herself in is reckoned to be the strongest you can get. We'll have the buggers coming from miles around screaming out for a stroking from Meg's hands. They'll pay any bloody amount for it, you'll see, missus.' He paused and eyed her speculatively. 'I'll tell you what, missus, you could do your ownself a bit 'o good as well. Iffen you brings anybody that you can find here, why, I'll gi' you half of what they pays. How does that sound to you?'

Now, at last, Tildy understood what he was talking about. The hands of someone who had died on the gallows, or who had killed themselves, were widely believed to possess strong curative powers. Sufferers from cancer, tumours, goitre, king's evil, wens and sores, would stroke the affected parts with the hand of the dead person in the belief that this would take away the affliction. Any disease that attacked the neck or throat was thought curable by the 'dead hand', and Tildy had even heard of the use of it as a remedy for a childless woman's curse of barrenness.

After her initial shock she was not unduly disturbed by what this man proposed doing. She had been very fond of Meg, but she lived in a world where terrible human suffering abounded. If the touch of Meg's dead fingers could relieve some of that suffering, then Tildy saw nothing evil in Mrs Tullet and Bocker Duggins acquiring money through it. Empty bellies do not nurture delicacy of feelings or undue sensitivity and tenderness of conscience. The living children of Mrs Tullet, rickety-bodied, scab-headed, already stunted by hardship and deprivation, needed nourishment and shelter. If the use of their dead sister's newly acquired healing powers could obtain some of those necessities for them, then Tildy was not prepared to condemn that usage. She sighed heavily, and sadly accepted that brutal necessity was a merciless taskmaster.

'I'll be on my way, Bocker,' she told the man. But for him she had already ceased to exist, lost as he now was in his feverish calculations of possible earnings, and so she left him to his engrossed thoughts.

Chapter Twenty

In the Fountain Mill the news of the tragedy was being discussed and argued over with avid interest. In general the dead girl was thought of sympathetically by the majority, but a sizeable minority self-righteously declared that while they were sorry for what had happened, it was God's own judgement on the girl for leading so sinful a life. After all, did not all tuppenny whores eventually come to a bad end?

During the day Josh Dyson listened to the various comments but voiced no opinion of his own.

Henry Milward senior was with his wife in the Fountain office when he heard the detailed story of the tragedy and the events which had led up to it from Arthur Conolly.

'So that's why that bugger Brompton never turned into work today. He was being questioned about tupping a young wench. Why, the soddin' old ram ought to ha' known better at his age,' he observed finally, then asked Conolly, 'Be they kicking up any fuss about it in the shops?'

The overlooker shook his head. 'No, Mr Milward, not at present, at any rate.'

'I'm wondering what 'ull happen when Brompton comes to work though?' Milward pondered aloud.

Millicent Milward, dressed in her working rig of old black dress, sack apron, floppy mob-cap and iron-shod clogs, didn't need to ponder. 'Some on the buggers 'ull be bound to have a go at him. That's guaranteed, that is.'

'Why so? Why should they do that? The wench hadn't

worked here for long had she, and they'd chucked her out from every shop but the lye wash, because her was no use to 'um. No, her was too yampy-yedded for anybody to feel that her was any great loss.' Henry Milward was not as callous as his words, but was simply stating the facts as he saw them.

'It arn't that they'll do it just for the sake o' the girl, is it, Mr Milward?' His wife was a very shrewd woman. 'The roaring boys 'ull kick up a ruction just because they'm always looking for sticks to beat the bosses wi'. You knows well enough what some on 'um be like, Master, any excuse to kick up a randy, and they'll jump at it.'

Her husband's plump face retained its expression of doubt. 'Mayhap a few o' the young 'uns might do that, Mrs Milward, but meself, I can't see the older, steadier people joining in any ructions against Johnny Brompton ... He's not disliked in the shops, is he?' He directed this last question at Arthur Conolly, who, being ever eager to make subtle criticisms of his colleagues, told him readily, 'Why no, Master. I should say that considering he's supposed to be an overlooker, he's very well liked by the people. They all reckons that he's very easy wi' 'um.' Inwardly he glowed with satisfaction as he saw that his employer had not relished the information that one of his overlookers was popular for being so easy-going with his workers.

'So, he bears the name of Jack Easy-Go, does he?' Milward observed grimly, making a mental note to investigate that aspect of the man very thoroughly.

'Does you think it wise to take Brompton back here at all, Mr Milward?' his wife queried. 'Arter all, whichever way you looks at it, the girl killed herself because of summat she got up to wi' Brompton, didn't her?'

Arthur Conolly perceived another opportunity to pay off old scores. 'I arn't so sure it was all because o' that, Mistress,' he put in. 'From what I'se heard, the girl was all right until that Crawford 'o man got ahold of her. It was Crawford who took the girl to the parson to make a complaint agen John Brompton, and o' course, when it come to it, the girl 'udden't say naught agen him, 'ud her?'

'That's Matilda Crawford, arn't it,' Henry Milward said thoughtfully. 'One way and another I seems to hear mention o' that young woman whenever there's any upset in these parts.' He turned to his wife. 'You helped her get her child back afore last Christmas, didn't you, and that after she'd had the bloody gall to try and take up pointing work?'

Millicent Milward, normally dominant in the marital relationship, was quick to resent her husband's accusatory tone. 'That's right, Mr Milward, I helped her get her child back, and I helped her to have that bloody tod-rotten husband of her'n whipped through the town, as well. And I'd gladly do the same agen, Master. I'm not going to stand by and see any bad bugger of a man ill use a woman just because her's weaker than him, not if there's aught I can do to stop him.'

Henry Milward, who was secretly afraid of his formidable wife, cringed inwardly. 'Jesus! I've started her going now,' he regretted silently.

Arthur Conolly shared his employer's sentiments, ruefully realizing that the figurative mine he had hoped to explode beneath Tildy Crawford had instead blown up in his own face.

'Tildy Crawford did right to take that Tullet girl afore the parson, if you wants my opinion of the matter.' Millicent Milward was in full spate now, and like some raging torrent nothing could stop her until she wished to stop. 'I arn't no noddle-pated gentry 'ooman! I knows what goes on in the mills and workshops hereabouts, ahr, and in this bloody mill as well. I'se spent my life in this trade, arn't I? All you bloody men thinks that you can make free wi' the factory-wenches just when you pleases. Brompton is just another dirty-minded bleeder, who can't keep his hands from reaching under women's skirts. But he's no worse nor the rest of you for that, is he — '

162

'Now, my dear,' Henry Milward essayed a placatory smile, but Millicent Milward refused to be placated.

'Don't you try and shush me, Master!' she shouted. 'I'll have my say, and be damned to all you bloody men!'

In stoic silence Arthur Conolly endured the tirade beating at his ears and inwardly accepted the fact that he would have to try and find some other means of getting even with Tildy Crawford.

Chapter Twenty-One

Tildy spent the rest of the day with her child, finding easement from her burden of sorrow and regret in his innocent artless prattling.

Like so many others, Mother Readman attributed the suicide of Meg Tullet to predestined fate. 'You mustn't fret yourself about it, my duck,' she admonished Tildy. 'Youm just being bloody stupid to do so. It's well known that when we'em birthed our span o' life is already written on our foreyeds. When our time comes, then God takes us, by fair means or foul, and there's not a bloody thing us mortals can do about that.'

'But how can I not blame myself in part for what has happened?' Tildy repeated over and over. 'I can't help but think that if I had not pressed young Meg to lay complaint against Brompton then she'd still be alive and well.'

The fat old woman's tallowy, brawl-scarred face was compassionate as she recognized the genuinely bitter remorse that Tildy was experiencing. 'I understands how you feel, my duck,' she said gently. 'And I understands that there's little or naught that I can tell you which 'ull alter your mind at present. But believe me, in time you'll come to see that I'm right in what I says, and what youm feeling now 'ull ease, and you'll be able to accept what's happened wi'out blaming yourself overmuch.' She paused, and then added grimly, 'Has you stopped to think on what Meg's life would ha' been iffen you hadn't gone to the parson?' The old woman did not wait for any response. 'That bastard Brompton would ha' kept on abusing the poor little cratur, and her would ha' got

164

pregnant by him just as sure as eggs is eggs. And once her was big-bellied, her would ha' bin sent to the poor'us. You'se bin in theer yourself, Tildy, you'se sin the pitiful craturs in theer. You knows the life they leads. And then, whether or not the babby had lived, when Meg had come back out Brompton would ha' bin at her agen until he'd filled her belly wi' another bastard, and so it would ha' gone on, and the poor cratur's life would ha' bin a grief and a torment to her, naught but misery. I'm spaking true, my duck. I'se sin it happen to more sad wenches than I likes to remember.' She slowly nodded her great mass of frizzed grey hair. 'So you remember, Tildy, Meg's better off wherever she's gone to now than she could ever ha' bin on this earth, and that's a fact you should draw comfort from.'

'Mayhap you're right in what you say,' Tildy answered quietly and with a heartfelt sigh added, 'I hope to God you may be so, for it's a terrible load to carry on my soul.'

Chapter Twenty-Two

At eight o' clock that night Josh Dyson laid aside his tools, rolled his apron up about his hips, put on his coat and left the Fountain Mill. He sniffed the night air appreciatively, enjoying the sensation of its cold freshness cleansing the fumes of oily smoke, burning charcoal and white-hot metals from his head. He walked alone up the rising road into the town, noting in passing that yet another dead donkey was lying on the edge of the big pool, the water supply, washing tub, sewer and general rubbish tip for the rows of houses around it.

'Dear God, and they profess to wonder why there is so much fever always in this town,' he muttered disgustedly, and to cheer himself up he reviewed his recent activities, and found satisfaction in that review. Will Stevens — Dyson grimaced and corrected himself, Will Stacey had found work in the finishing shop of the Heming and Bartleet Mill at the top of the Fish Hill. Up to now no one had queried his story of being an old army comrade of Josh Dyson's, and it seemed that his real identity was securely hidden.

Together they had by now recruited almost twenty men into their secret combination, the men coming from various mills and workshops around the district, and although they were few in numbers, Josh Dyson was well satisfied with their quality. Every one of them was intelligent and the majority, unusual in this day and age, could both read and write. Dyson flattered himself that owing to the extreme care both he and Stevens had exercised in their recruitment, not one of the men could be termed a 'tap room Radical'.

166

'No,' he smiled to himself. 'There's not one blowhard among 'um. They'll all prove good lads at six in the morn on empty bellies, I'd stake me life on it.' His smile became a wry grin. 'Come to think on it, that's exactly what I'm doing, staking me life on 'um. Just one informer among 'um and all the rest on us would soon be on our way to Botany Bay.'

Another aspect that he had carefully evaluated before approaching any potential recruit was if the man possessed any influence among his workmates. Dyson congratulated himself that indeed every one of them did exercise such an influence.

He started to whistle and thought of the coming night. Another meeting had been arranged at the brick kilns, and he hoped that there might be another new recruit to be sworn in as a member of the combination. He grinned to himself. This hoped-for new recruit would cause a stir of surprise among the rest of the lads. Mainly because she was a female. His grin widened. She didn't even know herself yet that she was going to be given the chance to join, but he'd wager that her dark brown eyes would sparkle with excitement when he told her what he proposed. Tildy Crawford had been constantly in his mind ever since their long conversation on the night of Shrove Tuesday, and he admitted openly to himself that her ideas had impressed him, even though at the time she had stated them he had not been prepared fully to accept their validity.

'I wonder how young Meg Tullet's death is affecting her, though?' He began to consider that perhaps it might be better not to tell her of his intentions to invite her to join the combination until he saw how the death of the girl had affected her. 'Mayhap she's too upset to think on anything else at present. Because she was powerful fond of that little simpleton, and no mistake.'

His footsteps slowed and he came to a halt on the road outside the arched entrance to the Silver Street, then, on impulse, he entered under that archway and walked quickly up the filth-thick narrow alley towards the Silver Square.

In the lodging house Tildy had just returned to the kitchen after settling little Davy to sleep. Nathaniel Farrel was seated by the fire when she came into the room, and he smiled in welcome and invited her to partake of his supper on the bench beside him, cold salted beef, pickled onions, bread and a flask of London gin. She declined politely. Tildy was uncertain of her feelings towards this man. He was always pleasant and quiet-mannered, and free with the money he appeared to have in abundance. He rented the small attic room next to Tildy's, but she heard little or nothing of his occupancy. Nothing was really known about him, despite his having spent some time in the lodging house, and his being ready enough to join in conversations. Whenever his personal antecedents were enquired about he always gave vague, smiling answers which disarmed his questioners, but at the same time left them none the wiser.

Mother Readman considered that he was in Redditch on some secret business which was probably illegal. But throughout the years so many strangers had passed through her doors who had things to hide that she cared little about yet another one to add to their number. She asked only that her clients pay their rents in advance and conduct themselves with a reasonable degree of decorum. What constituted a reasonable degree of decorum in Mother Readman's lodging house might well be regarded as outrageous licence in the more respectable quarters of the town, but as the old woman was fond of pointing out to her detractors, the standards of behaviour in her house were on a par with the goings-on at the court of King George IV, and what was good enough for His Majesty was most certainly good enough for her. So the Methody pisspots in the locality could think and say whatever they chose to about her lodging house, for she cared not a fart for any one of them.

Tildy sat down on her usual stool at the side of Mother Readman's now empty chair. She and Nathaniel Farrel were alone in the big room, but Tildy knew that shortly it would begin to fill up with the colourful nightly quota of tinkers and travellers and trampers and flotsam and jetsam from all corners of the land.

'I was sorry to hear about your young friend, Mrs Crawford,' Farrel told her, his light green eyes sympathetic.

By now Tildy had begun to come to terms with what had happened to Meg, and she knew that it was pointless to indulge herself further with useless tears and regrets.

'What will happen to the man, Brompton?' Farrel asked, his eyes speculative.

Tildy shrugged, and could not keep the bitterness from her voice. 'Not a thing, Mr Farrel. He'll go on his merry way, and it will be God help the next poor little wench that takes his fancy. If the gentry won't bring him to justice, then no one else hereabouts has the power to do aught against him.'

'It's a bad business,' Farrel agreed. 'There is no justice for the poor in his damned country, is there? It's a pity that her friends and workmates don't all join together to demand that the man be punished for what he's caused to happen.'

Tildy stared curiously at him. 'What do you mean, Mr Farrel, join together?'

'Well ...' He appeared to be giving his next words careful consideration. 'I suppose that I mean it's a pity they haven't got some sort of combination that would be strong enough to ensure that the man could be justly punished and mayhap to obtain some sort of compensation for the mother for the loss of her main support in life.'

'But combinations are forbidden by law,' Tildy pointed out.

The man smiled ambiguously at her. 'There are some

laws that are so patently unjust that they deserve to be broken, Mrs Crawford. I happen to believe that the Six Acts and the anti-combination laws are among them.'

'Them's dangerous thoughts to be giving voice to these days, Master.' Unnoticed by either of them, Josh Dyson had come into the kitchen in time to hear Farrel's last sentences. The Londoner appeared momentarily disconcerted by this unexpected intervention, and for a brief instant his eyes flickered uneasily towards Dyson. Then his easy smile returned and he spread his hands in appeal.

'I can only trust in my knowledge that you are not one of those who would enjoy running to the magistrates and reporting me for seditious speechifying, Master Dyson.'

The hardener looked searchingly at Farrel. 'How do you know me?' he challenged.

Farrel chuckled. 'I watched you at the backsword fighting, Master Dyson. I thought you were unlucky to lose.'

Dyson was not yet disarmed. 'Luck ne'er came into it, cully,' he growled. 'The parson is a bloody fine old gamester, probably the best in the Midlands, I shouldn't wonder. He beat me fair and straight.'

'You display generous sentiments towards a man who left you with a broken head, Master Dyson.'

Tildy thought she could detect a mocking undertone beneath the pleasantly spoken words, and saw by the angry gleam in Dyson's eyes that he shared that opinion. But his answer was civil enough.

'Well, you knows the old saying, don't you? That there's no use in crying over spilt milk, nor spilt blood neither.'

'Just so long as that milk is not deliberately spilt before starving people, nor that blood deliberately drawn from honest men by those who would tyrannize them,' Farrel responded, with a curiously provocative edge to his voice.

Despite the restraints of his innate caution, Josh Dyson's curiosity was now fully roused by this stranger and he asked, 'And who would you consider to be tyrannizing me?'

'Why, that's easy answered.' Farrel became serious in his manner. 'This unhappy land of ours has for many years now been tyrannized by foreign kings and their native-born lick-spittles, who daily sell their own countrymen's birthrights for selfish gain. The chorus of "rule Britannia" has long been rendered a nonsense believed only by fools, because Britons are truly only slaves in these modern days.'

For a long period Josh Dyson silently regarded the other man. Then he said quietly, 'I can't decide what sort of a man you am, cully. Brave, reckless, drunk, mad or just plain bloody stupid, to be going about saying such things so openly afore people that you can't really know much about.'

Farrel's ready smile flashed again. 'Oh no, Master Dyson, I'm none of those things that you've suggested. But I am a man who understands certain things about the very people that you tell me I don't really know much about.'

Josh Dyson's body visibly tensed, and he grated out, 'I'd advise you to tread a bit careful, cully. Because ice that you think to be thick enough to bear your weight sometimes is treacherous and breaks beneath you just when youm least expecting it to.'

The gathering threat of violence was to Tildy a tangible presence in the room, and she breathed a sigh of genuine relief when the tension was broken and the threat dissipated by the noisy entrance of Mother Readman dragging the volubly protesting Marmaduke Montmorency by his ear.

'Unhand me, woman! Or by God, I'll make a ghost of you!' the decayed actor shouted, and Mother Readman cuffed the huge, floppy tam-o-shanter from his long greasy locks with her free hand.

'Shut your bloody rattle, Montmorency! I'll not bloody tell you agen, you wicked old villain.'

171

> 'Too late I stayed
> Forgive the crime
> Unheeded flew the hours
> How noiselessly falls the foot of time,
> That only treads on flowers,

Montmorency declaimed piteously as the monstrous-looking old woman dragged him to the fireside, and Tildy could not help but giggle at the ludicrous contrast between the sonorous voice reciting poetry, and the spectacle of Marmaduke Montmorency struggling to escape from the iron grip of Mother Readman.

'Unheeded flew the bleedin' hours, did they, you worthless old muck-tip?' Mother Readman bellowed. 'Forgive the crime, must I? You thievin' old sod!'

'What's he done now?' Tildy smothered her laughter sufficiently to gasp out.

'What's he done?' Mother Readman demanded rhetorically. 'What arn't the bugger done might be a better question. He's the blight o' my fuckin' life, so he is. That's so, arn't it? Youm the blight o' my life, arn't you?' she demanded of the old actor and shook him by his captive ear until he screamed out in agony. 'Yes, that's right! Scream away, you bloody old shit-heap. I'll bloody well learn you your lesson yet,' she bawled furiously. 'You'll not be able to skrawk when I'se done wi' you, you wicked old bastard. Because you'll be fucking well dead! That's why!'

'Mercy! Show mercy! In the name of God and all His blessed saints, show mercy!' Montmorency pleaded, then caught Tildy's eye and winked broadly, and she erupted with helpless laughter, finding in that involuntary outpouring her own release from the bondage of her terrible day.

'I give this bugger a shilling to goo and buy some bread for me, and what did he do wi' the money?' Mother Readman shook the hapless man's head so violently that he cried out in fresh protest.

172

'Yes, skrawk, you bugger! Skrawk!' Mother Readman bawled. 'You spent my bread money on drink, didn't you, you worthless old baggage?'

'I merely followed the precepts of the good book, Madam,' he stated, with an air of one who is grievously misjudged. 'Does it not direct us to "Drink no longer water, but use a little wine for thy stomach's sake"? Who am I, a poor thespian, to go against the teachings of our Lord?'

'Oh, docs it now? Does it tell you that indeed?' Despite her temper the fat old woman was by now fighting to stop herself grinning in amusement. 'But don't it tell us also "Resist the devil, and he 'ull flee from you"?' A chuckle escaped her, and she released Marmaduke Montmorency's sorely reddened ear. 'Goo on, bugger off from me, you old sod, and don't show your face in here again!'

The old reprobate didn't wait to argue, but scurried quickly out.

Mother Readman laughed wryly. 'He'll be back tomorrow, large as life and twice as smelly just as though naught had ever happened today. Still, I'd miss the old sod if he warn't here. I can't help but like him, for all his roguery.'

Her fit of involuntary laughter had greatly cheered Tildy, and now when Dyson asked her how she felt she was able to tell him that she was much better and easier in her mind about Meg's death.

'Good.' Dyson smiled at her, and then advised, 'You'd best make sure that you comes to your work tomorrow though, Tildy. Your mates in the lye wash was telling me that Conolly warn't best pleased wi' you for not turning to. But seeing as what happened I doubt that you'll hear any more about missing your work, so long as youm there nice and early tomorrow morning.'

'I will be,' Tildy assured him. 'I can't afford to miss any more time or I'll not have wages enough to pay my way with this week.'

Dyson decided against mentioning the secret meeting of that night to her. He had also decided that he distrusted Nathaniel Farrel, knowing as he did from past experience that 'provocation men' would voice Radical opinions to inveigle others to follow suit, and would then hasten to inform on those others for reward. 'I'll see you tomorrow then, Tildy. Try not to brood over what happened today. I bid you all good night.'

After the hardener had left Farrel said, 'I would think that that man commands much respect and influence among his fellow workers.'

'Indeed he does,' Tildy confirmed warmly. 'And he is a good man in himself. I like him very much, and respect him greatly.'

Farrel was piqued by jealousy. 'He's too old to be your sweetheart, Mrs Crawford.'

Tildy shrugged. 'Does age matter so much between man and woman?'

'Well, winter and spring do not run side by side.' Although Farrel's tone was light, his eyes were very serious as inwardly he castigated himself for allowing his attraction towards this girl to affect him so powerfully that he felt jealous of her professed liking for another man. 'Think on,' he silently admonished himself. 'Have you not always mocked those who'd let a pretty face sway them? Who for the sake of a pair of bright eyes let themselves be hindered from forwarding their business? Think on, you damned fool. Think on!'

He was saved from betraying his feelings more openly by Tildy's announcement that she was going to her room to sleep. She lit a stub of tallow candle to light her way up the rickety staircase and left Mother Readman and Nathanial Farrel alone together.

The lodging house mistress looked keenly at the man and she told him, 'There's a good many men hereabouts who's got a fancy for Tildy Crawford, Master Farrel. But I'll tell you summat, it 'ull take a rare sort of man to win her, and that man 'ull be a rare lucky cove to have a wench like

Tildy at his side. Her's good as gold, so her is.'

The young man's eyes held an unfathomable expression, and when he spoke his tone was musing. 'She could bring a man to his ruin, Mistress Readman, by distracting his wits just when he most needs them to be sharp and concentrated.'

Chapter Twenty-Three

Seventeen men were crammed into the black-gloomed interior of the thick-walled, disused brick kiln, and Josh Dyson was satisfied with that attendance. Counting in the three others posted outside as sentinels and lookouts it was a hundred per cent turnout. He rose to his feet.

'Brothers, it looks as if everybody is here now, so let's begin. Now, we'se bin organized long enough, so I reckon it's high time we tested our strength.' A rustle of excitement greeted his words, and he grinned in the darkness. Since leaving Mother Readman's he had been thinking very hard about an idea that had occurred to him while there. Now he voiced that idea. 'Most of you has never acted in a combination afore, I know, and with the present situation as regards the law, then it's necessary that we must work secretly, but you needs experience of acting together as one union. What I'm going to propose now 'ull give you that experience, and it'll give you the confidence to know that we can challenge the masters and win, despite everything that's bin done against us by way of the Six Acts and the combination laws.' He paused to give them time to absorb that concept, then went on, 'I expect most on you has heard by now about that young wench throwing herself into the Forge Mill pool. Now I arn't going to be a hypocrite and say that I'm much concerned about what happened to her in one way or the other. But what I will say is that we can use her death to our advantage. It was an overlooker at the Fountain Mill who was partly to blame for what her done to herself. If Johnny Brompton is let to go back to his work by Henry Milward, then that gives us our opportunity to strike a blow agen the masters.'

'You arn't expecting us to strike from our work just because a tuppenny whore drownded herself, be you, Josh Dyson?' A voice growled from the close-packed mass, and was supported by half-a-dozen other voices.

'Us going on strike 'ull do naught for her.'

'No, it wun't bring her back from the dead, 'ull it?'

'We'll lose our wages for nothing.'

Josh Dyson scowled impatiently. Already the bane of combination was occurring: each man asserting his own views and protests without stopping to hear fully what was being proposed.

'Will you do me the favour of holding your peace until I'se finished, brother Tandy, and the rest on you,' he requested with laboured politeness. 'Arter I'se done speaking, then we shall act as true brethren, and take a vote on my proposals.' He paused, as if inviting further comments, but none were offered and relieved by that he went on, 'I'm not calling for any of us to strike from our work, brothers. What I'm proposing is that we uses the opportunity presented to us by this wench's death, to practise rousing the people and directing them to take action. It's obvious that we mustn't be seen to be doing this though, arn't it?'

'How does we do it then, Josh? Does we hide in the shit-house and shout directions from inside theer?' another man questioned facetiously, and there was a rumbling of laughter.

'Listen to me, brothers.' Will Stevens, or Stacey as he was now known locally, rose to his feet. 'It seems to me that some o' you be thinking that this is all a game. A bit o' sport.' His voice was hard and challenging. 'Well you'd best forget that bloody notion. We arn't playing games here, me and brother Dyson. We'em in deadly earnest. Both on us has seen friends hung or transported for what we'em doing right this minute. So forget any ideas any of you might be holding that you can walk away from this combination any time you feels like doing so because you'se had your bit o' fun, and you'se got tired of the game. You can't walk away from this combination ... ever!' His voice was a cold threat, and the atmosphere within the cramped, dark hole sobered. 'Each and every one of us here has took a solemn oath. And that oath is a hanging matter,' Stevens continued, and now there was no trace of facetiousness left in his listeners. 'Any judge who hears that you'se took such an oath is going to try and arrange a meeting between you and Jack Ketch just as soon as he can. So you listen hard to what brother Dyson is telling you now, and let's have no more fun being poked ... And another thing while I'm about it. This combination of ours is an honourable brotherhood, and that's why we addresses each other as brother. It's used as a mark o' mutual respect and unity, so in future I don't want to hear any one of you addressing each other while we'em in a meeting without using that title.'

He reseated himself on the brick floor and there was a brief, uneasy shifting and muttering amongst his audience which lasted until Dyson spoke again.

'My thanks, brother Stacey, that needed saying, and I hope that all present has accepted and understood what you've told them. Now, brothers, what I'm proposing to this meeting is that we waits to see if Henry Milward is going to let Johnny Brompton back to his work. If he does, then it's up to us to start up demonstrations agen him and make trouble for Henry Milward until he's forced to hand Brompton his sack. If needs be we must keep up this action until Brompton is driven from this district. Doing this will give us all the experience of how to use a mass of people to gain our own ends. Is there anything anybody wants to say about this proposal?'

'I does, brother Dyson.' It was Thomas Tandy who spoke. 'I works at the Fountain, the same as you, and Johnny Brompton had always bin a good mate o' mine. I don't relish the idea of driving him from this town just because he had a bit o' fun wi' a wench that we all knows was naught but a whore. But it arn't only that, brother Dyson. What youm proposing really means that from now on if any of us tries our hand wi' a woman in the mill, and that woman kicks up a fuss about nothing, well then, it 'ud be us next to be driven from the town.

'It arn't natural to expect that men be agoing to not try and shag all the wenches they fancies, and all us men gets a bit rough wi' our wenches at times, don't we? So I don't think it right that we should have a go against Johnny Brompton. It arn't going to do us any good that I can see. It'll just make the women more uppity than they be already.'

Josh Dyson sensed the strong undercurrent of agreement and sympathy with Tandy in the meeting, and he very carefully chose his words in reply. 'I can accept the justice in what you say, brother Tandy, but I reckon the times are such that all on us here must now realize that we can't any longer go on treating the wenches who works alongside us as just easy game. It's my opinion that one of the main mistakes previous combinations had allus made, is to have their members all men. I reckon it's high time we brought the women into the combinations as well, because remember, one of the things we hopes to gain eventually is a vote for every man. Just think if our womenfolk had a vote as well. Just think how our strength politically 'ud be doubled straight away.'

A concerted reaction of rejection swept through the meeting. To accept women as equals went against the inbred, indoctrinated chauvinism of every man present. Dyson himself, sensing that instant rejection and realizing that he had taken the wrong tack, instantly and smoothly changed course. 'Anyway, let's not trouble our yeds with such questions as that, brothers. Our brother Tandy here has pointed out that he's a good mate of John Brompton's and let me say that I applaud brother Tandy for speaking out so bravely and honestly, it does him credit and demands our respect. I sympathize wholly with the difficult situation this puts brother Tandy in. All I can say to him, and to you all, is that we are fighting a war here. A war against the masters to try and wrest from them what are the rightful possessions of all Englishmen: freedom, justice, and a fair share of the world's riches for each and every one of us. In this war we'em now fighting there will be times when we'll each of us be called on to make sacrifices. A lot of good men have already sacrificed families, homes, freedom, even their lives in this war, and before we achieves victory I don't doubt but that some on us here might well be called on to make our own sacrifices for this cause of our'n. To sacrifice a friendship 'ull be only a little thing compared with some that men have already made. But having said that, I want to make it plain that I don't expect brother Tandy to take any action himself against his friend. Whatever is necessary in the Fountain Mill, then I'll do it. All I ask from brother Tandy in this case is that he keeps the faith with us, and says naught to nobody concerning what the rest on us be about. Does you consider that to be fair, brothers?' A chorus of affirmation greeted his question. 'Brother Tandy, what say you?' Dyson pressed the objector, and the man nodded and said quietly, 'That's fair enough by me, brother Dyson. I can't bring myself to act agen a man who's allus been a good mate to me, but I understands what you mean when you say we'em fighting a war here. So I'll keep the faith. I swear on me babby's life to that.'

Muted applause for him came from all sides, and Josh Dyson was pleased that a potentially difficult situation had been defused so amicably. 'Remember, brothers, we has to seize each and every opportunity to carry our struggle forwards, and this is a prime chance to do so. About the question of women, I think meself that our best course of action is to goad the women into kicking up the randies against Johnny Brompton. Let's get them to shoot the bullets. So work through your wives and sweethearts and female kin, but do it cunning, so that they'll think it's their own idea. All in favour of my proposals, give voice.'

The 'ayes' were in the vast majority.

Well pleased with his stratagems, Josh Dyson told them, 'Wait for the word from me, brothers, and then act fast on it.'

Shortly afterwards the meeting came to a close and the company began to slip away into the night. While they waited their turn to leave, Dyson told Will Stevens, 'I've only got one worry now, Will, and that's if Old Henry buggers up our plans by handing Brompton his sack wi'out us taking any action.'

'Never fear,' his friend answered. 'He wun't. And if he does, why then it's been obvious tonight that Brompton has got a lot of mates in this town. We can always kick up trouble for Milward by saying that Brompton's been treated unjustly if he sacks him afore we wants him to.'

Chapter Twenty-Four

Tildy arrived at the Fountain Mill just as the great gates opened and the morning bell began ringing. Arthur Conolly, standing in his usual post under the big hanging lantern called her to him as she came into the entrance tunnel.

'Cummon here, you. Wheer was you yesterday? Does you think that you needs only come to your work when it pleases you to do so, Crawford? Does you reckon yourself to be bloody lady muck?'

Although Tildy disliked the man intensely, and knew that he knew very well where she had been, because by now the news of that tragic event was known by every man, woman and child in the district, she accepted that by deliberately absenting herself from work she had placed herself in the wrong, and so he had the right to tax her with her absence. So she answered quietly, 'I had to take young Meg Tullet to see Parson Clayton. You know what happened after that. By the time everything was done with it was too late for me to come. I'd not have gained entrance at that hour, would I?'

'Don't you be so sure that youm agoing to gain entrance now, my wench,' he shouted, and took pleasure as he saw the alarm in her eyes.

To be sacked from this job could have very serious consequences for Tildy, because at this moment in time she desperately needed even the paltry wages she earned here.

'But I've only lost the one day,' she stammered apprehensively, and was angry at herself for betraying that apprehension before this man whom she so despised.

'Stand over there,' he ordered, pointing to a spot the wags called 'execution dock', just inside the gates where workers waiting to be sacked or disciplined by the master always stood. 'You'll wait theer until I decides what's to be done about you.'

By now the workpeople were arriving in full stream, and Tildy's cheeks burned with embarrassment as some of the rougher elements among them jeered and made ribald comments as they saw her waiting on that spot, while those who were well-disposed towards her and her friends from the lye shop seemed to be made uneasy by the sight of her, and averted their eyes and hurried past, or offered only the briefest sidelong glances of sympathy.

His rotund body made even bulkier by his thick layers of clothing, the top-hatted Henry Milward passed majestically through the entrance and he frowned when he saw the young woman standing there against the wall, visibly shivering as the cold, biting wind gusted erratically, sending swirls of snow dust buffeting against her threadbare gown and shawl.

'That's that Crawford woman, arn't it?' the needle master jerked his several chins in her direction, and his overlooker confirmed her identity.

'I'se kept her here, Master, because I warn't sure what you wanted done wi' her, seeing as what happened yesterday.'

Milward was sorely tempted to tell his overlooker to sack the girl on the spot for the trouble she had already caused him; but aware of the consequent embroilment with his wife that that course of action might bring down upon him, because after all Milly had befriended this little bitch once and would most certainly spring to her defence now, he restrained that primary impulse. 'Keep her cooling her bloody heels theer, Arthur,' he instructed low-voiced. 'I'll have a think about what's to be done with her.'

At that precise moment Johnny Brompton came into the mill. He saw Tildy and his eyes glowed with triumph as he noted where she stood. Noting also that Henry Milward was nearby he said nothing to Tildy but went to the needle master who growled at him, 'Get in my office you bleeder. I'se got a bone to pick wi' you.'

When Josh Dyson saw Tildy he stopped and asked her, 'What's you doing here, Tildy? Be they agoing to sack you?'

She shook her head. 'I don't know, Josh. Conolly told me to stand here, but when Henry Milward saw me he didn't say anything. I hope they don't hand me my sack, because I really need this work.'

Dyson smiled reassuringly at her worried face. 'Don't you fret, my honey,' he murmured so that only she could hear what he said. 'I'll do my damndest to keep 'um from sacking you.' He walked on and halted again in front of Arthur Conolly. From the nearby office came the sounds of the needle master shouting abuse at Johnny Brompton, and Dyson chuckled grimly. 'I hear that Johnny Brompton's getting his breakfast served good and hot this morn.'

Arthur Conolly nodded, wary as always of this man before him. 'That's right, Josh. Still, better a bit o' tongue pie that to lose your work, arn't it?'

'What's to happen to the wench, then?' The hardener jerked his head back towards Tildy. 'Because I can't see as how Old Henry 'ull want to keep her here arter what she tried to do against Johnny Brompton.'

'I don't rightly know what's to happen to her,' Conolly told him. 'All Mr Milward said was to keep her here until he's had a think about it.'

Dyson nodded casually. 'Ah well, sooner her than me standing theer on a frosty morning. Be seeing you, Arthur.' He nodded and sauntered on into the mill.

In the lye wash shop Tildy's friends were also talking about her. Shame-faced because of the timidity each one of them had shown when confronted by her standing in 'execution dock', now the three of them were feeling an anger fuelled by that very sense of shame. Their anger lacked any definite focus, however, until William Kitchen came into the shop with his arms full of needle-purses and told them, 'Old Henry arn't half give Johnny Brompton a roasting. You could hear the old sod blaggardin' him all over the bloody yard. He buggered him up one side and down the other, so he did.'

'Has he sacked the bugger, though?' Sarah Farr demanded.

The youth grinned slyly. 'Nooo, o' course he arn't. Old Henry 'ull never sack an overlooker if he can help it, 'ull he? But he's agoing to sack Tildy for trying to cause trouble like she did yesterday.'

'Who says he's agoing to sack her?' Mary Ann Avery questioned aggressively, and the youth shrugged.

'Well, I heard it from Terry Wilkes, him who works in the hardening shop, and he reckons Josh Dyson told him, so it's got to be right arn't it, because Old Josh gets to know everything that's happening in this place, don't he?'

'Is this some more o' your bloody nonsense, you young bugger?' Mary Ann challenged angrily, and the youth reacted aggrievedly.

'Look, don't you start on me because your mate's getting her sack give her. It arn't my doing, is it? I'm only atelling you what I'se bin told meself.'

'It arn't bloody right, Old Henry adoing that,' Sarah Farr burst out. 'It arn't right to give Tildy her sack just because her was trying to help poor little Meg.'

'It's wuss than not right!' Mary Ann's normally placid, pleasant expression had become a mask of seething fury. 'He arn't sacked bloody Brompton, has he? And that's the bastard who should have bin hung up by his balls for what he did to poor little Meg.'

'It's allus bin the same, girls,' Old Tabby stated peevishly. 'The buggers 'ull allus put the blame on the wench, never on the bloody man.'

185

Mary Ann's eyes were blazing now, and for a few moments she stood as if uncertain of what she wanted to do. Then she pitched the purse of buckram she had begun to unlace into the copper, spilling great splashes of boiling, hissing water over its sides. 'Bollocks to this!' she declared. 'Let's goo and tell every woman in this mill what Old Henry's adoing. Let's all get together and show the old sod what we bloody well thinks o' the way he's treating poor Tildy. Let's get everybody out into the yard!'

Ever eager for anything that would bring some excitement and novelty into the grinding monotony of their day, the workers streamed from their various shops out into the courtyard and gathered there in a noisy crowd, partly serious, partly joking and horseplaying.

The overlookers from the shops went at a run to Henry Milward's office, where he was still berating the hangdog Johnny Brompton, and the needle master's face purpled with rage as he heard their spluttered words.

'What?' He emitted a strangled bellow. 'All in the bloody yard, be they? Laid down their tools, has they? Every shop stopped work, has it? I'll bloody well see about that!'

He stormed from the office and the overlookers trooped dutifully behind him as he went to confront the crowd.

Thomas Tandy moved to where Josh Dyson was standing against a wall watching the noisy gathering. 'Well now, Josh, you arn't wasted any time, has you?' He spoke in an undertone that contained a mingling of surprise and admiration.

The hardener smiled grimly. 'You should know by now, Tommy, that these buggers are like dry tinder, any spark serves to set 'um alight.'

Secretly he was amazed himself at the rapidity with which events had moved, and not too well pleased, because he realized that he was not in any way directing or controlling what was taking place here. Like a horse out of control, the crowd had taken the figurative bit in their teeth and had bolted away with it.

'How does we get word to the other lads?' Tandy asked, and Dyson, anxious to maintain the impression that he was in full control, answered, 'I'll take care o' that in due course, Tommy. There's no call to involve any other place yet. I wants to see what develops here first.' He was gratified by the respect in the other man's eyes and by his whispered reply, 'I'll tell you this much, Josh. I warn't too sure that you could do the business afore, but I bloody well am sure now all right. I'd never ha' believed you could ha' done this so quick if I hadn't ha' seen it wi' me own eyes.'

'Shush now,' Dyson instructed. 'Let's hear what Old Henry's got to say for himself.'

By now Henry Milward had mounted the stone steps onto the loading bay of the mill's storage shop, and the workers were crowding around the base of that platform. The needle master, timid when faced with his wife, was fearless when facing his employees.

'Now then, you buggers,' he bawled down into their upturned faces. 'What's all this about? If you've a grievance, then bloody well spake it now to me bloody face.'

No one answered at first, and Milward jeered, 'What's this then? Arn't nobody got the guts to spake out to me face?'

'It's about Tildy Crawford,' Mary Ann Avery called out, and instantly the people directly around her edged away, creating an open space in which she stood isolated. Milward's purplish features showed his surprise at finding that it was his normally meek and placid lye shop forewoman who was apparently leading this demonstration.

'Mary Ann? What's amiss wi' you?' he asked in genuine puzzlement. 'This arn't like you at all.'

'No, Master, it arn't like me, is it?' The woman was flustered and embarrassed by her physical isolation, but she spoke out clearly. 'We don't think that it's right what youm adoing to Tildy Crawford.'

The needle master frowned. 'What does you mean by that, Mary Ann? What arn't right?'

'It arn't right that you should be handing her her sack, just because she tried to help poor little Meg Tullet.' A rumbling of assent and encouragement came from among the crowd and, emboldened by these tokens of support, Mary Ann went on, 'It's that dirty bleeder Johnny Brompton that you should be sacking this day, Master. Not Tildy Crawford.'

'That's right!'

'You tell him, Mary Ann!'

'Sack the bugger!'

'Sack him!'

Again her supporters voiced their agreement.

Henry Milward, like most of his breed, was a very shrewd man when it came to his personal interests. His father had been a needle master before him, and Henry Milward had had a lifetime's experience of dealing with underlings. He could sense now the temper of the crowd, and knew that any wrong move on his part could well precipitate real trouble. He had witnessed many outbreaks of local violence during his life, and was well aware of the local propensity towards riot and mayhem. Thankfully there were only his own operatives here, none of the hotheads and brawlers from the other mills were present, but he knew that once trouble began, then like bees drawn to their hive those hotheads and brawlers would come flying to join in it. The tension in the atmosphere was mounting fast, and the crowd were beginning to simmer like a fused bomb ready to explode. He decided to defuse that bomb.

'You've got it all wrong, Mary Ann.' He smiled bluffly at the angry woman. 'The only reason Tildy Crawford is waiting in the entry is because I wants to see her afore she starts work. I wants to hear from her own lips the full account of what happened yesterday to poor little Meg. There's no suggestion at all of me handing the wench her sack.' He recognized another potential friction, and moved to smooth it away. 'She arn't going to lose any wages by being in the entry there instead of working. She'll still get paid her hours.' He paused, evaluating the effects of his words, then uttered reproachfully, 'God damn it all, Mary Ann! How many years has you known me, my duck? It's since we was kids, arn't it? Has you ever known me to be a cruel man? Does you really think that I'd punish a wench when her was only trying to help a pitiful cratur like Meg Tullet was? You knows that arn't so, Mary Ann. Now come on and admit that you knows it arn't so.'

After a momentary hesitation the woman nodded. 'That's true enough, Master Milward, you'se never had the name o' being a cruel man.'

'Maybe not, but he's always had the name o' being a bloody tight 'un,' a wag shouted from the crowd, and Milward roared with laughter, in which after a brief instant the crowd joined. The tension among them disappeared with the laughter, and Milward seized the moment.

'Now let's have you back to work, you buggers,' he cried jovially. 'Or I'll have no bloody money to be tight wi', will I? And none to pay the bloody wages wi', neither.'

Josh Dyson grudgingly gave Milward full credit for the masterly way he had handled a potentially explosive situation. Men, women and children were now going back to their work laughing and joking, all thought of Johnny Brompton apparently forgotten in the general amusement with the way the wag had so aptly scored off Henry Milward.

Thomas Tandy came to the hardener's elbow again. 'Well? What happens now, Josh?' His expression was puzzled, and he seemed to doubt the evidence of his own eyes as to what was now happening. 'I don't understand it Josh. One minute these buggers were all primed to go on a randy, and next minute they'm all going back to their work as merry as bleedin' crickets.'

'They'm going back merry because Old Henry is as

sharp as his own bloody needles, my bucko,' Josh Dyson told him. 'I got to admit that I underestimated the old sod. But ne'er mind, we'll get our chance yet.'

'When?' Tandy demanded glumly, and Dyson forced himself to grin confidently.

'Why, when I decides to manufacture that chance, Tom. That's when!' Inwardly he was consoling himself, 'Ah well, it all come too easy to be true, didn't it? I couldn't really have hoped for a riot straight off, could I? That arn't being realistic. But the chance 'ull come sooner nor later, I'll make sure of that.'

When Henry Milward went back to his office he dismissed Johnny Brompton with the parting admonition, 'You attend strictly to your work in future, my lad, and be thankful that I'm allowing you to stay on here. Because if them buggers out there had their way, you'd be looking for another job this very minute. The only reason that I arn't handing you your sack right now is because when I've promoted a man to be one o' my overlookers, I hates having to admit publicly that my judgement was mistaken. But if you so much as thinks about shagging any wench in this mill in future, then I'll have you through those bloody gates afore you can draw a breath. Now sod off, and earn some o' the wages I pays you, you stupid bastard!'

There were occasions on which Henry Milward could be brutally honest both with himself and with others. There were also occasions on which he could be a consumate hypocrite. He followed the latter course when he called Tildy into his office and smiling kindly at her gestured her towards the blazing fire.

'You warm yourself by there, my duck. You looks nigh on perished.'

In his heart of hearts he could have wished that she had indeed been frozen to death out in the entrance tunnel for bringing such aggravation to him.

'Now, my duck, while you're warming yourself, I want

you to tell me in your own words everything that happened yesterday, and what you think led to it.'

Tildy did as he bade her, shivering still despite the heat of the fire, for the long wait in the entrance had chilled her to her very bones. Trying to relate factually and calmly all that had occurred, she made no secret of her conviction that Johnny Brompton was mainly to blame for the girl's death.

The needle master listened gravely, and did not interrupt. When she had finished and fallen silent, he began to pace up and down before her, hands clasped behind his back, head bowed as if he was thinking deeply about what he had heard. Henry Milward was not a vicious or brutal man. He was something of a tyrant to those beneath him, but no more so that his contemporaries among the masters, and less so than many of them. He had felt some genuine pangs of sympathy as he listened to Tildy's story. But although he was absolute master here, he was dominated by unspoken mores. His station in life as one of the newly rising middle class demanded from him certain personal standards of behaviour and morality. Although he might secretly make mock of and flaunt these standards, the pressure of his peer group and of the higher gentry impelled him to conform outwardly to the postures expected of him. It was an open secret that immorality, bad language, cruelty and drunkenness were rife in the factories and mills, but still he must act as if the strictest of moral codes were enforced by him in his establishment. His hard-won middle class respectability demanded that. As a select vestryman and chapel warden he must set an example to others. He was fully aware of the sexual harassment many of his overlookers had practised, but he could not admit this to Tildy, just as he could not admit to her that he fully believed her story.

'It's a sad tale you've told me, young woman,' he halted to tell her. 'But what's done is done, and there's naught to be gained by stirring up more trouble than you have already. The parson has questioned Johnny Brompton, and so have I, and to both on us he has sworn that he used no force against the girl. He admits to having had carnal connection with her when he was drunk, and of course I'm of the opinion that that was a most sinful act, but it arn't a crime in the eyes of the law, Crawford.

'Parson Clayton is of the opinion that the girl was willing for the connection to take place, and he's a highly educated man with a vast knowledge of human nature. I for one would never dream of questioning the parson's judgement. When he states something to be a fact, then you may wager your life on it being a fact. And, of course, to me the most telling thing was that when the girl was given the opportunity to state her case she 'udden't utter a single word against Brompton, would her?

'I arn't blaming the poor wench for being what she was, Crawford, don't think that for one moment. But we all on us has to face facts, unpleasant though those facts might be. And the fact is that young Meg Tullet was well known as a tuppenny whore, as was her mam, and her mam's mam afore her. John Brompton has always held a good character. He wouldn't be one o' my overlookers if he didn't. And his parents were very respectable, God-fearing people as well.'

While she listened, Tildy was ravaged by a kaleidoscope of emotion. Bitter anguish for Meg. Bitter anger against Johnny Brompton. Bitter disgust for those like Parson Clayton and Henry Milward who refused to acknowledge the truth. But more bitter than any of these things was the knowledge that she also would be forced to fail Meg Tullet. Her desperate need to work here and earn sufficient money for herself and her child to survive on must take precedence over her burning desire to fight on and bring Brompton to justice. The needs of her living child must be paramount, no matter what terrible wrong had been done to the dead child, Meg Tullet.

'... so, young woman, my advice to you is to put all this out of your mind, and accept the fact that you were told a lot of lies by that wench. You just get on wi' your work now, and concentrate on your own affairs.'

The claret-bleared eyes of the needle master were fixed on her in anticipation, and with a sickening sense of shameful, abject surrender, Tildy nodded. 'Very well, Master Milward. I'll do as you say.'

Chapter Twenty-Five

At eight o'clock that night when Tildy left the Fountain Mill she found John Dyson waiting for her outside the great gates.

'I'll walk up to the town with you, Tildy, if you've no objection.' He smiled sympathetically at her. 'Everything bin all right today, has it? You've had no harassment from Brompton or Conolly?'

'No, Josh. I've seen neither hide nor hair of Brompton, and when Conolly came into the shop he never spoke a word to me.'

'Good!' Dyson let his hand rest on her shoulder. 'If either on 'um do start trying to give you a hard time on it, then you come straight and tell me.'

'I will, and thank you,' she told him gratefully. The ordeal of the previous day and her morning surrender to necessity had left her feeling weak and vulnerable, and she took much comfort from the reassuring presence of Josh Dyson and enjoyed the gentle pressure of his hand resting so lightly upon her shoulder.

For a while they walked in a companionable silence, each one searching for the right words with which to broach the differing subjects uppermost in their minds. For Tildy it was the galling realization that John Brompton to all intents and purposes had gone scot-free and unpunished for what he had done. Josh Dyson on the other hand was not unduly bothered by Brompton. What he wanted desperately was to draw Tildy into the combination. He had noted how popular she was with her workmates and how they had been prepared to challenge

Henry Milward on her behalf. He thought now that she would make a valuable and useful addition to the strength of the combination, and that she was brave and determined enough to take the inescapable risks inherent in helping to recruit and further organize this new-formed union. On a personal note he was also more than a little infatuated with her beauty and high intelligence and wanted to draw her closer to him.

It was the hardener who finally broke the silence.

'Do you remember what you and I talked about before all this sorry business with young Meg happened, Tildy?'

She thought for a moment, and then asked, 'Do you mean when we talked about forming a combination?'

'Ahr, that's it.' Instinctively he glanced all around to see if any of the other workers who were walking towards the town were close enough to overhear. Satisfied no one was, he went on, 'How would you feel now about belonging to such a movement?'

She gave the question grave consideration, then told him quietly, 'After what has happened here these last days, Josh, I'm coming to believe that it will only be by joining together that people in our station in life will ever obtain justice from those set above us. Yes, I would be prepared to join a combination. But from what I know of those that went before, no women were let to join them.'

'Times are changing, Tildy, and we must change with them if we are to achieve any progress. Myself, now I hold to the opinion that it's a necessity to bring the women into the combination if there's to be any chance of success.'

Tildy's smile was shadowed by sadness. 'Not all men think as you do, though, Josh. That's one fact that life has taught me well. It's a rare man who regards women as his equals.'

'Then it's about time you and me began to teach 'um different, arn't it?' Dyson grinned, and Tildy queried half-jokingly, 'Do we declare a mixed combination then, Josh?'

He sobered, and told her simply, 'There is a combination already in this town that you can join, iffen you've a mind to, my wench.'

She stared at him in surprise, but when she went to speak he took his hand from her shoulder and gently laid his finger against her lips. 'No. Say nothing yet, Tildy, only listen very carefully. There's a combination bin formed in this district that is only small as yet, but composed of men of high quality. There's no blowhards, no tap-room Radicals. Every man-jack in it has bin very carefully chosen and watched close afore being invited to join. It's a secret union, Tildy, every member is sworn on his dying oath to maintain that secrecy. There must not be even a whisper noised abroad that a combination exists here, until we decides that the time is right to let such whispers be put about.' He paused, studying the effects of his words upon her.

'Go on,' she urged softly. 'I'm hungry to hear more of what I am going to become a part of.'

He frowned slightly. 'Does you fully realize what becoming a part of it could lead you to, though, Tildy? If things were to go badly for us then you could end by being transported, or even hung.'

Her eyes were gleaming, and her voice throbbed as she declared, 'Of course I'm feared of transportation, and terrified at even the thought of Jack Ketch. But I'm convinced after what I've witnessed these past days that there's worse things in life than meeting the hangman, because at least that's quickly over and done with. But mayhap one day I'll marry again, and mayhap I'll bear a daughter. I'm not wanting to see her grow up in a world that could do to her what's been done to Meg Tullet. If your combination is prepared to fight to achieve a decent life for girls like Meg, then I'm proud to be a part of it.'

Again his hand rested on her shoulder and squeezed gently, and his eyes were warm and loving as he told her, 'I'm a happy man hearing you say that, Tildy. There's a meeting bin called just a few nights from now. I'll take you there with me and introduce you to your future comrades.

You'll take the oath as our first woman member. We'll become your brothers, and you will become our sister.' He hesitated a moment, then blurted out involuntarily, 'But in all truth, Tildy, I'd sooner have you as me sweetheart than as me sister.'

She came to an abrupt standstill, causing him to overstep clumsily. He stared anxiously at her.

'Has I given you offence, Tildy, by saying that?'

She shook her head solemnly. 'Listen well to me, Josh. Mayhap some day there could be such a bonding between us. I tell you frankly that I also am drawn to you in that way. But for now, for a multitude of reasons, all that can be between you and I is friendship. So please, do not press me for more than that at this time. I pray you to rest content with that.'

He forced a smile. 'I'll so rest, Tildy, I'll so rest. That I swear to you.'

The remainder of the journey was made in silence, but strangely, after the initial uneasiness caused by his declaration and her reply to it, the atmosphere between them eased to a warm, pleasant closeness, as if some invisible bonding had been forged which left to itself would inexorably grow and strengthen.

When they parted at the Silver Street archway, Tildy told him, 'I'll bid you a good night, Josh. Tomorrow, if you will, I'd like to hear more about your plans for the combination.'

He grinned happily. 'You'll hear more, my honey, never fear. In fact, you'll be hearing so much from now on that you'll begin to dread clapping eyes on me because of it.'

'No Josh,' she said gently. 'That's the one thing I'm certain sure of, that I'll never come to dread seeing you.'

She walked on up the narrow rancidness of the Silver Street and for one of those few times in her life so far, felt that she had met a man with whom, perhaps, she could share that life.

Chapter Twenty-Six

When Reverend the Lord Aston returned to his vicarage at Tardebigge hamlet four days after the suicide of Meg Tullet the coroner's inquest had already returned the verdict of 'self-murder' upon the tragic child.

Lord Aston walked with his curate, John Clayton, who had brought him that news, in the grounds of the big house with the slender spire of the church rising above them, and discussed with the young man what must now be done. John Clayton's ruddy face paled visibly when he heard what the course of action was to be, but presented no arguments against it. It was, after all, the established practice in such occurrences.

'I fear we might have trouble from the girl's mother, my lord,' he told his superior. 'She and her paramour have been badgering me constantly for custody of the corpse, and there is much local sympathy with them in that desire.'

His superior humphed contemptuously. 'They want the corpse only for their own profit, to take money from the damned fools who believe that the child's hands now possess curative powers. Rank superstitious nonsense! You were right to refuse to hand the body over to them, and to refuse them access to it. Let the locals caterwaul all they want, and be damned to them! I'll not countenance pagan practices in my parish. Where does the body lie now?'

'I have it secure, my lord. It's in one of the lock-up cells, and Cashmore holds the key with him at all times. No one can gain entrance to it.' He smiled mirthlessly.

'But I've two vagrants in the other cell at present who are complaining most bitterly that at night they can hear the girl wailing and moaning in her cell, and they swear that her ghost comes to torment them in their own cell on occasion.'

The other man belched. 'Damn this dyspepsia, I'm a damned martyr to it,' he grumbled sourly, then asked, 'Have there been any demonstrations in support of the girl's mother, or any directed against the man you questioned concerning those allegations made against him?'

'Brompton, my lord? No, none to my knowledge.'

'I'm glad to hear it,' the older man grunted. 'For I've worries enough at present with this damned combination that's supposed to exist in the parish. Have you discovered anything of that?'

'No, my lord. I've made what enquiries I could, exercising the utmost discretion, of course, but have been unable to ascertain anything. Frankly, I deem the whole matter a nonsense. This district's workpeople are not political, and never have been. There's scant sympathy for Radicalism in these parts.'

'Just so,' Lord Aston agreed. 'However, Peel's department seems convinced that such a combination has recently come into existence. Whilst I was in London I made enquiry at the office of the Home Secretary, and was assured that that damned spy they have sent here has reported that a combination definitely exists.'

'Has he also reported the identities of those involved in it?' Clayton's tone was mocking, and his companion's lower lip jutted petulantly as he complained querulously, 'If he has, then they did not deem it necessary to inform me of such. After all, why should they? I am only the chief representative of the law hereabouts, ain't I! But that fact appears to count for naught with those fine-feathered popinjays in London. All that they keep on repeating is that when the time is ripe their agent will make himself known to me, and I shall be expected to take immediate action on his recommendations. Damn them!' he spat out disgustedly. 'Anyway, let us leave that aside for now, John. I want you to dispose of the girl's body tonight. It must be done between the hours of nine o'clock and midnight, preferably nearer to the latter hour than the former — there are fewer people abroad by then. Take enough stout fellows with you to do the business speedily and naturally try and keep the whole matter as discreet as possible. Time enough tomorrow to have the news broadcast, these matters can cause a deal of trouble at times.'

'I understand, my lord. It shall be ordered as you wish.'

'I'll see to the necessary paperwork also.' The older man assumed a long-suffering air. 'God grant me some day a respite from my ceaseless labours, for I am sorely overburdened.'

John Clayton regarded his master's soft white hands and ample paunch with a sardonic gleam in his eyes, but made no reply.

Chapter Twenty-Seven

It was ten o'clock and clouds blanketed the moon so that the night was very dark. A thin drizzle fell, and the half-dozen men waiting outside the gothic doorway of the lock-up cursed their luck at having to be there instead of in their own warm beds.

From the direction of the chapel green a horse and cart came lurching and creaking and as the driver halted the vehicle by the lock-up the waiting men greeted him with curses for his late arrival. Will Vincent, the butcher, reacted angrily.

'I couldn't get here afore, could I? I had me work to finish.'

'Arn't we all had work that had to be finished?' William Brown, plumber, glazier, painter and deputy parish constable scolded. 'But the rest on us managed to get it done to time, Will Vincent. Anyway, ne'er mind that now, has you seen anything o' Joe Cashmore or the bloody parson on your way here?'

'Theer they comes now.' Another man pointed to the two figures momentarily illuminated as they passed through the light coming from the windows of the Fox and Goose Inn, opposite St Stephen's Chapel.

When he reached the waiting group Joseph Cashmore made a quick visual check and then questioned, 'Wheer's Tom Godfrey then?'

'His missus said he's bin took badly,' Will Brown informed, and the constable scowled.

'It's funny as how that bugger is always took badly when there's a bit of work to be done, arn't it? I'll go round to his house and see for myself arter we'se done for the night, and if he arn't real badly then he'll be paying out a few sovereigns for shirking his duties. Has the rest on you brought your tools?'

They lifted an assortment of mattocks, shovels and pick-axes to show him, and he nodded. 'All right, let's get on wi' it then.'

He unlocked the iron-studded doors and led the men inside the squat, castellated tower. When they reappeared they were carrying the long, narrow box which contained the corpse of Meg Tullet. The box was heaved onto the cart with as little ceremony as the tools which clattered against its sides.

'Where are the lanterns, Master Cashmore?' John Clayton spoke for the first time, his distaste at the present task causing him to speak more brusquely than he intended.

Cashmore bridled visibly at the clergyman's tone and grunted resentfully as he re-entered the black hole of the lock-up. When he returned he was carrying four lanterns, one of which he lit with flint, steel and tinder.

Sensing the constable's umbrage, Clayton said in an apologetic manner, 'We'll doubtless need the lanterns, Master Cashmore, because I fear the cloud will not lift sufficiently to give us moonlight to work by.'

Cashmore nodded, and then handed the lit lantern to the man nearest him. 'Here, you take this and goo ahead o' the cart. I don't want it getting a wheel broke in a pothole with what it's acarrying tonight.'

He placed the remaining lanterns by the side of Meg Tullet's makeshift coffin. There were two other items that he had brought out from the lock-up, but these he kept concealed in a cloth bag tied to his waistbelt beneath his caped greatcoat. He re-locked the great doors and said to the parson, 'Shall we set off then, Reverend?'

John Clayton sighed glumly. 'Yes, Master Cashmore, the sooner we get this sorry business over and done with, the better.'

'Amen to that,' the constable muttered in heartfelt agreement, and the small procession set off on its journey.

Outside the Fountain Mill another, larger group of people stood waiting silently. Some of them carried lighted torches made from lengths of thick rope which had been saturated with pitch. The flames spat smokily in the drizzling rain, and periodically the torchbearers would slap the lighted ends of their ropes against the mill wall to open the strands out and give the flame more purchase.

When Cashmore saw the silent crowd he cursed softly, and whispered throatily to the clergyman, 'Look yonder theer, Parson. I reckon we could have trouble wi' that lot.'

'I thought that I had impressed upon you the necessity for maintaining the utmost secrecy, Master Cashmore?' Clayton snapped pettishly, and the other man sneered defensively, 'Secrecy? In this bloody town? You was asking for a bloody miracle, Parson.'

'Don't take that tone of voice with me, my man,' Clayton warned angrily, but the constable was not the type to be easily intimidated.

'And don't you go spaking to me as if I was some sort of a bloody mawkin, Mister Clayton, for I'm not a man to be put upon by anybody, high-born or low-born.'

For a second or two the young clergyman's attractively ugly features suffused with temper, but he realized the basic injustice of his attack on the constable, and swallowed his ire.

'I apologize, Master Cashmore. I spoke too hastily, it was ill considered,' he offered as a peacemaker, and the constable in his turn subdued his own irate feelings.

'That's all right, Parson Clayton, we'em both on us not at our calmest with what we'em having to do this night. Do you reckon one of us should have a word wi' this lot?' He jerked his chin towards the dark mass by the mill wall.

Clayton considered for a moment, then shook his head. 'I think not, Master Cashmore, unless through some act of their own they force us to do so. Better to let sleeping dogs lie.'

'If you say so.' Cashmore gave apparently reluctant acquiescence, but kept his eyes fixed on the crowd and altered his grip on his crowned staff of office in readiness to wield it as a weapon if necessary.

The crowd maintained an eerie silence as the cart creaked past them; not even a cough or a whisper came from them, only the hissing intakes of their breathing and the splutterings of their torches sounded from their stillness. Then, when the cart and its escort had passed, the people silently filed after it, but kept a distance of some yards.

Cashmore fell back to the rear and kept on looking over his shoulder at those following. When the clergyman fell back to join him, he muttered, 'I reckon I should warn the buggers to get to their beds, Parson.'

The younger man had also been looking back frequently, and he sensed the growing nervousness among the men who were with him as the ominously silent crowd came after them, but an inner instinct restrained him from challenging the followers, and he told the constable, 'No, Master Cashmore. Leave them be. I don't think they will interfere with us.'

The bizarre procession continued on past Bredon and down the long slope of the Beoley Lane, through the treacherous ford across the River Arrow at the bottom of the lane, and on for a further half-mile to intersect the ancient Roman road known as Icknield Way. The cart made an abrupt turn to the north here and went on along the straight track for another half-mile to the crossroads at the foot of the steeply rising Beoley Hill, crowned by its ancient church and even more ancient hill fort.

'Whoooaaa! Whoooaaa now!' Butcher Vincent brought the horse to a halt in the centre of the crossroads, and Clayton stared about him, his eyes straining to pierce the darkness. He stamped his foot on the rutted, hard-packed surface of the track directly behind the cart's tailgate.

'Here, just here in the centre, this is the place,' he instructed.

The cart lurched forwards a few yards more. The men took the tools from it, and the rest of the lanterns were lit and placed to illuminate the area designated by the clergyman. Twenty yards away the followers had also halted and now stood watching, maintaining their eerie, ominous silence.

The diggers worked in short, intense bursts of effort, one spelling another in rapid succession to keep up the pace of the work; pick-axing the hard-packed stone, rubble and clay, cutting through the buried branches of the road's foundations, and burrowing ever deeper into the red marl clay of the subsoil, using long-handled shovels to clear the loosened soil, and taking up mattocks to shape the grave. Despite the chill air and the cold drizzle the toiling men sweated, and discarded coats and rolled up shirt-sleeves to give greater freedom for their muscles and tendons to exert full strength. Slowly the grave neared completion, and Clayton and Cashmore, fidgety and restless with strained nerves, kept vigil over the rough wooden box on the cart. While the work progressed the watching crowd was continually augmented by more and more silent, sacking-shrouded figures looming from the darkness until the mass of people could be numbered in their hundreds.

At last the grave was dug, and to John Clayton the yawning black hole seemed a fitting entrance to that bottomless pit of hell where he truly believed the soul of this tragic girl was bound. He shivered, made nervous by his own morbid fancies.

The long, narrow box was lifted from the cart and laid down at the side of the open grave.

'Get the top off,' Joseph Cashmore ordered, and in the pale light of the lanterns his face was deathly white and sheened with clammy sweat. 'Make the ropes ready to lower her quick arter I'se done, and you, Jack, hold the lantern so I can see clear what I'm about.'

The nailed-down lid of the box was levered off with mattock blades, the splinterings of the wood sounding preternaturally loud in the stillness, and the lantern was lifted so that its beam fell on the dead girl.

Cashmore stood with Clayton staring down at the pathetic corpse, still mud-plastered and wreathed with the slimy tendrils of water weeds. Cashmore's breath was a hoarse panting as he took the cloth bag from under his coat and lifted out its contents: a hammer and a foot long iron stake pointed at one end. For the first time a wave of restless movement and murmuring came from the onlookers, and Clayton stared apprehensively at them, then urged the constable, 'Best get it done with, Master Cashmore.'

The constable nodded mutely, then bent low over the corpse, placed the point of the stake directly above the heart, and with two sharp blows drove the iron deep through the dead flesh. As the hammer-head lifted and came down a long-drawn, keening, moaning wail came from the watchers, and with clammy sweat literally streaming down his face, Joseph Cashmore straightened, let the hammer fall into the box and ordered gutturally, 'Get this lid on, and get her put down.'

His helpers sprang to obey, and within seconds the crudely fashioned coffin was lying on the grave-bed and the first shovelfuls of stone and clay were thumping hollowly upon it.

Cashmore turned to the clergyman. 'I'm going across to spake to 'um.'

Clayton made no answer, only stood with tight-closed eyes, hands clenched together in front of his chest, his lips moving in silent prayer.

The constable's taciturn features twitched in a contemptuous grimace, then he walked to stand in front of the crowd and told them simply, 'The poor wench's spirit is chained fast now. She'll not rise agen until the day o' judgement. So I don't want to hear that any o' you are spreading scare-tales about poor Meg Tullet not being able to rest easy in her grave. Now go on back to your homes, all of you. This night's sorry business is over and done wi'.'

Almost wraith-like the silent crowd melted away into the blackness of the night, and soon all that could be seen of them were the scattered bobbing lights of their torches.

Cashmore was very calm and steady now, and his manner served to calm the strained nerves of the men with him.

'Ram it down real hard, lads,' he instructed quietly. 'Then spread dirt from the ditches all over the centre of the cross here, and run the horse and cart backards and forrards until the grave's well hid. We don't want no bloody resurrection men lifting the poor little cratur out agen ... May God forgive her and rest her soul.'

Tildy had been among that silent crowd and now, in company with Josh Dyson and the man known as Will Stacey, she walked through the drizzling rain back towards Redditch. As the constable had sneeringly informed Reverend Clayton, to hope for absolute secrecy in this town was to hope for a miracle. The first man told by the constable that his services would be needed for the burial of Meg Tullet had been the butcher, Will Vincent, and with many a sly hint and wink he had parcelled out that juicy item of gossip among his customers throughout the day. As always the news spread like wildfire, and so, together with those who had attended the girl to her grave to show their pity and to mourn her, there had come many, many others only to satisfy their lust for excitement and their curiosity.

The barbaric practice of driving a stake through the dead girl's heart, while physically nauseating and creating revulsion in some of the spectators, did not shock or horrify them, for they knew it was carried out to safeguard the living. It had been the custom since time immemorial to treat the bodies of suicides in that way and to bury them at a crossroads. The people accepted, indeed demanded, such safeguards against the tormented spirits of those who had committed self-murder. The iron stake was used to pin the spirit of the dead person to its corpse so that it could not wander abroad, and it was believed that the passage of so many feet and hooves and wheels over a crossroads served to erode gradually the strength of the imprisoned spirit, as minute fractions of its substance were carried away by those travelling feet, hooves and wheels to the four corners of the compass.

Like her companions, Tildy believed in the efficaciousness of the practice of suicide burial, and accepted its necessity.

When the trio had crossed the ford by means of the wooden footbridge and begun the long ascent of the Beoley Lane, Josh Dyson told Will Stacey of his plan to enrol Tildy into the combination. '... There's a meeting bin called for tomorrow night, so I'll bring her with me then.'

At first the crop-haired Stacey was doubtful, and he voiced objections: 'It arn't never bin the custom to have women in the combinations, Josh. And I don't reckon that women be any good for keeping secrets neither.'

Josh Dyson grinned sardonically. 'If that was the case, Will, then there 'udden't be the saying that it takes a wise child to know its own father ... And I wouldn't see so many men going around these parts wearing the horns their wives had fixed on 'um.'

Stacey chuckled appreciatively. 'I take the point, Josh, and I reckon the other lads 'ull take it likewise. It might be a good idea at that, to bring women fully in wi' us. So long as we'em very careful to pick the right 'uns, of course.'

Tildy made no contribution to their discussion, for her mind was filled with sad thoughts of Meg Tullet and the rankling torment of knowing that the man to blame for what had happened was even now probably swilling down liquor at some ale-house or other, and congratulating himself on his good luck. At last, unable to contain the anguish within herself any longer, she asked her companion, 'Does the combination intend doing anything about Johnny Brompton?'

The two men exchanged a knowing glance and Dyson winked broadly at his friend, then told Tildy, 'When youm a member of the combination, Tildy, you must bring the matter up at the meetings, and try and get summat done about him.'

'Ahr, that's so.' Will Stacey had a cunning gleam in his eyes as he advised her. 'What you needs to do, Tildy, is to start organizing the women to act together agen Johnny Brompton. It'll serve as good experience for you later on when we starts to widen our numbers hereabouts. But you must goo very careful about it, and make no mention of the combination. The way to do it is to get some of the others so riled up that they'm ready to commit blue murder, and then plant the suggestion of the way you wants 'um to goo in their minds. But you mustn't be recognized as having been the one who started all the ructions in the fust place. So that if trouble comes onto the women you can then deny any connection wi' whatever they'se done agen Brompton.'

Tildy frowned unhappily, as she mentally examined what he had said. 'That seems a very sneaky, underhand way of going about things, Master Stacey,' she told him. 'Surely if a person believes in something, then he or she ought to be ready to stand up and speak out in full view.'

'God strewth, Tildy!' Josh Dyson exclaimed impatiently. 'Arn't you learned your lessons yet? Arn't life taught you any bloody thing?'

Tildy's fiery spirit rose instantly, but she quelled it as quickly, realizing that she knew nothing as yet of how combinations went about gaining their objectives. She waited a couple of moments, then answered quietly, 'Yes, Josh, life has taught me much, but still I think there are some things that it does no one any good to learn; and one of those things is bringing to others grief without risking any personal harm. Ignorant I may be of many, many matters, but I do know one matter well, and that is that if you want people to trust and follow you then you have to be ready to stand up in full view and lead them.'

'God fuck me!' Will Stacey ejaculated in open disgust. 'This fancy-spaking wench o' yourn thinks that this is all

209

some sort o' fucking children's game, by the sound on it.'

'That's enough of that sort o' talk,' Dyson told him sharply. 'Tildy's a good-living girl, and she's yet to understand how we must go about things if we're to gain success. She'll learn and come to understand, only give her time.'

'Time's a commodity we arn't got a lot of, Josh,' the man muttered sulkily. 'Not enough on it at any rate to waste it on them who seems to think we'se got to act like bleedin' saints.'

'You'se said your piece, now leave it lay.' Dyson's voice held a note of warning, and Stacey subsided into a moody silence. The rest of the walk back to Redditch passed without further exchange. Tildy was glad of that, for she was struggling to come to terms with the unpalatable fact that she found the tactics advocated by Will Stacey as mean and dishonourable as those employed by the masters against their workpeople. She was also beginning to wonder if her present enthusiasm for the combination could survive if she should discover that the majority of her prospective comrades were of the same type as Will Stacey.

When they reached the Kings Arms at Bredon the two men went to knock on the door and gain entrance to the tavern despite the lateness of the hour, but Tildy refused Dyson's invitation to join them and continued on alone. Other groups of people who had attended the burial were also on the road, and Tildy could hear their loud discussions about what they had witnessed. Then there came the sounds of someone running hard behind her, and she turned to see Nathaniel Farrel.

'I thought it was you, Mrs Crawford.'

He was breathing easily despite his exertion and Tildy was impressed by his obviously good physical condition, for most men who had sprinted as he had just done would now be gasping for breath.

'I take it you've been to that poor girl's burial,' Farrel stated rather than asked.

'Yes, I have,' she confirmed.

He smiled boyishly. 'Truth to tell, I saw you there, in company with that man Dyson and his friend, er, what's his name now, it eludes me?'

'It's Stacey. Will Stacey,' Tildy told him without thinking.

'Ah yes. Stacey it is, to be sure. He's not native to this town, is he?'

Tildy shrugged. 'I know next to nothing about the man, Mr Farrel. But I think he is a foreigner here.'

Her companion looked keenly at her and then said, 'Judging by your tone, you don't like too well what you do know of him.'

Once more Tildy found herself impressed by this man, but this time by his display of shrewdness. 'You're a clever man, Mr Farrel,' she said, feeling a slight resentment that he could have read her so easily. She was remembering now that Josh Dyson was suspicious of Farrel, and she herself was beginning to share that suspicion. 'Tell me, Mr Farrel, what is it brings you yourself to Redditch?' she asked with a feigned casualness.

By this time they had reached the big pool, and even in the coldness of the night its dank, fetid stench hung on the air like a miasma.

Farrel ostentatiously sniffed the foul air, and laughed. 'Well one thing for sure, Mrs Crawford, I'm not here for the sweet odours of the place.'

His laugh was attractive and held an infectious quality, but Tildy resisted its disarming influence, and persisted, 'Are you here on business then, Mr Farrel? Are you interested in the needle trade?'

He smiled, and shook his top-hatted head. 'No, not exactly on business, Mrs Crawford, and I've not much interest in the needle trade, as such. I'm here rather because I am a man who seeks knowledge.'

'You seek knowledge?' Tildy repeated wonderingly. 'Knowledge of what?'

His smile widened, and he winked slyly at her. 'Why,

knowledge of my fellow human beings, Mrs Crawford ...
And now, regretfully, I must bid you a good night, for I
am going into the Horse and Jockey.' He indicated the
darkened inn which stood opposite the big pool. 'And
there I intend to broaden my knowledge of good London
gin.' He touched his fingers to the brim of his hat in a
farewell salute, and left her.

Tildy walked on, puzzling over what Farrel was really
doing in this town. Then she thought of what was to
happen on the following night. 'By this time tomorrow I'll
be a member of the combination.' She felt a frisson of
excitement shivering through her. 'And once I'm a
member, then I'm going to do my utmost to make the
combination bring Brompton to justice.'

Chapter Twenty-Eight

The night was again cold, an easterly wind gusting strongly and rattling the leafless branches of the trees in the Pitcheroak Woods. Nathanial Farrel shivered despite the protection of his thick, dark cloak, but consoled himself with the fact that at least it was not raining, and though the ground he lay on was damp from the drizzle of the previous night it was not soaking through his clothing. Beneath him the brick kilns appeared deserted, but Farrel knew that at least two sentinels lurked in the black oblong shadows cast by the moonlight, and other men were somewhere within the kilns.

As Farrel watched and waited for the arrival of the remaining members of the combination, he mentally reviewed his progress up to this point and was not too dissatisfied, although most certainly his task was proving much more difficult than he had anticipated. However, after last night he was now almost certain that he had definitely identified the man he sought as his main quarry. The man who now called himself Will Stacey. Farrel's teeth gleamed in a savage grin. He knew of Stacey under another name ... Stevens ... William Stevens, of Nottingham, and of the Pentridge uprising.

Farrel would have made his move as soon as he had identified his main target, when younger and less experienced, but the years had taught him caution, and he knew that to complete his present task successfully he needed to be absolutely sure of all of Stacey/Stevens's confederates. So far he had managed to identify almost a dozen of them, but there were still some whose names and faces eluded him. So, despite his impatience to bring his task to a close, he forced himself to wait.

'There's always the danger that if I only catch the big fish, and let the little fish swim free then those little ones might grow to be monster pikes.'

He took pleasure from the mental image of himself as a skilled and wary angler patiently waiting to strike home with the hook at exactly the right moment. His attention was caught by a dark figure emerging from the woodland and clambering down the steep clay slope of the pit. Again Farrel grinned savagely as he saw the man's clumsy progress.

'It's John Whateley,' he recognized. 'And drunk again, judging by the way he's moving.'

It was through Whateley that Farrel had first discovered that this location was used for the secret meetings. When in his cups, which was more often than not, the landlord of the Black Horse was prone to lose guard over his senses and tongue, and by carefully collating the snippets that Whateley let slip at such times, Farrel had discovered about the brick kilns. He was also able now to pinpoint with comparative ease the nights when the meetings were called. He spent much of his time drinking at the Black Horse, and by a judicious mixture of flattery and sympathy had become something of a confidant of Whateley's wife, Jean, who, thankful for such an understanding audience for her tirades against her husband, in all innocence let Farrel know when John Whateley would be away from his beer-house, thus making it easy for him to watch and tail the landlord wherever he went.

Whateley's approach to the kilns followed the normal pattern. The challenge, the hooded men coming forward to confirm the identity, the melting back into invisibility among the kilns.

'I fear it's going to be another dull night,' Farrel told himself, then his breath caught in his throat as two more dark figures appeared from the woods and descended the clay slope together. One of these newcomers was a woman.

'Jesus Christ! Is it Tildy Crawford, I wonder?' Farrel felt anxiety tug at him. 'Pray God it's not. I've no wish to see that sweet morsel put into any danger.'

'Who comes?'

'Seekers.'

'What is it you seek?'

'Freedom, justice, and fraternity.'

'Stand fast.'

Tildy experienced a compelling urge to giggle as Josh Dyson exchanged the low-pitched calls with the hidden voices, and when the two hooded figures came from the shadows and advanced towards them she was forced to bite her lips to stop from laughing aloud.

'Why, they're like children playing games,' she told herself with a mingling of amusement and disbelief. But when the hooded men reached her, her desire to laugh died abruptly and sheer terror momentarily gripped her as she felt the point of a knife jab into the soft skin of her throat, and the stinking breath of the man assailed her nostrils as he growled, 'Who the fuck be you? Spake out, or I'll shove this blade through your fucking throat.'

'Tildy Crawford,' she stammered out. 'My name is Tildy Crawford.'

'Who vouches for you?'

The painful pressure of the sharp point increased, threatening to pierce the skin and draw blood, and in her mind she cried out, 'Josh, why don't you answer them? Why?'

'I vouches for her.' As if in answer to her unspoken plea, Dyson spoke out, and the pressure of the knife-point eased a trifle.

'Does she seek fraternity, justice and freedom also?'

'She is so seeking freedom, fraternity and justice.'

'And what does she seek with us?'

'She seeks her brethren.'

The knife point was removed.

215

'Then pass in with her, brother Dyson.'

'If you will lead me, brother.'

'I'll so lead, brother Dyson.'

The hooded man walked back towards the kilns, and Dyson and Tildy followed, with the second hooded man bringing up the rear.

Tildy was completely bemused by the bizarre aspects of this confrontation, not realizing that this exchange of sign and counter-sign and carefully worded sentences were purposely structured so that if any member arriving in company with another person was acting under duress to that person, then he could, by altering the structure of the sentences, convey this knowledge to the hooded sentinels. Just as they, if they were being kept under duress by men concealed among the kilns with weapons, could convey a warning to the new arrival by the same means.

Once in the shadows of the kilns the two sentinels left them and resumed their careful vigil. Dyson took Tildy by her arm and led her inside the central kiln. Its interior was pitch-black and she was only made aware that others were already inside by the hoarse breathing and the sour acridity of unwashed bodies and clothes which fugged the air.

As they stepped into the kiln rough hands jolted them to a halt, and Tildy hissed in fright as yet another knife point came into painful contact with her throat. Yet another ritual of words took place between Dyson and an unseen man.

'Who has come?'

'Brother Joshua Dyson has come.'

'And who brings he with him?'

'He brings a seeker.'

'What name bears this seeker?'

'She bears the name of Matilda Crawford.' As Dyson spoke the name muffled exclamations of surprise came from the blackness.

'Be silent, brethren,' another voice commanded, and Tildy thought that this was Will Stacey, then the first man resumed his exchange of curiously archaic sounding sentences with Dyson and finished by saying, 'Be welcome here, Matilda Crawford.'

Flint and steel were struck and stubs of candle were lit to shed a pale, wavering glow. Tildy looked at the close-packed heads of the men squatting in the confined space. She saw Thomas Tandy and Elijah Buggins, who both worked at the Fountain Mill. Will Stacey was there also, and others whom she knew by sight, if not by name.

'Brethren!' It was Josh Dyson who now took command of the meeting. 'The first business afore us tonight is to swear in our new member, Matilda Crawford. I know that there's some of you who arn't too happy about enrolling females into this combination, but let me remind you that on a free vote at the last meeting, the ayes carried the motion by a fair majority.' His eyes raked across the clump of men. 'So, brethren, is there anybody who wants to say anything more on the subject afore we proceeds with the oath-taking? It's spake out now, or forever hold your peace.'

No one offered to speak and at a signal from Dyson a shabby Bible and a rusty-bladed old cavalry sabre were produced from somewhere. Another object was also handed forwards, and when Tildy saw it she again felt laughter bubbling in her throat. It was a human skull and, judging by its colour and condition, a very ancient one. She could not help but see the farcical aspect of these proceedings, but at the same time she recognized how seriously the men around her took them.

Dyson handed the Bible and skull to Tildy and she stood with one in each hand held before her chest. Stacey moved in front of her with the sabre and placed the point of it between her full breasts.

'Matilda Crawford, I'm now going to administer the sacred oath of this combination to you,' Will Stacey told her solemnly. 'You must repeat after me: — I, Matilda Crawford, of my own free will and accord ...'

Still battling with the laughter bubbling within her

which the spectacle of the crop-haired Stacey brandishing his rusty sword irresistibly invoked, Tildy repeated the words sentence by sentence: '... do hereby promise and swear that I will never reveal the name of any member of the combination, under the penalty of being sent out of this world by the first brother that may meet me. I furthermore do swear that I will pursue with unceasing vengeance any traitor that should arise, even though he fly to the verge of hell. And may that same hell swallow me and mine, and may I be eternally damned if I should betray any of my brethren in any way, manner or form. So help me God to keep this my oath inviolate.'

'Amen!' The men in the kiln intoned loudly, and Will Stacey swung up the sabre blade and told Tildy, 'Sister Crawford, you are now a member of the needlers' combination of Redditch. Our recognition sign is this, if you wish to discover if any of your brethren are in company you must raise your right hand to your right eyebrow. Any brother present will then raise his left hand to his left eyebrow. Then you must raise the forefinger of your right hand to the right side of your mouth. He will raise the little finger of his left hand to the left side of his mouth and will say, "What are you?" You will answer, "Determined." He will say, "For what?" Your answer will be, "For free liberty." Only then will you both freely converse. Have you understood?'

Tildy nodded, impressed despite herself with the deadly gravity all present were displaying, and with a burgeoning realization that despite the childish overtones of these proceedings she had in fact irrevocably committed herself to something that could very easily become a literal matter of life or death. All desire to laugh stilled within her and when she took her place sitting on the brick floor among her new-found brothers her mood was very, very sober.

The meeting proceeded very mundanely after the preceding drama of the ritual challenges and oath-taking. The question of finance was discussed and it was decided

218

that each individual member would contribute three pence a week into a fund to be used at the discretion of the officers of the combination to aid any member who got into difficulties through no fault of his own. Thomas Tandy was voted as treasurer of that fund.

The name of a possible new recruit for the combination was suggested and it was voted that careful enquiries should be made concerning that man and a close watch kept on him for some time to ensure that he was suitable to be approached for membership.

Then Josh Dyson asked various men what the feeling was in their separate mills and workshops concerning Johnny Brompton. As she listened to their replies Tildy's heart sank. Each man reported more or less the same thing. That the consensus of opinion now appeared to have swung in favour of Johnny Brompton. That the girl Meg Tullet had been lying. And that because of her mental instability she could well have killed herself at any time, so the man could not be blamed for that.

'I reckon we'll be flogging a dead horse to try and use Brompton now to stir up a randy.' Elijah Buggins appeared to speak for the majority present, judging by the murmurings of agreement that followed his statement.

'Has you got any idea for any other thing we can use at this time then, brother Elijah? Has any of you got any ideas?' Josh Dyson wanted to know. 'Because it's important that we test our strength.'

'Well, there's a rumour going about that Heming and Bartleet be thinking of cutting the rate for "straightening",' Thomas Tandy offered.

The 'straighteners' were the women and children who after the needles had been bent and distorted by the hardening and tempering process used small hammers and blocks to straighten the lengths by hand once more.

'When be the rates supposed to be cut then?' Dyson questioned, and Tandy shrugged.

'Like I said, brother Dyson, it's only a rumour as yet.'

'Then that's no good to us.' Dyson dismissed the

matter. 'Has anybody else got anything that we might be able to use?'

Tildy, although as a new member feeling shy and diffident, was driven to raise her hand.

'Well, sister Crawford?' Dyson looked at her enquiringly.

'If you please, brother Dyson.' The title came awkwardly from her tongue. 'I think that we should still stir up trouble over Johnny Brompton. He should not be let away scot-free for what he's done.'

Resentful mutterings at her forwardness came from all parts of the group and she blushed with embarrassment.

'You'se already heard, sister Crawford, that the feeling that was agen John Brompton exists no longer. Most folks now reckons him to be innocent,' Dyson told her.

Tildy stuck doggedly to her purpose and replied spiritedly, 'There was a time when most folks thought that the world was flat, brother Dyson, and they were all wrong as well, weren't they? I know without any doubt that Johnny Brompton is guilty of raping that poor child, and I think that we should take the lead in avenging her.'

'Who the fuck does her reckon her is?' a disgruntled voice uttered, and other voices followed the first.

'Her arn't bin here but a few minutes and her's already trying to rule the roost.'

'Cheeky bleeder, arn't her? Too much mouth for a bleeding wench.'

The audible comments caused Tildy to squirm inwardly and blush outwardly with embarrassment, but her stubborn courage was roused now and she refused to let herself be brow-beaten by this display of open hostility.

'I'm not trying to rule any roost,' she stated emphatically. 'And I don't reckon myself to be anything other than what I am. But I'm now a full-sworn member of this combination and as I understand it that gives me equal rights to have my say with the rest of you.'

'I told you we shouldn't ha' let soddin' women into this union,' a man spat out in loud disgust. 'I told you it 'udden't serve.'

Josh Dyson's first impulse was to spring to Tildy's defence, then he realized that if he did so he would be doing her a disservice in the long run. If she were ever to be fully accepted as an equal by the other members then she must earn that acceptance by her own efforts. She must demonstrate that she could hold her own in verbal discussion and dispute and be able to persuade others of the justness of her case. Willing her now to succeed, he watched silently.

She turned on the man who had last spoken. 'How can you say that my being in this union won't serve when you have not yet heard what I have to say?' she demanded hotly. In a single lithe, fluid movement she came to her feet and addressed the whole assembly. 'All I ask of you, brothers, is my right to state my case. Only hear what I have to say and then take a vote on it, and I will accept the verdict of that vote without further argument.'

Support for her came from an unexpected quarter.

'Sister Crawford has the right on it.'

Tildy's wide-eyed glance at Will Stacey showed her shock at his intervention.

'Let her hold the floor, brothers, and give her a fair hearing. Then we'll take a vote on it. That's the law of this combination.'

After a few moments there was a general grudging acceptance, and Will Stacey gestured to Tildy. 'Everybody's waiting to hear what you'se got to say, sister. So don't be bashful, but spake out loud and clear.'

For a brief instant she suspected a veiled sarcasm in his manner, but then disregarded the thought as being of no importance. What was important was that she convince these men. She coughed once with nervousness and then began to speak. To her amazement the words flowed from her as if of their own volition, without hesitation and with a ringing confidence that she inwardly wondered at because she was not really that confident.

'Brother Dyson has just told you that it is important to test our strength. I agree with what he said, but I think it's

important also to bring our fellow workers to an understanding of their own strength. All I've ever heard
throughout my life are people like us cursing their poverty
and the hardship of their lives, and praying that someday
the gentry might do something to ease the burdens upon
us.

'I've learned well that the gentry will do nothing to ease
our burdens unless they are forced into doing so, and the
only people who can bring that force to bear are ourselves.
Divided we have no strength. United we could become all-
powerful.' She saw in some of the faces before her a
dawning boredom and she exclaimed, 'I know you've
heard this sort of talk before and that you may well be
wearied of hearing it again. But it is a truth which we must
never allow ourselves to forget. Just as another truth is that
the gentry and the masters consider us to be nothing more
than brute beasts. They think of us as brutal, ignorant,
dirty, godless savages.' For the first time she hesitated and
drew a long breath, her courage momentarily wavering at
the thought of the possible reactions her next words might
provoke. But she steeled herself and went on, 'The gentry
and the masters are quite justified in holding us in such
low esteem, for we do behave like brutal, ignorant, dirty,
godless savages.'

An indignant outburst greeted her scathing strictures
and for the first time Josh Dyson intervened.

'Be silent and let her spake,' he commanded sharply.
'The truth is always hard to hear, but that's what she's
spaking now and in our hearts we all on us knows it is.'

Tildy flashed him a look of gratitude and declared
vehemently, 'We are savages in the way we treat each
other. The gentry and the masters see how many of our
menfolk ill-treat and brutalize their own women and
children. They see how simple-minded girls like Meg
Tullet are abused and degraded by the men who work
with them. They see the children left to run ragged and
neglected in the streets of this town while their parents get
drunk in the ale-houses. They see the wives with black

222

eyes and broken bones that their own husbands have given them, and those same masters and gentry despise us all because of what they know we do to each other.'

Now, for the first time since she had begun to speak, Tildy sensed a burgeoning disquiet in the minds of her listeners, and suddenly confidence enveloped her and she experienced a rush of elation at this discovery that she could influence an audience by her own eloquence.

'If we now let Johnny Brompton go unpunished for what he has caused Meg Tullet to do to herself then the gentry and masters will only count it as just another proof of how correct their views of us are.' A note of pleading entered her voice. 'Cannot you understand then how important it is that we demonstrate to those set above us that we can care for each other? That we can fight to avenge even the lowliest and most humble of our fellow creatures? That we are not the brute beasts, the dirty, ignorant, brutal, godless savages they consider us to be, but are people whose minds and hearts are capable of thoughts and emotions that are as elevated and as deeply felt as they consider their own to be.'

She swept her gaze across the faces so intent on her and knew that for this moment at least she had won some of them over to her way of thought.

'Let me say only one thing more before I finish. Let our fight to avenge Meg Tullet also demonstrate our cold courage. Let us not fill ourselves with drink before we act. Instead, let us do it in a sober state, so that the gentry and the masters cannot say that we only dare act when our bellies are full with drink and our minds made mad by it.'

She fell silent and would have reseated herself, but Josh Dyson gestured her to remain upright.

'Hold there for a moment more, sister Crawford. Tell us now, what would you have us do?'

Once again Tildy surprised herself when all her half-considered, vague ideas suddenly clarified and coalesced, and she stated firmly, 'I would have you support me in what I intend doing. Tomorrow at work I shall go among the women and try to rouse them against Brompton. I shall lead them in a body to petition Henry Milward to give Brompton his sack, and if he refuses to do so then I shall confront Brompton myself and to his face tell him that he must leave this district before twenty-four hours have passed, otherwise I shall try to get him tarred and feathered for what he did. If that fails then I shall attack him constantly with whatever weapons lie to my hands. I shall tell him that I'll not allow him a moment of peace while he stays in this town and that I'll not rest until he is in some way punished for what he has done.'

'When you say that you want our support, in what manner do you want it?' Dyson questioned gravely.

'I do not want the combination to be openly seen to act in this matter. Because I believe that if we were so seen to be acting then the authorities would claim that we were only motivated by our radical beliefs and trying to make a scapegoat of Brompton just because he is an overloooker and a loyal servant to his master. A political reason would be attributed to what we were doing, and people would say that we were only acting for our own gain. I do not want any suggestion of politics to be bandied about in this matter. For me it is a simple question of justice. So I would only ask of you all that you do not try to prevent any of your womenfolk from following me, and that instead you encourage them to do so.'

'But what then can the combination gain from all this? What advantages can it bring to us? For I can't see any at first hand.' Dyson was quite deliberately acting the part of the devil's advocate to test Tildy and allow her to show her worth before these men who were so prejudiced against the enrolment of females in their movement.

She answered confidently, 'What the combination will gain is that the women of this town will have seen how they can alter affairs by acting together. They will then be able to understand better what benefits combination could eventually bring to them. They will feel their own strength.'

'Have you thought about the harm that could come to you personally by being seen openly to stir up and lead the women?' Dyson asked next.

Tildy nodded solemnly and could not prevent a slight tremor entering her voice. 'Indeed I have, brother Dyson, and I've thought also of what might become of my child should anything befall me as a result of what I intend doing. I'll not try to hide the fact that I'm sorely troubled and feared by those thoughts. But there are times when we must all face our fears and try to conquer them. All I can tell you now in all truth is that I shall try with all my heart and soul to conquer my own fears and act as I see fit and right. Fear has ruled us all too long, has it not? It's time we refused to let it do so any longer without challenge.'

Quite spontaneously a man seated directly in front of Tildy clapped his hands applaudingly, and instantly the others joined in. Dyson grinned his delight at the slender young woman, now fiery-faced with embarrassment at this unexpected display, and he gently patted her shoulder.

'You'll do for me, Tildy Crawford,' he told her warmly, 'and you'll do for all on us here as well, by the sound on it ... Well, brothers?' He raised his voice. 'Has she got our support?'

All hands shot up simultaneously and Dyson laughed aloud. 'The ayes have it!' he declared. 'The ayes have it!'

Outside the sky had clouded over and the rain had begun to fall quite heavily. Nathanial Farrel cursed the weather and his own bad luck in having to be out in it. But for a time he made no attempt to move. He was determined to find out if the woman he had seen earlier was indeed Tildy Crawford. With the moon now shrouded by clouds, however, the night had become very dark and visibility was greatly diminished.

'It's no use my stopping in this spot,' Farrel decided. 'It don't serve now that I've lost the moonlight.' He pondered for a few moments. 'If it is Tildy then surely she'll go directly back to Mother Readman's once the meeting's over. She don't like being away from her child any longer than she has to be, and with this rain falling so heavy she'll go by the Red Lane as the quickest way. I could intercept her there and make sure it is her.'

He rose and moved stealthily around the edges of the great pit and took up a fresh vantage point between the kilns and the pathway that led into the Red Lane. He waited there until the first indistinct shadows began to move away from the kilns and then slipped away himself.

Half-an-hour later, hidden in the undergrowth in the dip of land where the Red Lane came into the outskirts of the town, Farrel watched Tildy go past him in company with Josh Dyson and the man known as Will Stacey.

'Goddamn it all!' With considerable chagrin Farrel peered through the darkness at the trio's backs as they began the ascent up the Unicorn Hill towards the town centre crossroads. 'Goddamn it, Tildy, why the bloody hell did you have to go and join their bloody combination?'

There was also considerable chagrin in Mother Readman's expression when the rain-soaked Tildy came to dry her clothing at the kitchen fire. The young woman was still elated from her triumph and talked excitedly to her friend and confidante.

'I've just been upstairs to see Davy. He's fast asleep, bless him. Mind you, he was already alseep before I went out and Apollonia looks over him like a mother hen — it's no wonder that he adores her so, is it?'

'No, it arn't any wonder, is it? But then he's seeing rather more of her than of you these days, arn't he?'

The sharpness of the older woman's reply caused Tildy to look anxiously at her.

'Is aught the matter, Mother Readman? Are you angry with me for something I've done?'

The kitchen was filled with the usual variegated transient and semi-permanent lodgers and the fat old woman looked carefully about her before lowering her voice to a gruff whisper.

'I'm vexed at you for what youm agoing to do, you silly little cow. Mark my words, you could find that you'll stir up a bloody hornet's nest about your ears.'

Tildy's eyes widened. 'How do you know what I'm going to do?'

Mother Readman's massive mob-capped head nodded towards a bench by the door. 'Look theer, Tildy, but do it real careful. Look over by the door theer. See that chap in the brown coat and the moleskin cap asetting on the bench next the door?'

Tildy's eyes surreptitiously sought and found the man, and his damp bedraggled appearance struck an instant chord in her memory. Despite the poor, smoke-fugged light in the kitchen she was sure that she had seen him at the meeting in the kilns.

Mother Readman confirmed the younger woman's unspoken thought. 'Ahr, I sees you knows him all right, Tildy. You saw him earlier tonight, didn't you, at the meeting?' she whispered. 'He's a member o' your combination, arn't he? His name's Billy Garner and he's bin alodging here wi' me off and on for a lot o' years now,' she went on conversationally. 'He has a lot o' trouble wi' his wife and her kinfolks and every so often he buggers off from her and comes back here to stay wi' me. I'se done him favours at times, so he tells me bits and pieces of anything he thinks I might be interested in knowing about.'

Tildy could not help but smile wryly. 'In other words he's another of your spies, isn't he, Mother Readman?'

The older woman cackled with wheezy laughter that seemed to bubble up from the depths of her huge body. 'You could call him that I suppose, my duck.' Then her mood reverted to its previous seriousness. 'Youm paddling in dangerous waters, Tildy. Has you stopped to think yet that if I knows all about what's going on up at the brick kilns because I got one o' my spies in theer then what's to stop others having their spies in theer as well? What's to stop the masters, or the bloody magistrates even, having their own men join that bloody combination that's supposed to be such a deep-kept secret?'

Doubt and apprehension assailed Tildy. 'Surely they cannot have? Josh Dyson and his friend are so very careful about who they enrol,' she muttered as if to herself, visualizing in her mind the faces that had been present in the kilns that night. 'They all seemed decent, steady men. I knew nearly all of them by sight, if not by name.'

'That's as may be, my duck, but you knows that money can buy nigh on anything and the best o' men can be bought, if not wi' money, then by other means. I knows a bit about this sort o' thing that youm mixed up wi', Tildy, and I knows for a fact that there's bin government spies and provocation men sent into this district afore now. There could well be suchlike men here agen ... and a likely prospect to be one on 'um has just come through the bloody door. So keep your mouth tight-guarded for now, my wench, and we'll talk later.'

Shaking the raindrops from the nap of his tall hat, his long cloak darkly-sodden, Nathanial Farrel came to the fireplace and seated himself on one of the benches fronting the vast inglenook. 'It's a foul night, ladies,' he remarked pleasantly and his light green eyes fixed shrewdly on Tildy's damp shawl and gown steaming wispily from the heat of the fire. 'I see you've been abroad in all this rain yourself, Mrs Crawford. I trust you did not have to journey far in it?'

With Mother Readman's allusions concerning this young man still ringing in her ears, Tildy only smiled and gave a non-committal reply. 'No, not far, Mr Farrel.' Then she fell silent and kept her gaze fixed on the flames licking around the base of the smoke-blackened, hanging iron cauldron.

The silence between the three of them lengthened and twice Farrel opened his mouth as if to speak to Tildy, but when she kept her gaze resolutely turned from him he closed his lips and said nothing. At length he ostentatiously yawned and stretched. 'Ahhh well, time for me to go to my bed. I'm falling asleep. I'll bid you both a good night.'

As soon as he had left them Mother Readman sniffed expressively and declared in a hoarse whisper, 'I don't trust that flash Cockney bleeder, Tildy, there's summat about him that arn't jannock.'

Tildy could not help but smile secretly to herself, wondering if a large portion of Mother Readman's new-sprung hostility towards Nathanial Farrel might possibly stem from the fact that she had not had her usual success in discovering his antecedents or his present purpose for being in the town.

'Now, young 'ooman, what's your intention for tomorrow? I hope you arn't forgot that my cousin Milly proved a good friend to you when your husband was trying to come the cunt last year?'

The old woman's cousin Milly was Millicent Milward, wife to Henry Milward of the Fountain Mill.

'I've not forgotten that,' Tildy assured her. 'And before I do anything I intend to go first to Mrs Milward and tell her what I'm about and my reasons for it. I know well that it's thanks to her I've got my Davy with me now, and I'd not return her a bad service for a good one.'

'But that's what youm really doing, arn't it, my duck?' Mother Readman's eyes were affectionate as they dwelt on the pale oval of Tildy's face. The girl's dark, luminous eyes became instantly troubled and she questioned anxiously, 'Does it really appear so, Mother Readman? Because truly, I've no wish to cause Mrs Milward even the slightest of upsets. But if I don't do something to hit back at Johnny Brompton then I'm certain sure that once he's got over the scare he's had then he's going to get hold of some other girl and serve her as he served poor Meg.'

'It's a problem, arn't it?' the older woman agreed sympathetically. 'Believe me, I knows how you feels,

Tildy, because if the bugger had done that to Apollonia then I'd not be able to rest until he was served out for it.' She paused, and then said disgruntledly, 'Mind you, that hot little bitch can't get enough prick to satisfy her. It arn't Johnny Brompton who'd ha' raped her, but her him. When her's on heat it don't matter a bugger to her whatever age or condition the man is in, just so long as he can get it up inside her.' She grimaced and shook her head resignedly. 'Ahh well, each to their own, I suppose. I just wish that Apollonia had liked summat that warn't going to land me wi' a load o' little bastards to feed and shelter. Because that's what it's agoing to be, Tildy, a child every bloody year I shouldn't wonder. As though I arn't birthed sufficient of me own through the years. At my age I'd have thought I'd ha' done wi' all that sort o' trouble ... Still, ne'er mind that now. What I wants to say, Tildy, is that you must do whatever you thinks is fittin'. And if, God forbid, you should get into trouble because of it, well, you'll always find a friend in me and you and your baby 'ull always find shelter beneath my roof.'

On impulse Tildy acted completely contrary to her normally reserved and undemonstrative manner. She leaned over and kissed the fat, tallowy cheek of the other woman.

'God bless you, Mother Readman,' she whispered with heartfelt sincerity and moved nearly to tears by the old woman's kindness she ran from the room, afraid that if she remained a moment longer she would make a spectacle of herself by bursting into tears.

Without a candle Tildy was forced to fumble her way up the dark staircases and along the narrow landings and passages that honeycombed the big old house, until she reached the floor directly beneath the roof-trees. Moving cautiously towards the door of her tiny attic room the toe of her clog hit a small, heavy object. Bending, she felt with her fingers and found it to be a leather pouch filled with coins that by the feel of their size and weight could only be sovereigns.

In her room she reached for her tinder box and lit the stub of candle. After checking that Davy slept comfortably she turned her attention to the pouch. She poured the coins it contained out onto her narrow bed and caught her breath in awed amazement at their shimmering, golden mass. There were more than two hundred sovereigns on the threadbare blanket when she had finished counting them. A tight-rolled sheet of paper lay among them and when she opened it she saw words printed in tiny, neat letters on its surface.

With a shock of fear she read out, 'Joshua Dyson, agitator in the Black Country ... William Stevens, alias Stacey, active in Nottingham and the Pentridge uprising ... Thomas Tandy, nothing known. Elijah Buggins, agitator in Birmingham ... Matilda Crawford, nothing known ...'

'Dear God, what have I found here?' she muttered aloud, her heart thudding painfully and her full breasts rising and falling furiously as she dragged in rapid breaths in her agitation.

There were other names also, and some she recognized as members of the combination. For a time Tildy could only sit and try to think what she should do. To her it appeared almost a certainty that the pouch belonged to Nathanial Farrel. His was the only other room occupied at present on this floor.

'It's got to belong to him,' Tildy decided. 'And with a list like that in his possession he can only be a spy. A provocation man!' This term sent cold shivers through her. Provocation men, paid by the Government to infiltrate the combinations and unions and Radical movements and provoke the hotheads in those organizations into seditious words and actions, which could then be informed upon and so bring those hotheads to their ruins.

The provocation men played a dangerous game, for they were regarded with fear and loathing by every working man and woman in the country and if discovered ran a very real risk of being killed in order to silence them.

Again and again Tildy scanned the list of names and the comments annotating them, imprinting it on her memory. By now her shaken nerves had steadied and she was thinking rationally and calmly. She must find some way of confirming that the pouch really did belong to Farrel, then, once she knew for a fact that it did, she could go to Josh Dyson and Will Stacey and tell them what she had discovered. The temptation to risk keeping the money, or at least a part of it, did rise within her, but she repressed it. Tildy's basic honesty was deeply ingrained in her character and she would have to be absolutely desperate before she could bring herself to steal from anyone, even a man she suspected of being a Government spy.

'And if Farrel is such then it's better that he should have no suspicion that I have discovered him,' she realized, and then thought worriedly, 'But if I return the pouch to him after confirming it's his then he will obviously suspect that I've opened it and read the list of names.'

After some reflection she resolved her quandary, deciding to sneak into his room and place the pouch on the floor there, so he would think that was where it had dropped initially. Tomorrow she would tell Josh Dyson of her discovery and then see what was his opinion of the matter.

Stealthily she opened her door and stepped to the door of Farrel's room. Pressing her ear against the panel she listened hard, but could hear no sound from within. With painful slowness she cautiously opened the door a crack and again paused and listened intently, but still there was no sound from within. She risked opening it wider and peeping round its edge and to her surprise saw that the room was empty.

'But he said that he was going to his bed to sleep?' she thought puzzledly, then quickly placed the pouch on the floor and closed the door upon it.

Back in her own room she lay awake for long hours, listening to the drum-beat of rain on the tiles so close above her head and listening also for any token of Farrel's return, her mind restlessly examining the possibilities of his whereabouts. Finally she drifted into an unquiet sleep which scant hours later was broken by the distant ringing of the factory bells summoning the people to their work.

Head aching and eyes gritty with weariness, Tildy rose and made her toilette, then with a sense of foreboding weighing upon her spirits she gently kissed her sleeping child and went out into the clammy darkness of early morning.

Chapter Twenty-Nine

The messenger from Reverend the Lord Aston arrived at John Clayton's house on the Fish Hill just as that young man was seating himself to his breakfast of coffee, fresh-baked bread, fried eggs and salted bacon.

'Youm to come at once to Tarbick, Parson Clayton,' the smock-frocked, red-faced countryman announced. 'Me lord says to tell you it's imper . . . impera . . . imper . . . He says youm to come straight off I delivers this message to you.'

'Very well. Do you return with me?' Clayton questioned brusquely.

'No, Sir, I has to goo and summons some o' the needle masters and Joe Cashmore as well as you, Sir.'

Clayton frowned thoughtfully, wondering why the needle masters and constable were also required, and considered that it was probably something to do with the alleged secret combination that his spiritual and temporal superior seemed lately to have become obsessed with uncovering in the district.

The young man sighed sulkily, for he greatly enjoyed his leisurely breakfasts.

'I'll attend on his lordship directly,' he dismissed the messenger, then hastily bolted his food and shouted to his manservant to have his horse saddled and ready by the time he had finished dressing.

As he rode over the muddy tracks towards the Tarde-bigge vicarage some three miles from Redditch town, John Clayton's thoughts turned once more to a matter that he found impossible to dismiss from his mind, much as he wished to be quit of it. The matter of the child Meg Tullet's suicide. Ever since that tragic event he had, despite his reluctance to accept it, experienced the nagging, gradually strengthening conviction that Tildy Crawford had been speaking the truth, and Johnny Brompton had been lying about what had happened in the Pitcheroak woods. Over and over again he had replayed in his mind the scene in his study when the Crawford woman had confronted Brompton, and with each replay his own sense of guilt had expanded.

'I should have pressed that man. Pressed him until he confessed to what he had done,' Clayton muttered now, and bitterly castigated himself. 'You're a damned stupid, pompous fool at times, John Clayton. You allow your prejudices to blind you. You allow them to cloud your perception of the truth. Damn and blast it, but I fear I erred greatly that day.' He suffered a genuine aching of remorse. 'Dear God, forgive me for my lack of charity towards that poor, benighted child ...'

Clayton was the first to arrive of those summoned by Lord Aston, and his superior came himself to the door to greet him.

'Good, I'm glad you've reached here before the others, John. I wish a brief word with you alone.'

He led the younger man into his sumptuously furnished drawing room and once there closed the door and locked it to ensure privacy, then pressed a sheet of notepaper into Clayton's hand.

'Quickly, John, read this.'

Clayton scanned the paper, noting the embossed seal of the Home Office at Whitehall that had been affixed to it, and then read the contents.

'Sir, A person well acquainted with the designs of the disaffected Radicals in the Western Midland counties will be visiting the needle district of Redditch and its surrounding hamlets. It is possible that he may obtain some information while at that place, the early communication of which to a magistrate on the spot may be of material importance. He will accordingly be entrusted with this letter which he will make use of as his introduction to you, in case such a communication should become necessary during his stay in the needle district. He is an intelligent man and deserving of your confidence.

I am etcetera,

R. Peel.'

John Clayton re-read the signature: Robert Peel, the Secretary of State himself ... 'How did you come by this, my lord?' he asked, and the older man excitedly bobbed his wigged head.

'In the early hours, John. The Government agent came here in the early hours of this morning. He confirmed to me the existence of a secret combination in this parish, a combination which has spread its tentacles of wickedness throughout the entire district.'

Clayton caught something of the infection of his superior's excitement. 'But who is this man, my lord?'

Aston assumed a conspiratorial air. 'I regret, John, that at this time I cannot yet disclose the Government agent's identity, even to you. I am sworn to absolute discretion.'

The young man was half amused, half irritated by the other's manner. 'Then, my lord, can you tell me more of this secret combination?'

Again Aston cast a watchful look round him, as though they were surrounded by eavesdroppers, and lowered his voice to almost a whisper, 'The man has imparted certain information to me, John, but again on this matter also I am sworn to an absolute secrecy. I can only divulge what I know when the time comes for us to take action against these cursed Radicals.'

Clayton's irritation briefly overlaid his amusement. 'If that is the case, my lord, then why did the fellow come to you now, instead of waiting until we could take action against them?'

Lord Aston's expression soured. 'Because he needed funds, John.' The vicar's notorious stinginess now became glaringly apparent as he went on peevishly, 'Damn it all, the fellow says he needs funds, and because of my position within this parish I was of necessity forced to advance him a sizeable amount. Naturally, I shall be able to reclaim my money from the Home Office, but still, it ain't good enough, is it, John? An agent of His Majesty's Government sent to do his work without sufficient money to complete that work with. I'll have a few harsh words to say about that when the time is right, I do assure you. Damn it all, John, I am a poor man! I cannot afford to finance the Government any more than I do already. It ain't good enough; in fact, it's damn disgraceful if you want my opinion on it.'

'Your pardon, my lord, for interrupting you.' John Clayton was by now eager to complete this interview. He had little liking for Lord Aston's company at any time. 'But with all respect, my lord, if the time is not yet come to divulge the identities of this spy and the people in the combination, surely you risk alerting these Radicals to their danger by telling the needle masters and the constable that the existence of such a combination here has now been confirmed by a Government spy? After all, Sir, some of the masters have a tendency to shout without prior thought, do they not?'

Not for the first time during their relationship, Lord Aston surprised his curate with his deviousness.

'God save me, boy,' he declaimed witheringly. 'Can it be that you really do take me for a fool, I wonder? Or have I not understood you correctly? I've not summoned those men here to tell them of this. Dammee, don't I know only too well that if I were to tell that set of loud-mouthed hucksters of this then it would be common knowledge throughout the district afore they'd even reached the end of the lane out there! What has passed in this room is solely between you and I. I kept the letter on loan from the man to demonstrate to you a positive proof that my suspicions of what was afoot in this parish had been proven correct.' He paused and stared ironically at his curate for a considerable length of time before continuing with a sarcastic inflexion in his voice. 'For I know well that from the Olympian heights of your intellect you look down upon me with a sense of pity for my senility of mind.'

Clayton wisely forebore to answer to that charge and instead only stared down at the carpet and flushed hotly.

'The reason I want to see the masters is because the earl is considering introducing a Bill of Enclosure for that piece of waste to the north-west of the Bridley Moor and I want to sound out what objections any of them might have to that. As for Cashmore, I want to see him about the robbery that took place at Webheath last Tuesday. I trust that your curiosity is now satisfied, young man? Or is there anything more that you need to be informed of?'

'No, my lord, I'm well satisfied, I thank you,' Clayton muttered, more than anxious now to be out of this hugely embarrassing situation.

The older man, smiling now that he had suitably chastised his subordinate, nodded in dismissal. 'I'll not detain you longer, John. Be off with you, and mind, keep tight-close all that I've told you.'

Chapter Thirty

At nine o'clock that morning when the bell at the Fountain Mill clanged out the signal for the breakfast break, Tildy left the lye shop and went in search of Millicent Milward. She found the master's wife in the work shop where the finished needles were sorted and packaged for transit and sale.

'Could I speak with you, Mistress?' Tildy could not suppress the tremors in her stomach at what she was about to do.

The large woman, who bore more than a passing family resemblance to her cousin, Charlotte Readman, nodded while her eyes evaluated this pretty young woman standing before her. Although clad in her normal working dress of old black gown, sack apron, floppy mob-cap and heavy iron-studded clogs, Millicent Milward was still a commanding presence.

Tildy swallowed hard and stammered, 'I haven't forgotten how good you were to me when I had that trouble with my husband, Mistress. And I don't want you to think that I'm deliberately returning ill for good, but . . . but . . . but . . .'

Millicent Milward snorted impatiently. 'Come on, my wench, spit it out. I arn't agoing to bite your yed off, even though I don't doubt but that it's aggravation youm bringing me.'

Tildy, angry at herself for her own timidity, gathered her courage and blurted out, 'I've come to tell you, Mistress, that I'm going to try and rouse the women against Johnny Brompton. I'm going to try and get him his sack.'

'Am you now?' The other woman accepted the statement with outward casualness. 'And how does you intend going about that?'

'I intend to lead a deputation to Mr Milward and ask him to get rid of that evil rapist. If he refuses then I'll try and get Brompton tarred and feathered if need be. One way or another I mean to see that wicked bastard punished for what he did to poor Meg Tullet.' Tildy's previous timidity had gone now and the flush in her cheeks was not caused by embarrassment, but by her own fiery emotion and determination.

Every man, woman and child who worked in that department was by now listening avidly to this exchange and, aware of this fact Millicent Milward's mind raced. She herself was faced with an inner conflict. In one way she sympathized totally with Tildy's aims. Her own personal inclination was to sack Brompton from the mill and see him driven from the town in disgrace. If it had not been for the fact that he had a wife and young children dependent on him she would have applauded his hanging, for she also believed him to have been guilty of rape. However, after examination the man had been declared innocent by those who controlled the legal powers of the town. Her husband had decided to keep the man in his employ, and although Millicent Milward had not turned her back on her own lowly origins, she still must always remember that she was a needle master's wife, and as such could not be seen to go against her husband's decisions, particularly where those decisions affected the business of the mill. In any confrontation between men and master, Millicent Milward in the final analysis was bound in her own interests to stand with the masters. This young woman was now openly stating her intention of challenging the right of a master to decide what he did with his own workpeople. Leaving aside all emotion and all question of abstract or actual justice, Matilda Crawford was in effect proposing to challenge the established system of power in the town.

If it had been someone else's mill or factory Millicent Milward would have secretly applauded the girl's boldness and enjoyed seeing what became of the battle. But this was not someone else's mill. It was her and her husband's business, and Millicent Milward was well aware that if she and Henry conceded defeat and handed Johnny Brompton his sack at the behest of this girl and her supporters then that defeat could well presage a whole host of other demands from the workers. God only knew there were more than sufficient abuses and exploitations for the workers to fight to have righted, and if once they gained a victory against the masters then it would very soon become a case of Jack thinking himself as good as his master, with a vengeance.

'If we give in now, then we'll lose all control of the buggers for good and all,' the woman thought fearfully. Outwardly she betrayed none of her feelings but remained calm and impassive as she listened to Tildy.

'. . . as I said before, Mistress, you have been good to me, and when I needed a friend, then you acted as such, and I'll be eternally grateful for that.'

'Then why be you trying to stir up trouble for me and Mr Milward now? Is that what being eternally grateful means?'

'It's not you I'm trying to stir up trouble for.' Tildy was almost pleading to be understood. 'It's not you or Mr Milward. But when Meg Tullet needed a friend, there was no one with any power in this town to stand up for her. Not one of the masters or the gentry cared one scrap what happened to the pitiful creature. Not one except for those like myself, who were only ignored and laughed at because we possess neither wealth nor position in life.

'It's wrong that this should be so, Mistress. Totally and wickedly wrong! It means that men like Johnny Brompton can do whatever they've a mind to do.' Tildy glanced at the rapt faces of her listeners and what she saw in some of those faces steeled her resolve to go on with what she intended doing. 'I'm asking only one thing, Mistress, and

241

that is that Johnny Brompton be given his sack, and when that happens then the whole district will realize that he really is guilty and that decent people will not employ him, and mayhap it will give pause to those others like him before they next serve some poor girl worse than they would serve an animal —'

'That's it, my wench! You'se got the rights on it,' one of the listening women uttered aloud, and a rustling of agreement came from those about her.

'Does you realize that you could get yourself into serious trouble, Tildy Crawford, if you leads a randy in this mill? You'll be breaking the law,' Millicent Milward warned.

Into Tildy's mind there came the memory of Nathanial Farrel telling her that some laws were so unjust they deserved to be broken. A sharp visual image of her child superimposed itself upon the previous one and her resolve momentarily faltered. But then she saw once more the pathetic, muddied, slime-tendrilled body of Meg Tullet being dragged from the mill pool and she knew that no other choice remained open to her.

'I know that there will more than likely be sufficient laws I can be charged with breaking, Mistress,' she replied quietly. 'But I've no other choice but than to break them if needs be.'

With a gleam of grudging admiration in her eyes, Millicent Milward told her, 'Youm a real rebel on the quiet, arn't you, Tildy Crawford? But you should remember that in this country the rebels never wins, my wench. They always gets a good hiding give to 'um.' She waved her hands indicating the listeners. 'All this lot here 'ull give you support wi' their tongues, Tildy, and there's a good many more in this mill who'll do the same. But when it comes to the crunch, girl, and the real fight starts, then you'll more nor likely find yourself on your own. There 'ull only be you toeing the mark when the blood and snot starts flying about.'

'Oh no, Milly Milward, not this time!' From the doorway Mary Ann Avery, Sarah Farr and Old Tabby advanced into the workshop, followed by half-a-dozen other women. 'We'em all on us determined in this.' Mary Ann's plump features were stubbornly set, and she pointed at Tildy. 'We arn't agoing to let this young 'ooman here, we arn't agoing to let her shoot the bullets for the rest on us, or stand to the mark by herself against you lot and your gentry cronies.' She spoke to Tildy directly. 'The women be gathering in the yard, Tildy, they'm waiting for you to come out and tell 'um what it is you wants 'um to do.'

Tildy stared bemusedly at her friends, who had acted completely without her knowledge in going from shop to shop haranguing all the women to gather in protest against Johnny Brompton. 'Oh, Mary Ann,' she murmured, as if distressed. 'I didn't want to act without first giving a fair warning to Mrs Milward here.'

To her surprise the large woman only laughed grimly. 'Don't you fret none about that, girl. I knew that summat like this was bound to happen sooner nor later. The only thing you should be worriting about now, Tildy Crawford is your own yed, because I fear you'se started summat which you arn't going to be able to stop. Take my advice, girl. Stay in here and let it all drop right now, because youm begining a fight which you can't win. That goes for the rest of you as well. I reckon you'll end by sorely rueing this day's work. I really does.'

Tildy shook her glossy head. 'I can't drop it, Mistress, not now.'

'Be it on your own yed then, girl, because if you don't drop it then I'll not stand as friend to you agen.'

Tildy sighed with genuine unhappiness. 'I'm truly sorry to hear you say that, Mistress.'

'Come on, Tildy, the rest on 'um are waiting,' Sarah Farr urged, and with a last regretful look at Mrs Milward, Tildy led her followers out into the courtyard.

As on the previous occasion the crowd had massed around the loading bay of the warehouse, but this time only the women and girls were there. The men and boys ranged along the edges of the yard, lounging against the walls or thronging the windows and doorways solely as spectators.

The overlookers had gathered in a body at the doorway of Henry Milward's office, and inside that office a hang-dog Johnny Brompton was enduring yet another tongue-lashing from his raging employer.

'See the bloody trouble youm causing me, Brompton. For two pins I'd give you your sack right now, you worth-less heap o' dung! Only if I did that then those buggers 'ud think that they'd frightened me into doing so, and I'll not let inferior scum like that ever frighten me. But you'se already cost me more aggravation than youm worth, you dirty bastard! You should have had that prick 'o yourn chopped off at birth. But you'll pay me back for this trouble you'se caused me, Brompton. I swear on my mother's grave, you'll pay me back somehow or other for what this is costing me. I don't care if it takes the rest o' your lousy stinking life to pay me back, but youm agoing to, that I'll swear.'

A burst of cheering greeted Tildy's appearance in the courtyard and as she mounted the steps of the loading bay many of the women shouted encouragement.

'We'em all wi' you, Tildy!'

'We'll all stand together, girl!'

'We'll stand wi' you, Tildy, don't you fret!'

Josh Dyson was keeping well back to the rear of the spectators. He felt a curious mixture of apprehension and elation as he watched Tildy turn to face the crowd.

Tildy herself was beyond any apprehension now. She was filled only with the fierce determination to finish what she had begun and was already mentally accepting that if it meant her being singled out for punishment by those in authority, then she was ready to dare that punishment.

The women quietened, their eyes expectant, and Tildy's voice rang out clearly so that all could hear her.

'I don't need to remind anyone why we're gathered

together now. Meg Tullet was raped and driven to commit self-murder by Johnny Brompton. Brompton must be given his sack from this mill and be driven from this district, so that others like him can take warning that the days when they could do as they wished with defenceless women and girls are gone. If we only stand together, and stand firm, then we can demand and achieve our rights. Our right to walk safely through the day or the night. Our right to be treated with respect by the men who work with us.'

The women cheered excitedly.

'That's it, Tildy!'

'That's what we wants!'

'We demands our rights!'

'Give us our rights!'

'We'll stand, Tildy, we'll stand firm!'

Henry Milward had come to stand outside his office door, flanked by his overlookers, and he listened to Tildy with an expression of derision on his plump features.

Tildy looked directly at the needle master, and called, 'Can I come and speak with you, Mr Milward?'

He nodded brusquely, and Tildy came down from the loading bay and through the crowd to stand face to face with the needle master.

'With all respect, Mr Milward, can I ask you to hand Johnny Brompton his sack from this mill?' she requested firmly.

Milward grinned with savage anger. 'Oh yes, girl, you can ask, but the only sack that's going to be handed out this day is your own bugger if you don't get back to your work this instant.' He raised his voice and bellowed at the crowd, 'And that goes for the rest on you as well. I'm the master here, and I'll not be dictated to by anybody, least of all them who relies on me to put the bloody bread in their bellies.' From his fob-pocket he pulled out a gold hunter watch and held it high above his head. 'Afore ten seconds have ticked off this watch you'd best all be on your way back to your shops, or you'll be going through these bloody gates for good.'

Tildy reacted to his threat with almost blind instinct.

'You can save yourself the bother of counting the ten seconds, Master,' she declared vehemently. 'Because every woman and girl in this mill is going to walk out of those gates right now and stay outside of them until you do what is right ad proper; until you give that animal, Brompton, his sack.'

Praying that she had not misjudged the women's mood, Tildy walked firmly through the tunnel entrance of the mill without a backwards glance. For brief seconds the others wavered uncertainly, and then Mary Ann Avery shouted, 'That's it, girls! One out, all out!' And with a roar of cheering the crowd of women and girls broke from their standstill and poured out of the mill gates.

Millicent Milward came to her husband's side. 'By the Christ, Master, you surely handled that like a bloody mawkin!' she spat viciously.

Shock and fury purpled Henry Milward's cheeks and he demanded, 'What else could I ha' done, woman? I couldn't give in to the buggers just like that, could I?'

'No, mayhap you couldn't,' Millicent Milward conceded grudgingly after a moment or two of reflection. 'But I fear this 'ull cost us dear.'

'Not as dear as it's going to cost that Radical bitch, Crawford,' her husband growled savagely. 'She'll pay a sore price for this day's work, I'll see to that.'

On the roadway outside the mill, Tildy stared at the excited, chattering, gesticulating women and girls seething around her, and a bombshell of panic exploded in her mind. Now that she had them here, what was she going to do with them all? At that moment Tildy wished with all her heart that she had not brought those women and girls out with her, and she longed desperately for someone other than herself to take command and tell her and the rest of them exactly what they must now do. Then she saw that Mary Ann Avery and Sarah Farr were staring at her expectantly, awaiting her instructions, and she realized that there would not be anyone else to take command. She was the elected and accepted leader here, and she must direct this unruly mob which had placed its trust in her. They had become her responsibility. She fought back the panic that was threatening to engulf her and shouted the noisy women to silence. Then, suddenly, it was again as it had been on the night of her enrolment in the combination. The words came through her mind as if from a source beyond herself and a heady confidence enveloped her.

'I'm going to divide you off into groups,' she said. 'Each group will then be given an area of this district to cover. You'll go to every mill, factory and workshop in your area, and you will tell the women there what we are doing. You must ask them for their support, and for anything that they can spare which will help us to continue this fight: money, food, clothes, anything. We'll not step foot again inside Milward's mill until he gives Johnny Brompton his sack. And if Milward employs black-leg labour to replace us, well then we'll persuade the other women in the district to do as we've done — to withdraw their labour from their own workplaces so that the other masters will be forced to bring pressure to bear on Henry Milward as well.

'Mary Ann, Sarah, Tabby, Jenny and Martha, you'll each choose an area and lead a group, as I will myself, so start selecting your people. Try and have women from the area you'll be covering so that they'll be known to the others there.'

While the groups were forming Tildy could not help but have a sense of wonderment at how events had so suddenly developed.

'It's as if it were meant to happen,' she finally decided, and experienced an eerie sensation of déjà vu. 'I was destined to do exactly what I am now doing. So there's no use me feeling afraid or regretful at anything, because it was all meant to be.'

'Tildy Crawford?' Millicent Milward had come out of

the mill and was shouting. 'Tildy Crawford? I wants a word.'

Tildy hurried to the master's wife. 'Yes, Mrs Milward, what is it you want to say?' She was pleasant and polite to the big woman, because even now she bore nothing but good feeling towards her for her past kindness.

'Be you hard-set on this, Tildy?' the woman wanted to know, and Tildy nodded.

'I am, Mistress. If your husband will not acknowledge Brompton's guilt by sacking him, then I'm determined to carry on this fight.'

'You'll be bringing a deal of hardship on these women's heads,' the big woman said gravely, and Tildy thought carefully before replying.

'I'm not doing this for any personal gain or for pleasure, Mrs Milward, and I'll not let myself feel guilty for any hardships that these women might suffer because of what we're about. Any hardships falling on them fall on me also. What we are asking of your husband is but simple justice, Mrs Milward. And you know yourself deep down that we are in the right.'

Millicent Milward's strong, yellowed teeth bared in a sardonic smile. 'Being in the right don't ever fill bellies, my wench, and it never has done. If you'll take my advice you'll come back to work right now, and make your apologies to Master Milward for the upset you'se caused already. No matter what you does now, it arn't going to bring Meg Tullet back, is it, or alter what's happened? You can't win this fight, my wench. The longest pockets 'ull win this, and we'se got them.'

Tildy's white teeth bit into her full red lips as doubt once more assailed her. She recognized the truth of Mrs Milward's statement, that this was a struggle with all the advantages held by the opposing side.

'Have I the right to drag these women and girls into such a hopeless contest?' she asked herself. 'Do I have the right to bring such hardships down on them?'

The question was answered for her. Mary Ann Avery

came to the two women and told Tildy, 'Right, my duck, we'se got the groups sorted, and the areas as well.' She smiled nostalgically at the needle master's wife. 'Does you know, Milly, this reminds me o' the bread riots, when me and 'you was young 'uns. I'se never forgot the excitement o' that day.'

'Is that why youm doing this then, Mary Ann, just for the bloody excitement?' Mrs Milward challenged, and the lye shop forewoman shook her head in emphatic rebuttal.

'No, Milly, that arn't the case at all. I'm not doing this for excitement, because at my age all I really wants is a bit o' peace and quiet. The reason I'm doing this is because it's time it was done. We should ha' done it long since when we was both still young. You'd ha' bin at my side then, my wench, not opposite me.'

Mrs Milward smiled wryly. 'Ahr, that's maybe so, Mary Ann. But them days are long past, and I'm a master's wife now.'

'Master's wife you may be, but to me you'll always be Milly Brough from the Silver Street, who was a good mate o' mine and who stood agen the constables and the volunteers when the children needed bread to fill their bellies.'

'You and your children's bellies have been filled well enough for a good length o' time now, Mary Ann. You earns good money in this mill,' Millicent Milward countered.

'I'm paid a fair wage for being a forewoman, I arn't gainsaying that, Milly. But I reckon it's time that all the women and girls in this mill were treated as people who needs more than just a full belly in their life. I reckon it's time they were all allowed to have a bit o' dignity in their lives as well. I'se held my peace for too many years, Milly. Too many years of seeing buggers like Johnny Brompton make free with other people's daughters. Oh, I know what youm agoing to say.' She lifted her hands as if to ward off any reply from Mrs Milward. 'You'll say that there's some on 'um who be nothing else but whores and sluts anyway and that they encourages the men to take liberties. But not all the wenches in this mill, or any of the other mills, be sluts and whores. The most part on 'um are decent, or at least they tries to live so. It's for them that I'm doing this now.'

Millicent Milward's heavy face was solemn, but not hostile, as she told them both, 'Well girls, I can't really wish you good fortune in what youm adoing, because it's my mill that 'ull suffer from it most. But remembering old times and what I was then, and what I had to put up wi' meself, then I'm not agoing to wish bad luck on you neither.'

She turned away from them and went back through the mill gates. Tildy kept her eyes fixed on her employer's retreating back, and said regretfully to Mary Ann, 'Do you know, I truly wish that it could have been anyone else rather than Mrs Milward that we were going against in this way.'

'Amen to that, Tildy,' her companion sighed resignedly. 'But there's naught to be done about it, my duck. And now we've begun to fight, well, we'd better make certain that we taps their claret for 'um, and makes a brave show on it. So, lets get these groups on the move, shall us ...'

Chapter Thirty-One

All through that day the small groups of women and girls trudged the district and, ever eager for novelty, the workers at the various mills, factories and workshops they called at welcomed them, listened to their news, and invariably promised to contribute towards their appeal for food and money. The masters were not welcoming, but forebore from trying to prevent their own workers from clustering about the callers. As if by telepathic communication and accord many of the employers rode their horses or drove their pony-traps into the town to the Fox and Goose Inn, opposite St Stephen's Chapel, which was the accepted meeting place and drinking haunt of the masters and minor gentry. There, over glasses of brandy and claret, pipes of tobacco and boxes of snuff, they gathered to discuss the situation.

Henry Milward went to the Fox and Goose just after the noon hour, and was greeted with a storm of questions as he entered the bar-parlour favoured by the company. He waved away all queries until he had drained two large bumpers of mulled brandy-punch, and then mopped the sweat from his forehead with his garishly coloured bandanna and announced, 'I've never seen the like on it, gentlemen. It's the bloody women and girls who are striking. None of the men seem ready to join them though, thank God.'

There were those among the masters in the room who were secretly pleased to see Milward's difficulties. The needle trade was highly competitive, and if a rival lost his production then there was always the possibility of stepping in to sell their own products to disappointed customers.

Others, more far-seeing however, were worried by this unusual occurrence. They were accustomed to trouble from the notorious pointers, but the women and girls were normally docile enough, and it was highly disturbing to see these usually submissive underlings now rising up to challenge their master.

William Heming, whose mill stood at the top of the Fish Hill, was one of these latter who felt concern.

'Tell me, Henry, do you think that if you were to dismiss this fellow, Brompton, the women would return to their work?'

Milward spread his hands and shrugged helplessly. 'Who can tell what the saucy buggers might do, William? Mayhap if I give the man his sack then the women might return sweetly enough. But there is another way o' seeing this, ain't there? Supposing I hand the bugger his sack, and then they're not satisfied with that alone. Once they see me give in to them and bow to their will, then what's to prevent them demanding more concessions, and then more still?'

Another man now rose to his feet. Middle-aged, bulky-bodied, red-faced, his hair queued and pigtailed in the style of the previous century, and looking like a small farmer in his blue smock-frock, leather gaiters, heavy hob-nailed boots and a billycock hat pulled low on his fore-head, Abel Morral, of the Green Lane, Studley village, one-time needle pointer, was now one of the largest and most influential needle masters in the trade.

'Right, gentlemen, we all knows what's afoot, the question is what be we going to do about it?'

'But what can we do, Master Morral? After all, it's naught to do with us, strictly speaking. It's Henry Milward's concern, not ours.' Uriah Lilly, bent-shouldered, drab-suited, sallow-faced and thin-lipped, spoke for several others there, judging by the instant agreement within the gathering.

'Don't talk so bloody sarft, Lilly.' Morral's brawl-scarred features were aggressive, and Uriah Lilly swallowed nervously, remembering the wild pointer youth of this man.

'Listen to me well, all on you.' Morral asserted an instant influence over the meeting by the threatening brutality of his manner. For the moment at least those who were not nervous of him and might have challenged his assumption of control were content enough to hear what he had to say. Whatever else might be said of Abel Morral, no one ever doubted his shrewdness or his cunning.

'The fust thing that we'se got to understand is that this upset at Henry's mill does concern us all. The only other time I can remember the women acting together in this way was back in the bread riots, and we all knows the damage they caused then, so let's not underestimate the buggers. What we must do is to give Henry our full support to enable him to last out and beat these women. To help him starve the buggers back to their work the vestry and the overseers must refuse any application for relief from any woman refusing to go to her employment. We'll make up his lost production from our own stocks. He can buy at cost price from us whatever he needs to meet his orders. You can re-pack the needles in your own wrappers, Henry, and they'll think your quality's improved,' he joked roughly, and Henry Milward grinned uncertainly, as if not appreciating such a joke.

'Well, do we all agree?' Morral asked, and when one or two of the men present were tardy in voicing agreement he rounded angrily upon them. 'Damn and blast your eyes! Can't you bloody well see that these women be threatening our own positions, and our rights as masters to do what we will in our own mills? If we lets 'um beat any one on us, then none on us 'ull be safe from their insolence. It'll be a case of the tail wagging the bloody dog, wun't it?'

It was Uriah Lilly who still hung back from agreement. 'Surely, Master Morral, these women are acting in concert, so why not report them to the magistrates for being in combination?'

'Because it 'udden't bloody well serve, Master Lilly.' Morral jeeringly mimicked the prissy tones of the objector. 'These women be acting in concert, so let's report 'um to the magistrates for being in combination ... Bugger me if you arn't talking like a bloody mawkin, Master Lilly!' he exclaimed, shaking his head as if bemused by such stupidity. The other man's sallow face darkened with resentment, but he was too physically nervous of Morral to display his anger openly.

'Of course we all knows that these women are acting in combination,' Morral announced. 'But if we tries to bring the law agen 'um, all they'll say is that they'm not acting in combination, and they'll point out that they'm not asking for higher wages, or shorter hours, or anything else from their master. All they'm doing is refusing to work alongside a man that they reckons is a bloody rapist ... And there's no law agen that to my knowledge, is there? Of course we can tell the magistrates that there's ringleaders among 'um. But are these ringleaders administering any oaths to the women? Be they meeting secretly? Be they drilling with pikes up in the woods theer?' He answered his own questions. 'You knows bloody well they arn't. The magistrates 'ud be forced to dismiss any charges we laid agen 'um, and you all knows that as well as me. So to my mind we can't really hope to bring the law to bear upon 'um, and in all honesty, I don't really want to do so anyway. Because personally I reckon that Brompton did force that wench. But mind you, I arn't saying that he's any worse than a good many others in this town that I could name, who's done their own share o' forcing wenches in their time. Still, that's neither here nor there. The thing now is that we can't let Henry be made to give way to the women's demands, so we must all stand together ourselves and act in combination until we'se won this fight. Then, once we'se won it, Henry can kick that bastard Brompton arse over tip from his mill for the trouble he's caused us. But that must wait until we'se beat the women, which shouldn't take too long. Their menfolk wun't appreciate losing their beer-money, that's for sure, so they'll be pushing them back to their work afore more than a week's passed, I'll wager. So gentlemen, does we all help Henry, or are there any more objections to that?'

This time acceptance was complete. Even the sour-faced Lilly nodded his agreement.

'Good! That's settled then,' Morral gusted in satisfaction. 'All you needs to do, Henry, is just sit tight and let us know what amounts o' needles you requires, and all this 'ull very soon be behind us.'

Chapter Thirty-Two

Tildy was very footsore and weary when she arrived back at the lodging house that evening. Before anything else she hurried to see her child, and as he came running to her arms her heart was heavy at the dread of what could happen to them both because of her activities. She fetched water from the pump and heated it on the kitchen fire, then carefully bathed Davy, and fed him with bread and milk she had bought out of the pitiful stock of coins she had left to her.

Mother Readman sat in her great chair and watched the mother and child, smiling at the tenderness the young woman displayed towards her son.

'How went the collections, Tildy?' As always, the old woman knew what was happening before practically anyone else in the town.

Tildy made a moue with her lips. 'Promises by the score, but next to nothing actually given us,' she said tiredly. 'But then, working people have little enough to live on themselves. We can't expect much.'

'Do you think you'll win, my duck?' Mother Readman looked concerned, and Tildy forced a smile of confidence that she did not really feel.

'We'll win, Mother. We have to win, don't we? But I'm hoping that the men have planned well how to aid us. Still, I'll find that out for myself presently.'

'There's a meeting bin called for tonight then?'

'Yes, Josh Dyson sent a message to tell me we must be at the brick kilns by nine o'clock tonight.'

'I popped down to see cousin Milly this afternoon,

Tildy. She arn't best pleased with you, my wench.' The old woman's cheeks and jowls quivered as she blew out a noisy gasp of air. 'No, her arn't pleased at all! Her reckons youm returning bad for good, after the way she helped you out afore.'

'I can't blame her for feeling that,' Tildy said sadly. 'After all, in a sense that's exactly what I'm doing, isn't it? But knowing my reasons, do you think that I'm acting badly, Mother Readman?'

It was a cry for comfort and reassurance, and the old woman answered it by touching Tildy's smooth cheek with her swollen, arthritic fingers. 'Youm acting from a good heart, Tildy, I knows that, and that's what I told cousin Milly. Youm not fighting agen her, but only for the memory of poor Meg Tullet.'

'I'm worried about paying you my rent, though.' Tildy's face became drawn as she thought of that debt mounting, but Mother Readman dismissed her concern with an airy wave of her hands.

'Don't you fret none about that, my duck. We can keep a count, and when things improves for you, why, you can pay it all back to me then, can't you?'

'I'm truly grateful.' Tildy spoke from the very depths of her feelings. 'I don't know what I've done in my life to deserve such a good friend as you.'

'Don't think on it, girl. You'd do the same for me, 'udden't you, if positions was reversed? I don't want to hear any more nonsense about it from you, or you'll make me bloody angry, so you will. Now you goo upstairs and put that babby to his sleep, and rest yourself for a while as well, because you looks to be knackered out. Arter you'se rested a bit, then come down and ate some supper. At least you can goo to the kilns wi' a full stomach, even if your pockets be nigh on empty.'

Tildy cradled her drowsy child in her arms and took him upstairs to her attic room. Once there she cuddled and kissed him for some time, listening to his childish prattlings and glorying in the fresh, innocent sweetness of

him. Then she put him into his small cot and sang softly
to him a lullaby which she herself had learned as a child.

> 'Baby, baby, naughty baby,
> Hush, you squalling thing, I say.
> Hush your squalling, or it may be,
> Bonaparte will pass this way.
>
> Baby, baby, he's a giant,
> Tall and black as Rouen steeple,
> And he dines and sups, rely on't
> Every day on naughty people.
>
> Baby, baby he will hear you,
> As he passes by the house,
> And he limb from limb will tear you,
> Just as Pussy tears a mouse ...'

Her soft voice ceased as she saw Davy's eyes close in
slumber, and she yawned and stretched her arms wide to
ease her aching muscles.

'Mayhap I'll just snatch a few winks,' she decided, and
laid herself on her own narrow bed. Then there came a
soft, insistent tapping at the door. Reluctant to call out in
case she woke Davy, Tildy rose and went to the door,
opening it to find Nathanial Farrel standing there. He was
dressed for outdoors, with his dark military cloak around
his shoulders and his tall hat on his head. He smiled, and
whispered, 'I know you've just settled Davy to sleep, Mrs
Crawford, I heard your lullaby. Can I speak with you? It's
urgent that I do.'

She glanced back over her shoulder to see if Davy was
being disturbed, and Farrel whispered, 'We can step into
my room and close the door. He'll not be able to hear us
in there, and we'll not risk waking him with our talk.
Please, Mrs Crawford, if it were not of the utmost importance I would not be so importunate at this time.'

'Very well.' She surrendered to his urgings and

followed after him the few steps to his room.

'Please to seat yourself, Mrs Crawford.'

He indicated a three-legged stool against the wall, and she was glad to sink down on it, for her legs were trembling with her tiredness.

The young man removed his hat and placed it on the bed, then seated himself beside it so that he faced her on the same eye level. His thin face was sombre, and his light green eyes troubled, and Tildy felt a clutch of foreboding at her heart.

'I beg of you to hear me out without interruption, Mrs Crawford,' he said quietly. 'For I have that to say to you which I fear will cause you considerable disquiet, if not distress.'

Tildy's heart was thudding fast now, and she nodded. 'Go on, Mr Farrel. I'll not interrupt.'

He bent forward so that his elbows rested on his knees and gripped his hands together in front of him. Keeping his eyes fixed on his entwined fingers, he told her, 'Mrs Crawford, I know that you are a sworn member of an illegal combination.'

She emitted a faint gasp, and his eyes flicked to her blanched face. 'Don't be feared of my knowing, Tildy,' he said quickly. 'I'm no provocation man.' He smiled wryly. 'Oh yes, Tildy, I know well what certain people have been saying of me in this town. But I swear to you, by all that I hold sacred, that I am no Government spy.'

Tildy's thoughts were whirling. Events had moved so rapidly that day that she had had no opportunity of telling Josh Dyson about her discovery of the list of names in Farrel's possession. She had intended to tell the hardener that night at the forthcoming meeting.

'Then who, and what are you, Mr Farrel?' The fright she had received imparted a strained, harsh edging to her soft voice.

'For the present it is only necessary for you to know that I am someone who has the best interests of your combination at heart, and I am here as the representative of others who are equally strong for the rights of the common man.'

'Is that why you carry a list of our names with you?' Tildy blurted out without stopping to consider, and instantly regretted it as he scowled in shock and anger.

'How do you know that? Have you been making search like some thief in the night while I slept?' he demanded harshly, and she shook her head and sought to protect herself from any possible unpleasant repercussions of her blundering revelation.

'Never mind how I came to know, Mr Farrel. But be warned that if I know, then my friends know also, and if something should happen to me, then they will also know who to blame for it.'

'Don't rattle like some stupid addle-pate, Tildy,' he told her angrily. 'I'll never harm you. But I must know who else you have told of this list. If the wrong person should have been told of it then it could bring ruin on your head, and on the heads of your friends.' His tone became urgently pleading. 'Please Tildy, for all our sakes, I must know whom you have told of this list.'

Tildy's head seemed to spin dizzily, and she did not know what to believe. Desperately she sought to clarify her confusion, and appealed to him, 'Mr Farrel, I'm sorely confused. Cannot you tell me more, so that I can come to a clearer understanding of what is happening with you and our combination?'

He appeared to give deep consideration to her appeal for a considerable length of time, and Tildy sat miserably watching him, cursing herself for not having told Josh Dyson of her discovery. Josh would have known what to do, and would have been able to tell her what she must do also.

At last Farrel appeared to reach a decision. 'All right, Tildy,' he said quietly. 'I will tell you all that I safely can. But in return I must then be told the names of all those who know of this list. Is that agreed?'

He waited in silence until Tildy reluctantly gave her

assent, then smiled reassuringly at her troubled face.

'Don't worry, Tildy, you and your friends face no danger from me. I wish only to help you. For many years now I have been active in the Radical and Reform movements in this country, the Hampden Clubs, the Spencean Society, and various unions and combinations.' He grimaced bitterly. 'Our cause seems hopeless, does it not? Up to now we do not seem to have achieved one iota of success in our aims. However, the fight must and will go on. As I see it, one of the greatest curses to afflict us are the damned Government agents and spies, the provocation men. Castle, Edwards, Oliver, these men are widely enough known by now, Tildy, but there are many, many others of the same evil breed, and it is one of them that brings me to this town. I want to unmask him and any accomplice he might have here before he can bring ruin down on you all.'

'But who is he?' Tildy's whirling thoughts had steadied somewhat, and she was now beginning to think rationally again. Suspicion of this man before her was rampaging through her mind, because up to now he had told her nothing verifiable about himself, and his story of a spy within the combination seemed highly unlikely to her. These were men known locally for many years, and vouched for by their peers. Curiously enough, despite her suspicion of Farrel, Tildy felt no physical fear of the man. It was as if her subconscious mind knew that he would not offer her any personal violence. That this man was a paradox she had no time to consider now.

For his part, Farrel once more appeared to be pondering a decision concerning her last question.

'If I tell you his name, Tildy, will you in return give me your word that you will not reveal it to your comrades until I tell you to do so?'

'But that would be risking their necks needlessly, would it not?' she protested. 'For me to know of a traitor among us and to say nothing would be a madness.'

'Madness or not, Tildy, that is my condition,' Farrel

told her adamantly. 'I must allow this man sufficient rope to hang himself with. At this point I could tell your friends the name of this man, but without actual proof would they believe that he is a provocation man? You yourself are experiencing a difficulty of belief in me, are you not?'

His verbal thrust caused Tildy to blush in momentary confusion, and he chuckled with genuine amusement.

'I do not blame you for so doubting me, Tildy. If our positions were reversed, I would be equally doubting of this wild story. Provocation men in Redditch! Government spies! Who could easily believe it? I could not myself, did I not know it to be a fact.' He paused, studying her face closely, then went on soberly, 'As to the matter of your own belief in me, Tildy, I would not have revealed myself to you so precipitately if events had not begun to move so quickly this day. I consider that at this moment you are in no personal danger of arrest. The protests you are leading are not motivated by any apparent desire for personal gain, and as I understand it you are making no demands other than asking for this man Brompton's dismissal. So long as that remains the same, the magistrates will not move against you. The masters were gathered together in the Fox and Goose this afternoon, so doubtless they have made their own arrangements. Left alone without outside interference it's safe to assume that this protest of yours will collapse of itself within a few days.' He winked slyly. 'And doubtless Brompton will have his sack handed to him very shortly following that collapse, for being the cause of such aggravation and loss of profit to his master. So you will have won, but to gain that victory you must first be publicly seen to acknowledge your defeat.'

Tildy was staring at him in fascination. 'How can you make such prophecies?' she whispered, enthralled by the authority with which he spoke.

Again he winked and smiled. 'I have read many times a book written by a man named Machiavelli, Tildy. You should also read what he has to say. He was a very wise man indeed, even though he was a foreigner.'

Greatly impressed, despite her own doubts, Tildy urged softly, 'Go on, Mr Farrel. I feel you have more to tell me.'

'Indeed I have, Tildy.' He was very serious. 'And you would do well to give full credence to what I am going to say. From what I have seen of the combination you belong to, your organizer is a shrewd and clever man. I would think that he will be using the opportunities created by these present events to manipulate the protest and so gain advantages of some sort for the combination. What I greatly fear however, is that the provocation man will also try and manipulate this situation to bring the combination to ruin.' At a tangent, he asked, 'Has there been a meeting called?'

'Yes. For tonight.' Tildy felt no hesitation in answering and Farrel noted that he was now gaining her trust to some extent.

'Very well then,' he murmured, and in a louder tone said to her, 'Tildy, I know something of how this particular provocation man goes about his filthy business of entrapment. I can practically guarantee that at tonight's meeting he will be urging some act of violence or other to be perpetrated against the masters. I'll venture that he will advocate this act of violence as necessary support for the women's protest. He will argue that such an act will frighten the master involved, Henry Milward, into acceding to the demand made of him. His further argument will possibly be that when the people hereabouts realize that there are men prepared to use such violence, men who are shadowy unknowns, then the fear engendered by the notion of these bogeymen will enable the combination to exert an influence out of all proportion to its numbers in any future confrontations with the masters.

'Once the provocation man succeeds in swaying the meeting to his plan, then he'll proceed quickly. The tools necessary for violence will be brought to the next meeting, and it's then he'll have the magistrates prepared to act.

They'll come with the constables and the Yeomanry Cavalry, and when they take up the combination lads in possession of instruments of violence the provocation man's purpose will be accomplished. He will be the chief witness for the crown, and he'll receive his blood money as reward.'

'How can you be so sure of this?' Tildy desperately wanted to know.

Farrel's thin features twisted in a rictus of grief. 'I know this, Tildy, because that is how this evil bastard entrapped my own brother. And my brother was transported for life, only his life did not last long once he was out in Van Diemen's land. He died there, broken by hardship and ill-treatment.' Farrel drew in a long shuddering breath, then looked at Tildy with eyes swimming with unshed tears, and grated out, 'I'm not doing what I do solely to serve my fellows, Tildy. I'm doing this for revenge, and I spit on those who would tell me that I am un-Christian and a wicked sinner for seeking blood for blood.'

Now, for the first time, all Tildy's doubts concerning this man's veracity left her, and she found herself believing him implicitly.

'I've told no one of the list you have,' she stated bluntly. 'No one knows except me.'

By now he had regained control of his emotions, and he nodded his satisfaction. 'Good, I'm more than pleased to hear that, Tildy. Because it means that I can still act against this provocation man without him suspecting that he is discovered. What I propose now is to try and give you certain proof of the truth of what I've told you. I shall write the man's name down and place it in a sealed envelope. Go to your meeting tonight, say nothing of what has passed between us, and watch and listen carefully for some one of them to act as I have forecast they will. Only then, after you have left the meeting, open the envelope and read the name I have written down. You'll be convinced then, I'm certain of it. Say nothing concerning me to anyone. Anyone at all,' he emphasized, then, making sure she would not overlook him, he used a quill pen and ink to write the name, and with his candle melted sealing wax to fix the envelope, and scrawled a hierograph upon the red wax lump. 'Here, you can see that there can be no question of trickery. Until that seal is broken you cannot know what name is written there. I must be abroad myself tonight, but please, if it is possible stay awake until I come to see you on my return.'

'I will,' Tildy promised, and with mingled trepidation and excitement went back to her own room.

Chapter Thirty-Three

'... and I say that the only way we'em ever going to beat the masters is to put the fear o' Christ into 'um.'

In the dull, diffuse light of the horn lantern the speaker's face was a mask of wolfish ferocity.

'We'se got weapons easy to hand, brothers. Pitchblend and oil, flint and steel, gunpowder and slow-match. If we sends a few workshops up in flames, then the masters 'ull listen all right. They only ever laughs at soft words and humble pleas, but they'll not laugh when they sees the sparks flying and the smoke gushing and roofs collapsing in storms o' fire.'

'That's so.'

'Ahr, youm right!'

'Let's burn a few o' the bastards out!'

Tildy shivered as she heard the growling voices, and marvelled at the uncanny accuracy of Nathanial Farrel's predictions. The breath caught in her throat and her stomach twisted queasily as she stared at Will Stacey and listened to his exhortations.

'We all on us knows, brothers, that the masters 'ull combine to starve the women from the Fountain Mill back to their work. The laws of combination don't apply to full-bellied rich men, you see, they only applies to empty-bellied paupers. But there's other laws, brothers, that you won't find written down in any books, or prated of by any judges. And one of them laws is "Fear is the greatest persuader". Once we strikes fear into any one o' the masters, then the rest on 'um 'ull very soon crumble. Fear will very soon break their bloody combination, that I can guarantee. Fear o' losing their property and wealth 'ull soon cause them to fall out among themselves. And once the common people see that our secret combination has forced Henry Milward to give Brompton his sack, then they'll start believing that we'em very powerful indeed. They'll think that there's hundreds, even thousands of us spread throughout this district, instead of just the few on us there really is. Because that's what the common people enjoys to think, brothers. Deep down in their hearts they wants to believe that there's a secret organization of poor men like themselves, who arn't feared of the bloody Government, or the gentry, or the masters, or their bloody Yeomanry Cavalry. Secret organizations of poor men who stand ready to fight back at those who oppress the poor and the weak. This can be just the beginning for us, brothers. We can become very powerful, if only we shows our courage now.'

Josh Dyson rose to stand by the speaker's side. 'We'll take a vote on it, brothers, as is our practice. The motion is, does we strike at the masters with fire, or does we just sit back and do nothing and let 'um ride roughshod over us, like they'se always done? All in favour of the fire, give voice.'

'Aye. Aye. Aye. Aye. Aye. Aye. Aye.' Man after man raised his hand and assented, and Dyson nodded.

'The ayes have it. The motion is carried. We use fire!'

The soft, insistent tapping came on her door soon after midnight, and Tildy slipped from her room and followed Nathanial Farrel into his.

'Well?' he questioned, and finally she brought herself to do what she had been unable to do until now: to open the sealed envelope she had carried with her and read the name written on the piece of paper inside.

Dreading that it still might be Josh Dyson, with trembling hands she held the piece of paper before her eyes. Bold and black in the candlelight the name burned itself into her brain.

'William Stevens, now called William Stacey.'

A soft moan of relief escaped her and Farrel, mistaking its reason, murmured sympathetically, 'It's always hard to discover that a man you trusted is a traitor to you, Tildy. Now then, firstly give me the names of every man in the combination, his place of work, and where he dwells. I'll need to know so that I can be sure of warning each of them in time. Secondly, give me the details of any plans made tonight.'

He seated himself on the bed, placed a flat board across his knees and readied paper, quill-pen and ink.

Tildy sighed heavily, and began. 'Josh Dyson, the hardener at the Fountain Mill, he dwells in the New End cottages. Thomas Tandy, finishing shop in the Fountain, he dwells ...'

Chapter Thirty-Four

For Tildy the next few days and nights were a torment of divided loyalties. At a further meeting of the combination she had been one of the handful who had argued against the use of arson. Her negation was not motivated solely by her belief that the proposal was a deliberately baited trap for her fellow-members, but more by her inner conviction that the act was wrong in itself.

The projected target was to be the property of the Milward family, and Tildy could not bear the thought that after Mrs Milward's kindness to her she would now be party to actions which could well bring the woman's family to bankruptcy. But naturally, Tildy felt loyalty towards the combination and had sincerely taken the oath to protect its secrets and struggle for its objectives.

Then there were her personal feelings towards Josh Dyson which were also influencing her. She greatly respected and admired the man, and was both physically and mentally drawn towards him. In her mind was also a niggling disquiet about Nathanial Farrel. He seemed reluctant to act quickly on what he already knew. She had told him of the latest plan to attack the Milwards' property and had urged him to let his identity be revealed to Josh Dyson and Thomas Tandy, so that they could then take concerted action to neutralize Will Stacey's schemes for entrapment. But Farrel only made vague excuses and prevaricated when she pressed him, and Tildy was beginning to wonder if in fact he himself secretly wished to see the Fountain Mill in flames. After all, he was now openly expressing his virulent hatred of the ruling establishment to Tildy and his lust to see them over-thrown.

'Could it be,' she wondered, 'that he is prepared to let the arson attack take place before he moves to lay Stacey by the heels?'

Yet another factor was also adding to her worries. Already, after so brief a time, the women and girls of the Fountain were grumbling bitterly at the lack of any manifestation of concrete material support from their fellow workers throughout the district. Some of the weaker-willed among them were openly advocating a return to work, even though it would be an abysmally early surrender. Tildy was sadly realizing that actions on impulse rarely maintained their initial impetus, and that without the necessary preliminary depth of dedication they could not be sustained for anything but the briefest of periods.

Tired and dispirited after another long, weary day of trudging about the district trying fruitlessly to collect food and money to support the Fountain women, Tildy faced those with her on the bank of the filthy, stinking big pool. There were only two of them, both young girls, and now they sought strength and encouragement from her.

'Does you really reckon that we can win, Tildy? Because we'em getting nothing to help us except empty promises.'

Tildy forced herself to speak with confident assurance. 'We'll win all right, just so long as we stick together. And we'll get help, you'll see. It's early days yet.'

'Well, I thought it 'ud all be over a couple o' days arter we'd walked out,' the eldest girl said despondently. 'I never reckoned on it lasting for a full week.'

Tildy struggled to hide her own despondency. 'It's not been a full week yet, has it? There hasn't been time enough for our supporters to get organized. When the next payday comes round, then they'll see that we get enough to live on.'

'I hope they does, Tildy, because if not then me dad

says I've got to go back to work and forget all this nonsense. He says he can't afford to keep me in bed and board, and he can't see why he should slave his guts out and goo short himself when there's work waiting for me.'

Tildy kept the false smile of confidence on her face, even though the effort to do so was almost intolerable. 'You'll have money enough to give your dad for bed and board, Abby. Come next payday we'll be rolling in it. If we only get a half of what's been promised to us, then there'll be enough and to spare.'

'Promises!' the short, stocky youngest girl snorted disgustedly. 'Promises be only made to be broke, Tildy!'

Tildy suddenly felt that she could not bear to listen to any more grumbling and complaining. Her body was weak with hunger, and her head was throbbing painfully. As it was, she was already being tormented sufficiently by a burgeoning guilt at having dragged these youngsters into what was now increasingly becoming apparent: theirs was a lost cause. Now she hungered to get away from their miserable faces and whining voices, to get away from everyone if only for a few minutes, and seek some solitary peace and quiet.

'I'll see you tomorrow,' she blurted out, and almost ran from them, acting so precipitously that both girls remained staring after her in bewilderment.

Unable at that moment to face the rowdy uproar of her lodgings, Tildy hurried on past the Silver Street archway and went on across the chapel green and down the Fish Hill. She was heading to her favourite walking place, the peaceful Abbey Meadows.

Sitting in his study facing the roadway, Reverend John Clayton saw the pretty young woman hurrying past his house and on down the steep hill. On impulse he rose, pulled on his coat, and wigless and hatless went after her.

The last thirty-six hours had also been a troubled time for John Clayton. Early the previous day his master, Reverend the Lord Aston, had once more summoned him urgently to the Tardebigge vicarage. What the older man had told him then had been worrying the young curate ever since.

The provocation man had visited Aston again, coming stealthily in the night, as before. This time he had brought information of plans made by the secret combination to carry out arson attacks against certain manufacturers in the district, purportedly to support the women of the Fountain Mill in their demand that John Brompton be dismissed from his employment. The man had refused to disclose the projected locations of the attacks, and had again refused to name any members of the combination until he was now paid a substantial proportion of his hoped-for reward money in advance.

Clayton frowned. 'Reward money? Better call it blood money! For that is what it is.'

According to Lord Aston the provocation man had coolly informed him that he did not trust the authorities to pay him in full once they had the members of the combination in custody. It had happened before that after he had given information against other Radical conspirators, the authorities had refused to pay him the sums he wanted from them. So, despite all Lord Aston's entreaties, blusters and threats, the man had steadfastly refused to name names until he had received a substantial sum in gold.

He had even been insolent enough, Lord Aston spluttered indignantly, to remind his Reverend lordship coolly that the rewards paid for arsonists were higher than those paid for common or garden combination men. So he didn't care if half the town went up in flames; it was greater profit for him.

Tildy was looking over the mysterious mounds and hollows which spread across the Abbey Meadows, and musing on what lay beneath the shrouding green turf that covered them, when she became aware of the oncoming John Clayton. She waited with mixed feelings for him to

272

reach her. She believed him to be a good man at heart, yet they invariably clashed whenever they met, and now, in her present mood, she grimly readied herself for further conflict. But to her surprise his first utterance when he reached her was an apology.

'Forgive me for intruding upon you in this way, Tildy Crawford. I pray you allow me but a few moments of your time, and then I'll leave you in peace once more.'

She nodded wordlessly and, almost diffidently, he went on.

'I feel that I also owe you an apology for what passed between us on the day of poor Megan Tullet's death. I will frankly confess that I now believe myself to have erred greatly on that day. And because of my error, I feel that I am much to blame for the succeeding unhappy events that have taken place.'

As she listened and sensed the deep sincerity with which he spoke, Tildy softened towards him and, swayed as always by the basic warm generosity of her nature, tried to comfort him in his obvious distress. 'Please, Parson Clayton, there is no need for you to apologize to me. Or for you to shoulder blame where none should fall upon you.'

He shrugged. 'No matter. I felt myself in honour bound to tell you what is in my heart. And I'll not play the hypocrite in what I next say to you, Tildy Crawford. Because I must tell you frankly that if you should divulge to anyone my name as your informant, then I shall vehemently deny any such complicity.' His voice became rueful. 'I shall be forced to do so, because pauper that I am, I must ensure my own survival as a cleric, my dear.'

For the first time since she had known him, Tildy found herself liking the clergyman.

'What I am going to tell you now, Tildy Crawford, I tell you because I feel guilt. I blame myself in part for the unhappy state of affairs at present in this district. If I had perceived the truth when it was told to me, and had not allowed my own prejudices wilfully to blind me, then there would be none of this present discord, and mayhap the tragic death of Megan Tullet would not have occurred.'

When Tildy would have spoken out, he told her sharply, 'No! Say nothing! Only hear me, girl!' His voice became snappish as his own conflict of loyalties gnawed at him, but now he had embarked upon this course of action he would not allow himself to be deflected from it until he had purged his own conscience.

'From my own past experience of your character, Tildy Crawford, I know that whatever I may urge upon you, you will still only act as you choose to. You have always been a deal too stubborn and wilful for your lowly station in life. However, be that as it may, I ask you, indeed beseech you, to trust absolutely in the truth of what I shall now tell you. For truth it is, upon my honour as a gentleman.

'There is a Government agent abroad in this parish, Crawford. A spy. He has confirmed to my lord 'Aston the existence of a secret combination of working men here in Redditch. My Lord Aston has received information from this agent that arson attacks are to be perpetrated. Those attacks are to be made purportedly in support of the protest you are leading the women of the Fountain Mill in making.

'I need hardly remind you what will happen here in this town if such attacks should be made. We, the representatives of authority, will bring the full powers vested in us into play, and when we catch those responsible for such criminality, then we shall ensure that they are punished with the utmost rigor the law allows.

'I urge you therefore, Crawford, to abandon this protest against your master, Henry Milward, and to do your damndest to ensure that all those other misguided and deluded females return to their lawful employment forthwith. If that happens, then the would-be arsonists can have no pretext other than their own wickedness for carrying out their acts of violence.' He paused and regarded her speculatively.

Shock and fear at hearing him declare his knowledge of the secret combination had struck Tildy like a physical blow, and it took all her self-discipline to maintain an impassive façade before the clergyman's searching regard.

'It may well be that you yourself have some knowledge of this combination, Crawford,' he observed shrewdly, and a wild desire to flee coursed though her, and for a moment her barely-maintained impassivity threatened to crumble. Then that moment passed, and he frowned with what she imagined to be anger at her lack of response.

'Mayhap, Crawford, you are even acquainted with someone belonging to it? You have always been partial to the company of rebellious spirits, have you not? But if you should know such a one, then I would most strongly advise you to press upon them the wisdom of instant abandonment, both of their membership of an illegal organization, and of the criminal violence they threaten to inflict upon this parish. Because if they do not abandon their present course, then they will most surely end upon the gallows.' He drew a sharp breath.

'There! I have done what I intended, and I now regard my moral debt to you to have been paid in full. Consider well what I have said to you, Crawford, and believe me when I tell you that I have said it in your own and your child's best interests. Now I'll bid you farewell.'

Alone again Tildy remained motionless, convinced that if she relaxed her rigid stance she would dissolve into moaning wails of despair. She forced her mind to struggle to comprehend fully the fearful implications of what John Clayton had told her. Little by little controlled reasoning returned to her.

The provocation man had made himself known to the magistrates, and had disclosed to them his knowledge of the secret combination and of the planned arson attacks ... But why then had no one yet been arrested? Why were the magistrates allowing the members of the combination to walk free? Rack her brains though she might, she could arrive at no satisfactory answer to this. 'I'll need to go and see Josh,' she decided. 'For there's naught I can do alone. I'll wait by his cottage for him to leave work.'

Another tremor of apprehension shivered through her. 'My God, he'll be so angry with me for not confiding in him sooner . . .'

Josh Dyson was angry with her for not telling him sooner. Very angry. But he refused to allow himself the luxury of wasting valuable time in upbraiding the white-faced girl facing him in his austere cottage.

'What's done is done, Tildy. I only hope that I still have time enough to rescue something from this mess.'

Once more he took her through her story, and in the candlelight his face appeared to age visibly with despair.

'If the magistrates know of us, then we can forget all our hopes of achieving anything,' he muttered dolefully.

'If the magistrates know of us, then why haven't they had us arrested, Josh?' Tildy questioned. 'Why do they still let us walk free?'

'That's easy answered, my wench. There's more blood-money to be got if we're caught burning places down than if we'em only forming combinations. It's the same system for these provocation men as it is for the Bow Street runners, Tildy. The runners will go on letting a young thief go on robbing to his heart's content, they'll even supply him with news of likely places to crack sometimes, and they won't touch him until he commits a crime that makes him worth more reward money. They'll only get a few pounds for a sneak-thief or sheep-stealer, but they can get forty pounds for a house-breaker or a coiner.

'That's what this provocation man is holding back for. We'll easy be forty pounds value apiece once we've set torch to something. It's almost certain sure that he's not give any names to the magistrates as yet. Because if he had they'd have us arrested straight off for combining. By keeping our names to himself the bugger's protecting his own blood-money. We might still have time to shut his mouth for good, I reckon.'

His tone sent a shiver of dread through Tildy. 'How? How would you shut his mouth, Josh?' she stammered nervously, and the kindly man she knew was replaced by a ruthless, ferocious stranger.

'By cutting his bloody throat, girl. That's how.'

'Oh nooo,' she moaned. 'That would be murder.'

'And what is he going to do to us, girl, if it arn't to murder us? He's planning to get all our necks stretched on the bloody gallows. Anyway, don't piss your britches,' he told her brutally. 'Because you'll not be asked to wield the knife.'

'I've never seen you like this, Josh,' she stated wonder-ingly. 'I feel that I don't know you any more.'

'I'm like this because I has to be like this, you stupid little sod!' he burst out furiously. 'I told you afore, Tildy, that this arn't some kid's game we'em playing here. It's life or death. Our lives, and our deaths. That fucking provocation man means to get us all topped, and that includes you as well. So as far as I'm concerned, it's him or me for the chop. So make up your mind to that, girl. Because if you arn't ready to fight for your life by fair means or foul, then that babby o' yourn 'ull be a bloody orphan afore too many more meals introduces theirselves to his belly. If you'd only told me what was going on afore now, then perhaps we shouldn't be in this bloody mess. So don't you keep looking at me as though I'm some sort of evil madman now.'

Tildy could accept the justice of what he said, but still the prospect of a man being deliberately murdered to silence him filled her with a sick horror.

'The question now is how does I get to Farrel and do the business? Is he always armed, I wonder? Bound to be ...' Dyson seemed to be speaking to himself, and Tildy stared at him in bewilderment.

'Farrel?' she questioned. 'Why do you say Farrel? William Stevens, now known as Will Stacey, was what was written on that paper.'

The man looked at her and chuckled with bitter

amusement. 'By the Christ, Tildy, but youm a bloody innocent! Farrel's the provocation man, not Will Stevens. He's gulled you good and proper, arn't he, girl? Made a right yokel booby out o' you. No wonder the bloody Cockneys thinks we'em all mawkins in the country!

'But Farrel's agoing to learn the truth of an old saying we'se got in these parts, and that is "if you wants to be certain of finding a cunt in the country, then you must bring your own cunt wi' you."'

'But you can't be sure that it's Farrel and not Will Stacey who's the provocation man,' Tildy argued vehemently. 'After all, how long is it since you last saw Stacey before his coming here to Redditch? Not since 1817! That's five years ago. How can you know what he was doing all those years, or how he earned his bread? He tells you that he spent them in America, and you say that you had a letter from him there. But was he really there? Or did someone else send the letter for him? You call me a yokel booby and tell me that I'm easy gulled, Josh, and maybe I am both those things, but think now, how well did you know Will Stacey before? Did you know him well enough then to trust him with your life now, five years after?

'From what you have told me concerning him, he was only one of many that you knew briefly. You were never close to him, were you? I'm not saying that Stacey is the spy, Josh, because I don't know. But how can you know so surely that Nathanial Farrel is a spy?

'All I'm asking of you is that you make certain who is the guilty man before you stain your own soul with murder. Be certain, Josh. I beg of you, be certain.'

For a lengthy interval he only stared blankly at her, until Tildy began to fear that his sanity had suddenly become impaired. Then, to her relief, the old kindly Josh Dyson broke through the ferocious mask of this new-come stranger.

'It's a sorry business, arn't it, my duck?' he said gently, and smiled. To her mortification Tildy's emotion at his

278

metamorphosis was such that she burst into tears.

Instantly he took her into his arms and rocked her as if she were a distressed child, stroking her hair and murmuring soothingly, 'There now, honey, don't weep. I'll protect you, don't worry. You and your babby are going to be safe, I promise you. Come what may, you and little Davy will be safe. Hush now ... Hush, my honey ... Hush ...'

Gradually her sobs stilled and the shudderings of her body eased. She wiped her eyes and blew her nose, and tried to apologize to him. 'I'm sorry for acting so silly, Josh,' she began, but leaning swiftly towards her he kissed her mouth.

'Be quiet now, Tildy.' He smiled. 'There's much to be done, and little time to do it in.'

'What are you going to do, Josh?' she questioned anxiously, and he hugged her briefly.

'It don't matter now what I'm intending doing, girl. But you must do exactly as I tells you. Now, is that agreed?'

Wordlessly she nodded, too spent and drained to be able to argue further.

'You women are meeting again at crack o' light tomorrow morn, arn't you?'

'Yes, by the big pool,' she confirmed. 'But I fear most have lost heart already.'

'That's all right then, because youm going to tell them anyway that the protest is over and done with, Tildy. I'll see to it that Henry Milward makes no trouble about letting you all start back to work. Mind you, I don't doubt but that you'll have to ate a big slice of humble pie, but that won't kill any of you.'

He saw the sparks of protest leap into her eyes, and gravely shook his head. 'No Tildy, it's done with. Take it from me that this fight is a lost 'un. We drew weak battle-lines, Tildy, and attacked too soon, afore we were properly prepared. And there's naught to be done now, except retreat in good order.

'When I was a soldier I was in a few retreats, honey. It arn't naught to be shamed of, so long as you'se made a good fight on it afore that retreat. And you and the other women have done that all right, girl. You can all be proud of yourselves. And another thing, as of this minute the combination is disbanded as well.'

Again protest surged within her, and again he shook his head in negation. 'I'm the general of this army, my love. It's me who says when it's disbanded, and I'm saying that now it is. But don't grieve about it, because it'll muster and march again some day, and we'll be marching wi' it, you and I. That, there's no doubt of. But for now, it's done with.'

He kissed her again, this time with a tender passion, and Tildy savoured the warm, moist pressure of his lips, the hard, muscular feel of his shoulders beneath her fingers, the clean scent of him in her nostrils and his taste in her mouth. Then, gently, he put her away from him.

'Go now to your babby, Tildy. He'll be pining for you. And remember to do exactly what I've told you, and remember as well that you and your nipper are going to be safe. Go on now.'

Trusting him, she left him standing in the candlelight in the austere, monkish room, and hurried through the darkness towards the Silver Square.

Alone in his cottage Josh Dyson murmured her name, 'Tildy, my sweet Tildy,' and smiled with mingled sadness and regret, then took his long-barrelled fowling-piece from its hooks on the wall and checked its flint and trigger mechanism. 'And now I think it's high time I sorted out that bloody provocation man,' he muttered savagely.

Although his head was swimming from the effects of the gin he had been drinking, Nathanial Farrel's eyes were able to decipher the scrawled note he had found pushed under the door of his room when he returned from the Black Horse at midnight. It was terse and brief.

'Come to my house immediately on receipt. Aston.'

Farrel grinned triumphantly. 'The old bastard's going to pay me in advance. I knew the bloody chaw-bacon 'ud give way in the end.'

Without pausing even to snuff his candle he hurried down the stairs and out into the Silver Square. His heady satisfaction, coupled with the huge amounts of liquor he had drunk, made him careless, and he failed to notice Josh Dyson watching him from the shadows ...

Chapter Thirty-Five

At seven o'clock in the morning the vastly pregnant Apollonia came waddling into the kitchen and announced to Mother Readman, 'That fuckin' Cockney's done a bunk, Missus. Took his traps and gone. He never even left a bloody candlestub, but let it burn away to nothing.'

The old woman hawked and spat into the fire resignedly. Runaway lodgers were a very common occurrence in her world.

'The bastard owed me two nights and a bowl o' stew,' she grumbled. 'I never learns, does I, Apollonia? It don't matter a bugger how regular they bin wi' the rent, I should always take it in advance. I should ha' collared the flash bleeder yesterday afore he went out. It's me own fault, so it is.' She shrugged her massive shoulders dismissively. 'Ah well, there warn't anybody else wanting the room for them nights anyway. So at least I arn't lost double.'

Chapter Thirty-Six

The heaped needles glowed red-gold and Josh Dyson nodded with satisfaction and tipped them into the tub of cold water. The water hissed and bubbled and seethed thick clouds of steam.

Henry Milward came into the shop and stood at the hardener's elbow. 'How's this new batch of Dortmund then, Josh?'

'It arn't good, Mr Milward, but it'll serve.'

'I'se took all them daft wenches back, Josh.' The needle master's fat, florid face was petulant. 'I hopes you'll think on that the next time you starts blaggardin' me wi' being a cruel, hard master.' He coughed as if to cover a sense of unease, and then said, 'I'm going to have to get rid of that bugger Brompton, though. I could smell the drink on him again this morning. I don't begrudge anybody having a few pints at their work, but he's taking liberties wi' me now. Comes in half-drunk, and goes home blind-drunk.'

'Well, Mr Milward, you know your own business best. If the man's not conducting himself in the proper manner at his work, then he should be got rid of. I doubt that anybody in this mill 'ull blame you for getting rid of him.'

'I don't give a bugger whether anybody blames me or not,' Henry Milward blustered. 'I'll run my own mill as I see fit to run it. I'm going to kick Brompton's arse through the gates right now. I'll not tolerate drunks in my mill.'

Puffing and snorting, the needle master stamped out and Josh Dyson watched him go, an ironic smile playing about his lips.

Then the smile disappeared as he thought of the provocation man, Nathanial Farrel, and how he had planted the fake note in the room at the lodging house to flush him out from cover. 'Ah well, it had to be done. I needed to be absolutely certain that he was the spy. And I was that once I'd stopped him on the Tardebigge road and found those letters from the Home Office in his pockets. Then the bugger had the cheek to try and buy me off. Promising me half the blood-money. Bastard! Nearly had me cold with that knife of his.' Dyson winced, as his fingers touched the thickly bandaged wound Farrel's treacherous knife-thrust had inflicted on his ribs. 'He was a tricky bugger all right. Dangerous as a trapped rat, so he was.' Then Dyson's thoughts turned unhappily towards Tildy Crawford. 'What will she think of me now, I wonder, if she ever finds out what I've done? In her eyes I'll be no more than a murderer. But what else could I do? If I hadn't used my gun he would have slashed me to ribbons with that bloody knife of his. Nearly did for me the first instant as it was. And Farrel was going to hang all on us, including Tildy, warn't he? I've seen too many good comrades killed in battle to lose any sleep over the killing of a dirty, sneaking bastard like him. I'd do the same thing again if needs be.

'Good job the brick kilns were firing last night though, otherwise I could have had trouble getting rid of the body. He's just smoke in the sky now though, and all his lists and information with him. It doesn't matter what the magistrates might think, they'll not be able to prove anything against anybody now. We'll be able to form another combination afore too long.

'And Tildy? Well, she'll find he's gone missing soon enough. But I'll just tell her that I frightened him off and that she must put all thoughts of him from her mind. I mean, what else could I have done with that bastard, but kill him? It was him or us, warn't it? Him or us ... Him or us ... Him or us ... Him or us ...'

Final Chapter

In the lye shop the acrid steam billowed and the oily needles shed their filth into the tubs of boiling water.

Mary Ann Avery grinned at Tildy. 'Well, at least we'se had a bit of a holiday from this, arn't us, Tildy?'

Tildy smiled back ruefully. 'I could have wished for a longer one, Mary Ann.'

Sarah Farr looked up from the purse she was unlacing. 'Old Henry was quite civil really, warn't he, all things considered? I mean, all he did was moan a bit and keep on about how good he'd bin to us in the past, and how bad we was for repaying him by going on bloody strike.'

Mary Ann winked at Tildy. 'Ahr, he's so bloody good to us, he'll put all our wages up next, you'll see.'

'Ahr, put 'um up our arses, you means,' Old Tabby cackled.

Tildy listened to the badinage, and could not help but feel a thankful relief that no harm had come to her friends and workmates as a result of her own hotheaded actions. Strangely she felt no worry about any future repercussions. Josh Dyson had told her she need not worry, that she and her baby would be safe, and she believed him.

Sadness touched her as she thought of Meg Tullet. 'I'm so sorry, Meg,' she whispered in her mind. 'I'm so sorry that I failed you in the end. But at least I tried, Meg, and one thing I'll promise you is that I'll try and try again to gain justice for any poor girl who get's served the way you were served ...' Tildy's spirits rose suddenly, and she smiled to herself. 'Oh yes, I'll be trying again, Meg, of that there is no doubt. I'll never stop trying again.'